'What kind of ... me for? A rogu...

'Leave him out of it, if you pl...

'Gladly. But answer my question.'

'I cannot!' she retorted, squirming against him. 'All I know is that you have your orders and that's why you're here. How should I know what kind of a man you are, my lord? You must have heard how skilfully I form opinions in *that* direction.'

'Yes, I have. Stop struggling and listen to me. This is not what you believe.'

'You will never convince me of that, my lord. If I did not own something you'd been told to get hold of at any cost you would show no more interest in Lord Benistone's scandalous daughter than in any other widow.'

Juliet Landon's keen interest in art and history, both of which she used to teach, combined with a fertile imagination, make writing historical novels a favourite occupation. She is particularly interested in researching the early medieval and Regency periods, and the problems encountered by women in a man's world. Her heart's home is in her native North Yorkshire, but now she lives happily in a Hampshire village close to her family. Her first books, which were on embroidery and design, were published under her own name of Jan Messent.

Previous novels by the same author:

THE WIDOW'S BARGAIN
THE BOUGHT BRIDE
HIS DUTY, HER DESTINY
THE WARLORD'S MISTRESS
A SCANDALOUS MISTRESS
DISHONOUR AND DESIRE
THE RAKE'S UNCONVENTIONAL MISTRESS
MARRYING THE MISTRESS
SCANDALOUS INNOCENT
   (collaboration with the National Trust)
SLAVE PRINCESS

MISTRESS MASQUERADE

Juliet Landon

Published in Great Britain 2014
by Mills & Boon, an imprint of Harlequin (UK) Limited,
Eton House, 18-24 Paradise Road, Richmond, Surrey, TW9 1SR

© 2014 Juliet Landon

ISBN: 978 0 263 90941 8

Harlequin (UK) Limited's policy is to use papers that are natural,
renewable and recyclable products and made from wood grown in
sustainable forests. The logging and manufacturing processes conform
to the legal environmental regulations of the country of origin.

Printed a ... by Black ...

AUTHOR NOTE

The Regency, a period between the years 1811 and 1820, was dominated by George, Prince of Wales, eldest son of King George III and Queen Charlotte. He was a man of many facets, both attractive and ugly.

In 1811 George was required to take over his father's duties because of a severe illness showing similar symptoms to insanity, projecting the young man into a situation he was unable to manage to anyone's satisfaction—not even his own. This was not all his fault, but he was not a strong leader in any sense, preferring lavish displays of wealth and waste that drained the coffers dry at a time when funds were needed for the wars against Napoleon.

My depiction of him as an art-lover is fact, for he did indeed employ knowledgeable friends like Lord Hertford to act as buyer for his 'newest toys', Carlton House and Brighton Pavilion, on which he poured vast sums of money while at the other end of society thousands lived in terrible poverty after a series of bad harvests and severe winters.

In an otherwise intelligent and cultivated man, his insensitivity on a personal level was breathtaking, and it seemed to me, as a writer, that to include him in a story of this kind I must choose whether to concentrate on the sadness of his position or on his utterly reprehensible behaviour towards those he had once called his dearest friends. To allow Annemarie to rediscover her natural compassion I chose the former.

Emma Hamilton was one of those Regency characters whose colourful life needs no embellishment. Her story of 'rags to riches' both fascinates and repels us at the same time. It is an astonishing saga of how she exploited every attribute and talent she possessed to survive in a man's world, becoming the mistress of several men in the process, including Lord Nelson. There is no evidence that she and the Prince Regent were actually lovers, but they were close friends—until Emma's difficulties and demands became too much for him, when he failed to respond to her pleas for help.

Selfish to the last, George felt no responsibility to those he had once loved, though he kept thousands of love tokens, letters and mementoes. Again, one cannot help but find some sympathy for a woman like Emma Hamilton, so ill-used by her family and all those she had helped, who had taken full advantage of her generosity. Her ambition, apparent greed and amoral behaviour sometimes appear at odds with her naivety, innocence and longing for approval while expecting the same kindness from those she loved. I truly believe she could not tell her friends from her enemies most of the time. And that, sadly, was one of the greatest tragedies in her life, for she lived in the heart of a political and greed-ridden society whose loyalties dissolved faster than hers. Combine those expectations with a man like the Prince Regent and there is a recipe bound to collapse—like his protestations of eternal love.

Two such complex characters, so much to like and admire, so much to despise; their true stories are indeed stranger than fiction.

My main sources of information were *The Prince of Pleasure* by JB Priestley, which is now out of print, but there is plenty about George to be found in Ian Kelly's brilliant book *Beau Brummell*, published by Hodder and Stoughton in 2006.

Kate Williams's book, *England's Mistress*, is all about Emma Hamilton and is excellent reading, published by Arrow in 2007.

Chapter One

London. June 1814

Lowering his morning newspaper with a loud crackle, Lord Benistone put down his magnifying lens and stared vacantly at the pot of marmalade, then across at his three daughters. 'Poor unfortunate woman,' he muttered. Two of them knew by the way he spoke that he was more likely to be thinking of their mother at that moment than the woman who featured, yet again, in *The Times*.

'Obituaries?' said Annemarie, his second eldest.

His eyes warmed at her assumption. 'No, love. Not obituaries. Lady Emma Hamilton again. Another sale. She can have little more to sell now. You should go, Annemarie.'

'To an auction? I think not, Papa. All the world will be there.'

'I could request a private view for you. I can send a note to Parke at Christie's. He'd allow it. I know you'd like something of hers, wouldn't you? A memento? As an admirer?'

He'd got it wrong. Words of feeling were not his strong point. 'Not so much admiration as sympathy,' she said, 'for the way she's been treated since Lord Nelson's death. All those wealthy friends and greedy relatives, and not one of them willing to help her out of her debts. She must be desperate by now.'

Her younger sister Marguerite's opinion was only to be expected, particularly on a subject about which she knew little. At sixteen-and-a-half, she had still not learned the art of discretion. 'I shall not be wasting *my* sympathy on a woman like that,' she said, pushing her half-eaten breakfast away. 'She's brought it all on herself.'

It took much to make their father angry, but this hit a raw nerve and his hard stare at his youngest daughter would have made a bold man quake. 'Marguerite,' he said, softly, 'I wish you would try to acquire the habit of thinking before you speak before it's too late to make a lady of you. For one thing, no woman brings it *all* on herself. And for another thing….tch! Never mind. You wouldn't understand.'

Even Marguerite knew then that he was thinking of their mother.

Oriel, the eldest sister, glanced at her sideways and pushed the plate back into place with one finger. 'Unladylike,' she said. 'And I think an apology is called for.'

'I'm sorry, Papa,' Marguerite whispered. 'I spoke rashly.'

'No harm, child,' he said, nodding. 'No harm.' The morning sun caught the top of his silvery hair as he looked again at Christie's announcement. 'You go and take a look, Annemarie. I don't know whether she'll have saved the best or the rubbish till last, but you may find something to take down to Brighton with you.' At sixty-eight he was still a handsome man, in spite of the lack of exercise.

'What are you looking for?' said Oriel. 'I wouldn't have thought anything of Lady Hamilton's would be to your taste. A little too flashy, perhaps?'

'I've no idea. Something small, I suppose.'

Annemarie saw the flicker of amusement pass across her father's face at that. There was barely a square inch of space at their Montague Street home that was not occupied by his well-known collection of antiquities, and he knew as well as she that by sending her to Christie's auction rooms in his stead, his own curiosity would be assuaged without the temptation to buy. Even Lady Hamilton's last pieces would reveal something of quality, if not rarity, for she and Lord

Nelson had been presented with gifts from every corner of the world. Annemarie was due to return to her own house at Brighton the next day, so it seemed like a last chance to find something that would fit. Something small.

Only one hour later, a note was delivered to Montague Street assuring Lord Benistone that Mr Parke, Christie's senior valuer, would be delighted to show Lady Annemarie Golding over the most recent acquisitions.

So it was that, by mid-afternoon, she had chosen not the small thing she'd intended, but one of a pair of matching bureau dressing-tables made by the elder Chippendale, no longer in the height of Regency fashion but exactly what she needed for her bedroom. She would have bought its twin also, but did not need two of them as Lady Hamilton and Lord Nelson apparently had. Widows such as herself only needed one of anything. The generous price of it, however, was certain to relieve the poor lady's acute embarrassment more than all the other clutter she was selling, except for its twin which Mr Parke assured Lady Golding he would sell for at least as much. Even so, he pointed out that he knew of no one who would want to purchase the pair and was relieved to have got one of them out of the way so quickly.

* * *

It was delivered to Montague Street that very same day and, smoothing a gnarled hand over the rosewood surface, Lord Benistone bent to examine the delicate inlay, the pretty brass handles, the honeyed tones of the veneer, his fingertips reading the patterned woods as if they were words. 'I'll have it packed straight away for you,' he said, 'and ready for the wagon first thing in the morning. Will that do?'

'Thank you, Papa,' Annemarie said, glancing round the great hall where the brown bureau looked so ill at ease amongst the white carved reliefs and contorted stone figures, the smooth busts of Roman matrons, the urns and plaques. There was no point in repeating the countless invitations to go with her to Brighton. He would never leave his beloved collection, not even for a few days of bracing sea air, especially now when the whole of Europe was flocking to London for the end-of-war celebrations. The possibility of meeting other antiquarians was too good to miss. She could hardly blame him when she was using the same reason to escape to deserted Brighton where she was unlikely to meet anyone who knew her.

The other reason, she had to admit, was that the beautiful house on Montague Street had become more like a museum than a home and she longed for the white-and-pastel space of her own elegant rooms where she was not swamped by sculpted pieces of enormous proportions or paintings covering every vertical surface. They were even stacked against the furniture now, finding their way into the bedrooms, preventing the housemaids from cleaning and the housekeeper from keeping order. Entertaining had been out of the question for years unless the guests were fellow-collectors, making for some very one-sided conversations. It was not difficult for any of them to understand why their mother had left last year, although the manner of her leaving was another thing entirely. That would be even harder to understand and not a day passed when Annemarie did not feel the wound it had left.

They never spoke of it, papa and his daughters, but now it seemed as if something had tweaked at that raw nerve again as the day of Annemarie's departure drew nearer and his usually clear voice faltered as his hands ceased their caress of the rosewood. 'This thing will be all right,' he whispered, 'but it's you I'm concerned about, lass. You've been more affected by what happened than your sisters and, at twenty-four years old, it's time you found somebody else to take care of you properly. Holing yourself up by the sea is hardly the right way to go about it, is it? And when I'm no longer...' His voice trembled on a sob as the thought took over. 'I ought to have seen it coming, oughtn't I?'

Annemarie had not seen him like this before. Taking him into her arms, she hushed him with mothering sounds and felt him tremble as if a cool breeze had ruffled him. Then he was still again, composed and dignified, determined not to be seen caring too deeply for his loss. It was affairs of the heart that had been his undoing. That, and a disastrous misdirection of his attention. Perhaps there was more of him in young Marguerite than he cared to admit.

Withdrawing from her comfort, he sniffed and pushed a tear away with a knuckle, smiling thinly at the unusual lapse. 'You're so like her,' he said, touching her cheek. 'Oh, I don't mean like *that*. I mean in looks. The way she was when I first saw her: same glossy black hair, velvet skin, amethyst eyes. A beautiful creature.'

She smiled. What loving father did not think his daughters beautiful?

Later, she tried her persuasions on Oriel. 'I wish you were coming with me,' she said as they watched Marguerite disappear with a swirl up the wide staircase still in a state of agitation from breakfast.

'And I wish you were staying here with us,' Oriel said, tucking her hand through her sister's arm. Upstairs, a door slammed and her soft grey-blue eyes rolled heavenwards before turning to Annemarie's.

'She means no harm, love.'

'She doesn't have the sense to *mean* anything,' said Oriel 'That's the problem. We never know what she's going to say…or do…next. That's why it's best if I stay here to keep an eye on her. Besides….'

'Yes, I know. You have Colonel Harrow. I would never drag you away from him, just to keep me company.'

Oriel blushed, her smile lighting up her serenely lovely face like sunshine on water. Annemarie picked up the hand that was through her arm to check on the sapphire-and-diamond engagement ring. Colonel Harrow was fortunate to have won her and not for the world would Annemarie have claimed priority when the couple had so recently been reunited after his return from the Peninsula Wars. Oriel's relief to find him unharmed after so much hard fighting against Napoleon's forces had moved them all to tears of joy, especially after Annemarie's own late husband had fared less well. As a couple, Oriel and William were now able to take part in the celebrations that would last for months, if the Prince Regent could find the funds to pay for them.

Oriel shared in the study of her ring. 'It's not only that,' she said. 'It's Father too, isn't it? He prefers it if one of us is here to show his visitors round the collection and Marguerite is no help because she doesn't know the first thing about it. At least we can tell Egyptian from Assyrian.'

Giggling at the mental picture of Marguerite's carefully cultivated ignorance, Annemarie could not suppress the uncharitable retort, 'Yes, and the longer she refuses to learn, the less likely she'll be asked to help. She knows that, the little minx. And Papa knows it, too. He should take a stronger line with her.'

'He did at breakfast though, didn't he?'

'He should do it more often.'

'She takes notice of Cecily,' said Oriel, wiping a finger over the stone curls of a Roman's beard. 'This one hasn't been dusted lately.'

'Thank heaven for Cecily. She's a saint.'

Father's widowed cousin Cecily was in a perfect position to visit their London home as one of the family while keeping her own luxurious house on Park Lane as an escape from the comings and goings of visitors to their papa's "museum". Quite often, Marguerite would stay overnight with her when a chaperon was required for an evening event, an arrangement that suited them all for a variety of reasons. Cecily had been the one to sponsor Marguerite's coming-out ball last summer, and now she was just as likely to appear at the Montague Street breakfast table as Marguerite was at hers.

'You ought not to be travelling down to Brighton on your own, though,' Oriel said. 'You know Father doesn't like it above half. Won't Cecily go with you?'

'I would not want her to,' Annemarie replied. 'I'd rather she stayed where Marguerite is, while she's flitting about from party to picnic every day. She's quite determined to go to Lady Sindlesham's ball tonight, you know, and Papa doesn't seem at all concerned. Cecily is needed here. Anyway, love, I shall hardly be on my own with a maid and two coachmen, shall I? I'm not likely to come to any harm between here and the coast.'

'You're getting to be a recluse, Annemarie. It cannot be good for you.'

'It's best,' she said, not wanting to explain.

'Think of all the evening dresses. You know how you love dressing up.'

'Don't, Oriel. It doesn't help.'

But it was true. To wear the newest fashions had always been one of her weaknesses, but without that *frisson* of excitement at the admiration they caused, the exercise seemed pointless when the stares she received would be laced with pity and curiosity to see how she was surviving last year's scandal. She was not prepared to face that. Not yet.

Oriel's arm squeezed hers, understanding. When Mama was with them once again and Annemarie began to show signs of taking her

place in society, she and her handsome colonel
would name a date for their marriage. It was typical of her that she would not put a seal on her
own happiness before everyone else's was assured. But never once had the two older sisters
doubted that, one day, Mama would reappear
and that their lives would then begin a return
to normality.

It gave her sister no pleasure to keep them
waiting, but for the life of her, she could find no
way forwards.

The well-dressed delivery man touched the
brim of his top hat. 'Thank-ee, m'lord. Very generous, m'lord. Any time.' *A real swish beau, that
one,* he said to himself, watching the long stride
disappear round the corner. It was one thing to
be in such a cove's good books, but that man
could do some serious damage if the opposite
applied, if those shoulders and that deep barrel
of a chest were any indication, yet the blue su-
perfine sported not one crease. Pocketing the
gold coin, he patted the embroidered lettering
on his black-velvet lapel that said, 'Christie's of
London' before climbing up on to the wagon to
sit beside his mate. 'It don't get much easier than
that, Rookie,' he grinned.

'Blabbermouth!' replied Rookie, good-
naturedly flipping the reins. 'Giddup!'

Returning to the front of Christie's Auction

House, the admired beau climbed into his own conveyance, a cream-and-black curricle of exquisite delicacy, took the reins and whip into his gloved hands, nodded to his groom and moved away along King Street heading northwards, quite unaware of the admiration he had aroused.

Montague Street, he said to himself. That would be Benistone's place, of course, a collector better known for his Greek and Roman artefacts and old masters than furniture. One of the best collections in London, so the Prince Regent believed. Sadly, Lord Benistone had suffered some notoriety over the loss of his beautiful ex-courtesan wife who had run off with the suitor of one of his daughters last year. He himself had been away in the Peninsula with Wellington at the time, so knew little of the details. The elderly father had never been a socialite, and what the daughters were like he did not know, though he'd heard that one of them had her mother's looks, which might explain why that shortsighted worm Mytchett had taken what was on offer. His curiosity sharpened.

At Number Fourteen Montague Street, Lord Benistone's butler was apologetic. The master was not at home. He was across the road in the British Museum. He liked to take a look at least once every two weeks. Would Lord Verne like to return tomorrow? Leave his card?

No, Lord Verne thought he could do better
than that, though it would not do to betray his
impatience. In the marbled hall lined with art
objects, he had detected a white pedestal that
had moved, very slightly, in a shadowy corner
by the staircase. He took a chance. 'I wonder…
is Lord Benistone's daughter at home? I have not
yet had the pleasure of the lady's acquaintance,
but His Royal Highness the Prince Regent…ah!'

The pedestal moved forwards very slowly into
the light and became a tall shaft of creamy-white
flowing muslin topped by a scoop of peachy
skin, a long neck unadorned except by wisps
of escaping hair that curved on to her shoulders, the remainder of which was piled up into a
gloriously untidy mass of glossy blackness that
had obviously been set up there without mirror
or abigail.

There were very few times when Lord Verne
was bereft of speech, being an erudite man
known for his ability to handle any situation with
astonishing efficiency, but this was one of those
times. Aware that his incredulous stare would be
taken for incivility if he didn't utter some kind
of sound in the next three seconds, he let out his
breath on a narrowly avoided whistle. 'Miss…
er…Benistone?' he said. 'I hope you'll forgive
my intrusion.'

Her black-rimmed gemstone eyes glared at
him from beneath finely curved brows, one of

which was cleft by a loosened ringlet that on any other woman would have signified untidiness, but on her was sensational. So, *this* could be the jilted daughter. If the mother looked anything like this, Verne thought, who could have refused her? But the amazing eyes remained stony and one could not have said that her welcome was even lukewarm as she stayed well out of reach. 'No, we have not met, sir. I am Lady Golding, Lord Benistone's second daughter. And you are?'

'Lord Verne. At your service, ma'am.' The use of his title, he thought, was justified on this occasion.

'Then, in the absence of someone to introduce us, I suppose that must suffice. How do you do?' Gracefully, she inclined her head in what he knew to be the precise degree demanded by etiquette and not one jot more. His own slight bow matched hers. He had no intention of offering more in civilities than she did. She adjusted a frill over her other wrist before clasping her hands beneath the high bodice of her gown.

The butler bowed and took Lord Verne's hat and gloves and placed them on a vacant corner of the book-piled hall table before leading the way to a morning room that had now become a repository of treasures. There was very little room for manoeuvre, yet he was both surprised and amused when the butler, without being prompted, propped the door wide open with a gigantic plaster cast of a foot before leaving them alone. If one could be alone in such exalted company.

'Casts of Michelangelo's *David*,' said Annemarie, noting his interest. 'Here's his nose and one of his hands.' She blew a cloud of dust off it. 'May I ask your business, my lord?' Still no smile.

He decided to press for one. Foolishly, in retrospect. 'Yes,' he said, looking about him, 'it would be difficult to get the rest of him in here without chopping him into further little bits, wouldn't it?'

'You mentioned the Prince Regent just now. Was there a reason for that?' she said, ignoring his attempt at levity. She obviously did not appreciate having to deal with visitors, even noble ones, who turned up on the doorstep without a ticket expecting to be shown round individually. She would expect them to apply for the usual days: Mondays, Wednesdays and Saturdays. 'Does his Highness wish to see the collection, perhaps?'

Verne accepted defeat. She was not going to thaw. 'I mentioned the Prince Regent, my lady, because he has commissioned me to find something for him.'

Annemarie glanced sideways at the dusty piles of books, vases and body parts waiting to be catalogued. 'Really. And would you know it if you saw it, my lord?'

So, she needed to be told that she was not talking to an ignoramus. Idly following her glance, he was needled into a retort. 'Well now, I'd know that the hand you've just dusted off is by Bernini, not Michelangelo, like the nose. And I'd know that this bowl here is sixth century BC Attic and that you should put it somewhere safe. It's a very rare piece. And behind you is an El Greco, if I'm not mistaken.'

'It is!' Annemarie retorted sharply. 'What is it you're looking for?'

Right. Now we're level, Lady High and Mighty Golding, née Benistone.

'For a Chippendale bureau. Oak, mahogany and pine, mostly.'

'As you see, my father is not a collector of furniture. That is why I cannot ask you to sit. Most of our chairs are used for…other things…'

'Yes, quite. But I was led to believe, my lady, that a Chippendale bureau was delivered to this address only today. The day before the Hamilton auction.'

A quick frown shadowed her face. 'Mr Parke *promised* me—'

'It was not Parke who gave me the information,' he said. 'I did not even ask him for it. One does not need to go to the horse's mouth to find things out, if you'll excuse the expression.'

'I'm familiar with the Christie organisation, I thank you. I can guess how you made your discovery But you are wasting your time, my lord. There is no bureau here. Where on earth would we put such a thing?'

'His Highnesss will be very disappointed. He's offering a good price for it.'

'Well, that's not my concern. Why does he want it so much?'

'The Prince's buyer visited Christie's auction rooms at mid-day and found that the pair had been split up. His Highness was very put out. He wants the pair, you see, and at the moment he has only one. He sent me to search for it's twin.'

Angrily, she looked away, making it clear that knowledge of who had purchased the bureau was the very thing she had wished to avoid. Verne noted the angry flush and felt a moment of sympathy for this ravishing creature hiding herself away in this museum-like cavern with an ageing father and a heart growing cold with bitterness.

As if summoned by the butler, a well-dressed middle-aged lady appeared, entering from the hall with plenty of warning and looking from Annemarie to her visitor with a smile. One glance at the fair ringlets, the plump figure and the brightly rouged cheeks warned him that she was probably not one of the sisters.

'Cecily, my dear,' said Annemarie, 'allow me

to introduce Lord Verne. Mrs Cardew, my lord.
My father's cousin.'

'Ma'am.' This time, his bow received a smile
in return.

'My lord. You were hoping to meet Lord
Benistone? Oh dear. He's late.'

'I was hoping to find Lord Benistone *and* a
certain bureau, ma'am.'

Annemarie's quick frown would have cracked
a Greek urn, but it went unheeded. Mrs Cardew
preferred him not to leave without some discussion. She was never usually so blind to Annemarie's signals. 'Oh, *that*,' she said. 'What a pity
you've just missed it. It's just been loaded on to
the—'

'That's what I told his lordship,' said Annemarie, stepping in quickly to stem the verbal flow,
'that it's not here.'

'It's going down to Brighton, you see,' continued Mrs Cardew, brightly. 'It's for Lady Golding's personal use.'

'And it's not for sale. Now, if you'll excuse
me, my lord, I have things to do.'

'Ah, so it *was* here,' Verne said, determined to
persevere rather than be sent off with the flea in
his ear that Lady Golding had in mind for him.

'That is quite irrelevant, my lord,' said
Annemarie, sending him a withering look. 'I've
said it's not for sale. Naturally I am *mortified*
that his Royal Highness will be disappointed.

Indeed, I shall probably lose a week's sleep over it. I hope he soon recovers and finds something else he cannot live without. A diamond-studded horseshoe, for instance? A gold-plated handkerchief? A hair from the Great Chan's beard? Poor man. So much wealth to get rid of.'

'Annemarie, you must not say such things. Lord Verne and the Prince are sure to be close friends.'

'Yes, I imagine they must be if all they have to do is to chase round London after things they can't have.'

Taken aback by Annemarie's sharpness, Mrs Cardew responded to a sudden clatter in the hall that heralded the arrival of the one who could save a difficult situation: Lord Benistone himself. She went off to investigate.

Lord Verne, however, placed himself between the door of the morning room and Lady Golding. He'd be damned if he'd let her have the last word. His voice was little more than a growl meant for her ears alone, spoken while their eyes locked together like cold steel. 'I rarely chase after things I *can't* have, Lady Golding. When I see what I want, I pursue it. And I usually make it mine.'

She could be in no possible doubt about his meaning, which had nothing to do with the bureau. Her eyes read his, down to the last letter. 'Oh? With or without permission?' she said.

'Both,' he replied, watching her eyes flinch.

If his answer held a hint of ambiguity, he was certain she understood him well enough.

Her tongue was sharp, but not sharp enough to find a clever reply before the cousins returned, introductions were made, connections and interests defined. It was always a joy for Lord Benistone to find another man who shared his passion, and this man, working closely with the Prince Regent himself, had the best of credentials. Each had heard of the other.

Annemarie kept herself apart, fighting the temptation to run upstairs and shut herself away until he'd gone, her head echoing to his words, a statement of intent more than a challenge. After almost a twelvemonth, it was not what she needed to hear from any man hoping to find favour with her. Perhaps he believed that, after such a public disappointment, she would be desperate to regain her former standing in the fickle world of the *ton*, or that she was waiting for some bold knight to rescue a woman left desolate and pining. Nothing could be further from the truth. She wanted nothing any man had to offer, not even the nonsense about pursuing and owning. And for another thing, he was one of the Prince Regent's set, and that condemned him in her eyes as irrevocably as all the rest put together.

All the rest? That tall athletic presence, too?

The smooth doeskin breeches covering long muscular thighs, the matching waistcoat, under a creation that must have come from Weston of Old Bond Street, covering a deep chest. No padding or lacing there, she was certain of it. The impeccably arranged neckcloth and white cuffs, a single diamond pin and gold fob-watch on a fine chain were the kind of elegance that Mr Brummell advocated. Nothing to attract attention. That trend-setting gentleman, however, had no say over a man's physique or natural comeliness, and heaven knew she had seen enough men to know when one was several cuts above the rest. His long unmannerly stare had given her time to do the same and, although her scrutiny was not meant to approve, her reluctant conclusion was that his was the handsomest countenance she had ever seen.

She had also taken note of the ruthlessness there, too, the square chin and steel-grey eyes, the quick lift of his head when he'd sparred with her, determined not to be bested. His dark hair was a tangle of deep waves that had obviously resisted any attempt to tame it and there was a streak of white from his brow that disappeared into the rest, like foam on the sea. She had seen the manicured nails, the dusting of dark hairs on the backs of his strong hands, an unsettling detail that reminded her of how dangerous such a man could be.

Still, there was one comforting thought: he would not be getting her bureau for any price, so he might as well go quietly and leave her alone. As for Cecily's contribution, that was one of those annoying but forgivable mistakes, a result of her natural friendliness and her longing to re-establish Annemarie's connection with the *beau monde* that had been allowed to lapse.

This time, Cecily's enthusiasm was somewhat misplaced when she added her voice to Lord Benistone's invitation. 'Yes, indeed, my lord, *of course* you must dine with us. Miss Marguerite and I will be leaving for Lady Sindlesham's ball later on, but Lord Benistone loves nothing more than to hear who has acquired what. Annemarie, my dear, will you allow me to go and speak to cook?' A response seemed to be superfluous when Cecily was already halfway to the door, leaving Verne wondering exactly who was mistress here, Mrs Cardew or Lady Golding.

Cecily's unique position within the family caused such anomalies to happen occasionally. She meant well, but what annoyed Annemarie more was the almost indecently brisk acceptance by which the tenacious Lord Verne took advantage of her father's craving for men like himself to converse with. In no time at all, the two of them were away into Lord Benistone's inner sanctum, talking nineteen to the dozen as if they had known each other for years instead of minutes, all protests about not being properly dressed for dinner dismissed with a wave of the master's hand. 'No matter, dear boy. Neither shall I be. No time for that. Never have. Nobody minds here. Come and tell me if his Highness has a bronze like this.' And away they went without a backward glance, leaving Annemarie fuming at her own impotence.

Somebody *did* mind. *She* did. She preferred it if people dressed for dinner. What else would they dress for if not for the evening? She could hardly blame her father for latching on to a man so closely involved with the Prince Regent's treasures, but she knew that *this* man had come here for something he was sure he could get, one way or another. And Lord Benistone was such a generous and obliging man, far too willing to say yes because it took less effort than to say no. With the latter, explanations were usually needed.

After their acrimonious introduction, it would have been quite unrealistic for Lord Verne to expect anything from Lady Golding except a polite frostiness, which is exactly what she delivered, even though etiquette demanded that they sat next to each other. Obviously, she was not inclined to exert herself for his sake, but no one seemed to notice when the youngest sister

was intent on making enough effort for both of
them with her girlish chatter.

Dressed in her white ballgown, the young lady
looked astonishingly pretty with dark brown
curls framing features that, in another year or
two, would become more classically beautiful,
though never as stunning as her sister. She did
not possess anything like Lady Golding's intelligence or depth either, her eagerness to please reminding Verne of a puppy that went into raptures
at the sight of an audience. Especially a male audience. The eldest sister, Miss Oriel Benistone,
was dining out that evening so he was not able
to compare the siblings further, but the father
and his cousin kept up a stream of conversation
between them that made Lady Golding's studied
silence seem piquant to Verne. Even enjoyable.
It was some time since he'd met such tangible
hostility and never from a lovely woman. The
situation was intriguing, all the more so when
his brief was to get results at all costs.

Inevitably, the conversation turned to the
elusive bureau wanted by the Prince Regent for
Carlton House, the ongoing renovations of which
were so much over budget that he was having
to petition Parliament for extra funds for their
completion. Miss Marguerite Benistone aired
the question her father was too polite to ask.
'Doesn't the Prince have enough funds of his
own, Lord Verne?'

Verne smiled indulgently at her. 'His Highness never has enough funds. The Pavilion at Brighton is another half-finished project costing huge sums in improvement and decoration.'

'Not to mention,' said Annemarie, unexpectedly, 'the cost of entertaining the crowned heads of Europe this summer after a war that has drained the country of every spare penny. No wonder Lady Hamilton is having to sell her effects to make ends meet. We shall all be doing the same if his Highness insists on covering the rooftops of his Pavilion with fancy Indian domes.'

'You don't approve of the Prince, I take it?' said Verne, goading her.

Before she could answer, Mrs Cardew stepped smartly into the breach. 'Ah, but think of all those celebrations in the parks since Bonaparte was taken into custody, all the dances and routs, all the returning militia to entertain. Did you serve in the King's army, my lord?'

'Until a few months ago, ma'am. I was in the Peninsula Wars with the Prince of Wales's Own Regiment.' He knew that would only confirm Lady Golding's assumption that, as one of the Prince Regent's cronies, he was sure to be as unprincipled as the rest of them. The 10th Hussars were best known for glamour, wealth, women, drinking and riotous behaviour, amongst other things. The knowledge would do nothing to

endear him to her, he was sure. Idly, he wondered where Mrs Cardew stood in the scheme of
things. Did she live here with Lord Benistone as
dedicated chaperon, or was she simply an obliging cousin? Would it be worth cultivating her
help to get what he wanted? He touched his forehead just below the white streak. 'I have found
that making a study of antiquity is safer than
pursuing angry Frenchmen.'

'Oh,' said Marguerite, 'but you must know
how *all* English ladies simply hero-worship
Napoleon Bonaparte, Lord Verne. Such a stern,
scowling face must send goose-pimples…what?
Oh!' A look from her father, and Mrs Cardew's
gentle hand on her arm, stopped the gushing
tribute in mid-flow as she directed her limpid
brown eyes towards Annemarie's stony expression. 'Oh…yes, of course. Sorry, Annemarie.'

With the slightest shake of her head, Annemarie dismissed the gaffe without explaining its significance to Lord Verne. But Verne had already
made the connection, during his two hours with
Lord Benistone, that Annemarie was the widow
of Sir Richard Golding, one of Wellington's best
officers, killed by French sniper fire early in
1812. Married less than a year and known to
everyone as a brilliant man, his death had been
a great loss. Her grief must have been terrible,
but obviously not enough to penetrate the con-
sciousness of her younger sister.

Grasping at any subject of mutual interest, Lord Benistone reverted to buying and selling. 'So this bureau you're after, Verne. How much did you say his Highness is prepared to pay for it?'

'No, Father!' said Annemarie before Verne could reply. 'It belongs to me, remember? It's not for sale. Not at any price. If his Highness wants a pair, he can easily have one made to match and, in any case, if he's as short of money as all that, he ought not to be offering to buy an expensive piece of furniture, ought he?'

Her father, blinking in guilt at his daughter's pertinent reminder, gestured vaguely with his dessert spoon 'Well then, there you are, Verne. If you want to get to the bureau, you'll have to get to Annemarie first, eh?' The shocked uncomfortable silence lasted for what seemed like an eternity until, to ease the embarrassment, he continued. 'I was speaking in jest, of course. The bureau will be on its way to Brighton first thing in the morning and so will Annemarie. His Highness will have to find something else, won't he?'

Mrs Cardew's contribution, meant to ease the tension, did not have quite the desired effect. 'Lady Golding's other home is in Brighton, you see,' she told Verne, who had seen that some time ago and had been thinking ever since how strange it was that he'd never met her there. 'She does not care for the London crowds.'

'I think you need not explain for me, Cecily dear,' said Annemarie. 'Lord Verne has more important matters to occupy his mind than where I choose to spend my time. May we drop the subject now and talk of something else?'

But her father's idea of dropping a subject was not hers. 'Look here, Annemarie. What was I saying to you only today about travelling all that way on your own? Eh? Now why don't we ask Verne to accompany you, just to keep an eye on things?'

'No, Father! Absolutely not! I prefer my own company, thank you.'

Lord Benistone heaved a sigh, waved his spoon again like a white flag of surrender and plunged it into his baked apple and clotted cream. 'No, of course not,' he said. 'What am I thinking of? Verne will be tied up with the Prince's business from morn till night. A busy time for you, young man.' The spoonful disappeared into his mouth and the conversation swung away smoothly to less contentious matters concerning the mammoth task of accommodating the European royals, some of whom had other ideas about staying with the Prince Regent whose interminable meals bored them to tears.

It was no hardship to Verne to feed delectable snippets of harmless royal gossip to fasci-

nated ladies and, although the one who interested
him most refused to respond, the pleasure he de-
rived from sitting beside her lifted the exercise
to a different level, knowing that she listened,
weaving him into her own thoughts. She would
be thinking, naturally, that he was ingratiating
himself with her father in order to obtain the bureau through him. In her present defensive mode,
seething with resentment and distrust of men,
she would be planning how to shake him off,
how to keep him at a distance, how to strengthen
the shield that guarded her damaged heart which,
after a death and a desertion in the space of two
years, would still be aching, to say the least.

He could try the leisured approach, but that
would take more time than he had. Then there
was the other kind, more of a risk, intended to
unsettle her, to provoke her into doing something
rash and to remind her that she was desirable.
The choice was easy.

Once the meal was over, Mrs Cardew and
Marguerite took their leave of the company, giving Verne the chance to make his excuses also.
In the deserted hall, he lingered to speak alone
with Annemarie, who had watched her father's
retreat with barely concealed alarm. His blunt
question was intended to catch her off-guard,
though it was less than successful. 'You are still
annoyed with me, my lady? For coming to your

table in my topboots, or for pursuing my duty to the Prince Regent?'

'Your duty, my lord, appears to have been pursued with some tenacity. What his Highness will say when you return empty-handed I refuse to speculate. That's *your* problem, not mine. As for the boots…' she looked down at the twinkle of candles on the immaculate leather '…I suppose one must be thankful they're not covered in mud.'

'Your father assured me I would be excused, my lady.'

'My father would find an excuse for a fox eating his best hen, my lord. He obligingly believes his code is good enough for the rest of us. He's never needed to justify anything he does, which can be endearing, but at other times not so.'

'Then I can only apologise. I could easily have gone to change. My home is in Bedford Square, only a five-minute walk away.'

'So close? I did not realise.'

'Or you might have insisted? Well, if I'd realised who lived only a five-minute walk away from *me*, my lady, I would have called here months ago.'

'On what pretext? To find something else his Highness cannot live without?'

'No. This.'

His move towards her was too fast for her to see or avoid and before she could step backwards, his hand was gripping through the short frill that sufficed for a sleeve, his other hand slipping round to the back of her neck, bringing her mouth to his for a searching kiss that went far beyond a polite farewell. She was too astonished to protest or retaliate before the softness of her beautiful mouth gave way under his. Her hand came up to push at his shoulder, but by then it was too late. He had timed it to perfection. He prepared himself to catch the blow she would be sure to aim at his head , but it did not come. Her eyelids flickered before opening wide like windows to send out a fierce glare of concentrated fury then, with one hand to her mouth, she turned and whirled away towards the staircase, almost colliding with the butler who had come to pass him his hat and gloves before letting him out.

Chapter Two

Lord Verne had not been exaggerating when he'd told Annemarie that his home on Bedford Square was only a five-minute walk away but, striding out with some urgency, he managed it in three-and-a-half. Taking the curving staircase two steps at a time, his coat, breeches and vest were in a heap on the bed before Samson, his valet, arrived to assist, showing not the slightest surprise at his master's decision to go out again immediately, wearing evening dress. After eleven years in Lord Verne's service, Samson had become used to the mercurial changes of direction, plans made and unmade, instructions implied rather than specified. His master was to attend a ball, that much was clear, though hardly a word was exchanged between them.

Lady Sindlesham's house in Mayfair was not unfamiliar to Verne. On that night, it was transformed for the benefit of her royal guests, and others, who had cause to be thankful that General Bonaparte was at last in safe custody. With one ear tuned over the general hum to the rise and fall of various European languages, Verne chatted to his hostess, nodded and bowed to the foreign dignitaries and their wives who sparkled and shimmered beneath twinkling chandeliers while his sharp eyes sought out his employer, the Prince of Wales, who had been appointed Regent three years ago during his father's serious illness. Verne sauntered across to meet him, awaiting the royal attention. Then, a few quiet words, a smile and a nod, a gentle pat on the shoulder from the pudgy royal fingers, and Verne moved away again, this time to ascertain the whereabouts of a certain Mrs Cecily Cardew with whom he had dined only that evening. Biding his time until young Marguerite Benistone had been drawn into the set by a uniformed Prussian officer, he approached as if quite by chance and, with an impeccable bow, took the lady's jewel-laden hand in his. 'Mrs Cardew, what a delight. Such a crush.'

Her surprise was only to be expected, but she concealed it well behind a quick survey of the immaculate long-tailed coat, white vest and knee-breeches that Lady Golding would have preferred to have seen earlier. 'Lord Verne, you've just missed her. Look, there she is. Over

there.' She waved an outsized feathered fan towards Marguerite and Verne caught the ice-blue
flash of diamonds on Mrs Cardew's ear-drops
that almost reached her shoulders.

'Enchanting,' he replied. 'May I procure a
glass of punch for you?'

She knew at once that this was not a chance
meeting. 'Might be a little dangerous with so
many jostling elbows. I expect you know most
of these people, my lord?'

Her silver-grey gown rippled softly as he led
the way to a covered long seat between two massive curtains where tassels hung as big as chim-
ney pots from cords like ships' hawsers. As they
sat, she inclined her head towards him as if she
knew the reason why he'd sought her out immediately after his briefing from the Prince Regent.
Here was a man she could trust, at last, an ally in
her quest to bring some light into Annemarie's
shadowy life. Mrs Cardew missed little that went
on around her. Even now, Marguerite's every
move was being monitored.

'Many, not most,' Verne said. 'Sindy's good
at this kind of thing, isn't she?'

'She's had plenty of practice.' Realising how
that might sound, she shot him a mischievous
blue-eyed smile. 'Oh, I don't mean it that way.
Sindy and I are old friends. Her granddaugh-
ters are Miss Marguerite's age. They go about

together, you know. That's why she was so determined to be here.'

'Or she would have gone down to Brighton
with her sister?'

'Oh, I doubt that very much, my lord. There's
too much going on in London this year. Marguerite would never miss all that just to keep
Annemarie company. It's perfectly understand-
able. She came out only last year and the purpose
of that is to make contacts, not to hide oneself
away…'

'In Brighton?' Verne said, stepping into the
pause.

Cecily's sigh could hardly be detected over
the music. 'You were away when all that happened,' she said, 'or you'd have known about it.
Most people have put it quite out of mind now,
after a whole year, but Annemarie believes it
has ruined her, you see. To her, it's still happening, in a way.'

Verne decided to take the bull by the horns,
time being in short supply. 'Apart from yourself,
ma'am,' he said, 'there is no one else I would ask
and, even now, I am aware that an event such as
this is hardly the time or place to be discussing
such matters. But…'

'But perhaps it's better to hear uncomfortable things at first hand rather than the embel-
lished accounts of others. Don't you agree? At
least then you'll be in possession of the facts

before you…well, I was going to say before you begin manoeuvres, but that sounds rather too military. Annemarie may have fallen short of her duties as hostess this evening, but that's not to say she was unaffected by your presence. I've never known her use the wrong knife to butter her bread roll before.'

'Slender evidence of regard, Mrs Cardew.'

'I know, but it's in the eyes too, isn't it? Hers *and* yours.'

'Mmm,' he said. 'So may I ask what *did* happen, ma'am?'

'Indeed. You may already have heard that Lady Benistone was once a very lovely and successful courtesan. Well before your time, young man.'

At thirty-two, Verne could recognise an older woman's kindly flattery when he heard it. 'I had heard something to that effect,' he said.

'She was twenty-two years her husband's junior. I say *was*, but of course she still is. We don't know where she is. Even your employer, before he became Regent, pursued her without success. Lord Benistone kept her in some style and eventually she agreed to marry him. The trouble was…' she said, lowering her voice.

'Please don't continue if you'd rather not. I shall understand.'

'The trouble was…well, you've seen how things are there, haven't you? It's no kind of mess to keep a lovely woman and their three daughters in. She was a top-drawer courtesan, so you can imagine how she felt. Collecting was, and still is, my cousin's passion. He's not going to change now. No shortage of money. He's always been able to buy anything he wanted.'

'Including his wife.'

'Even Esme Gerard. And she loved him, too. But only for so long. He gives his entire attention to his collection and then wonders why he's lost the only woman he ever loved. Everyone can see it but him, although I think he's coming to realise his failings more now. Lovely man. Wrong priorities.'

'It's not uncommon, ma'am.'

'Unfortunately, it's not. Lady Golding... Annemarie...was widowed only a year when it happened. Not long out of mourning and being courted by a smooth-tongued young rake who promised her the world.'

'Sir Lionel Mytchett.'

'Yes, him. And if her father had taken the trouble to investigate him, he'd have seen what was happening. The young blackguard! Playing on her emotions.' Cecily's voice lowered again, this time in anger. 'Wooed her for close on three months and led her to believe he was about to make an offer for her.'

'So she was in love with him?'

The pretty fair curls shook in denial, but the

reply was less certain. 'Who knows? I believe it was too soon after Richard. I believe she was probably more in love with the idea of being a married woman than with Mytchett himself. I had offered to hold Miss Marguerite's coming-out ball at Park Lane. Well, they couldn't possibly have held it at Montague Street and I'd done the same for Annemarie's wedding. What none of us had quite appreciated was the growing attraction Mytchett had developed for Lady Benistone and what *I* think,' she said, emphasising her own interpretation of events, 'is that he'd seen in the mother something he could get without bothering to marry the daughter, if you see what I mean.'

Verne nodded. Mytchett was just the kind to take advantage of that situation. What a pity Lord Benistone had not looked after his family better.

'Annemarie,' Cecily continued, 'was a twenty-three-year-old widow and Esme was as eager as she was to get away from Montague Street and live a normal kind of life. That's what they both wanted, but it was less troublesome for him to take Esme than Annemarie. They disappeared at Miss Marguerite's ball. He knew exactly what he was doing, but I doubt very much whether Esme had thought it through. She's a creature of impulse, is Esme, like Annemarie was before this happened.'

'A double loss,' said Verne, watching Marguerite smile into her partner's eyes.

'A triple loss, my lord. Husband, beau and mother. She's become embittered. She won't allow her friends near and won't socialise at all. Rejection is a terrible thing. It changes perfectly delightful people into avengers.'

'It's clear she wants nothing to do with men, after that.'

'I'm afraid so. Any man hoping to make an impression on Annemarie will have to be very patient, with no guarantee of success. But if you would like some advice on the matter, my lord…?'

'Anything you can offer, Mrs Cardew.'

'Then you might begin by finding the mother,' she said so quietly that Verne had to lip-read. 'I doubt very much whether Lady Benistone would stay long with that scoundrel and I would not be surprised to learn that she'd already left him, though I cannot imagine how she'll live without support. Women like Esme are not good at that, you know. And the family are miserable without her. All of them.'

Again, Verne's attention was drawn to the swirling figure of Marguerite, her happy smile and arms outstretched to her partner. 'So you don't think Lady Benistone would return uninvited?' he said.

Cecily's sideways glance was full of forbearance, as if only a man could ask such a question. 'Pride, my lord. That's a terrible thing, too. It stops people doing what they ought to do and it makes them do things they shouldn't.' For the last closing bars of the music, Cecily's sad conclusion was left unanswered. 'Ah,' she said, 'the dance has ended. 'Shall you stand up with her before you leave, my lord? We'd take it as a great favour.'

Obediently, and without a trace of reluctance, Verne rose to his feet, understanding that he would be expected to pay for the help he'd just been given. 'Indeed I will, ma'am. It will be my pleasure.'

'And I shall be happy to receive you at Park Lane, my lord.'

'You are more than kind, Mrs Cardew. I shall take up your invitation.'

Two hours later, he was back in Bedford Square with a head too full of information to say much to Samson except that they'd be going down to Brighton tomorrow.

'Very good, m'lord. Marine Pavilion, is it?'

Grunt.

'Will it be the curricle or the phaeton, m'lord?'

'Oh, don't ask so many damned stupid questions at this time of night, man. I'll decide in the morning.'

'Certainly, m'lord. Only…you see…one trunk fits best on the curricle and the other fits on—'

'Prepare me a bath. I need to think.'

'Pleasant ball, was it?'

The deeply expressive groan warned Samson
that he had ventured too far and, being usually so
responsive to his master's every whim, saw that
he had better produce the required bath without
delay and in silence.

Soaking in the hot water by candlelight, Verne
watched the clusters of swirling soap bubbles
while trying to connect the day's events right up
until the dance with Miss Marguerite Benistone,
which he would normally have deemed too expensive a payment by half had he not discovered
so much from her chaperon to make it worth his
while. Miss Marguerite's cup had truly runneth
over when his friend George Brummell came
to the rescue. He had taken some persuading
to keep the girl occupied and Verne had had
to promise him another hefty 'loan'. The Lady
Benistone saga fitted in with what he'd heard,
but to have the approval and assistance of Mrs
Cecily Cardew, a member of the family and self-
appointed fairy godmother, had given him an advantage he needed in his pursuit of the avenging
angel from whom he'd stolen a kiss that evening.

Cecily would not have been too surprised to
learn that her cousin's wife, Lady Benistone, had
already left the scoundrel with whom she disap-

peared last year during Marguerite's coming-out ball, having discussed what they had discovered about his character and motives beforehand, though not the plans that Lady Benistone had devised to avert a disaster. Or so she thought. But never in her darkest dreams could Cecily have imagined the circumstances in which the flight would take place for, if she had, she would have stopped Esme from taking matters into her own hands. In Cecily's mind, Esme Benistone, with her experience of men, knew how to look after herself and, if she was less than competent in her understanding of financial affairs, she more than made up for it in her understanding of men. Even a confirmed bachelor like Lord Benistone, all those years ago, had lost his heart to her and she to him, to everyone's astonishment.

Last summer, Esme Benistone had devised a scheme, which she had kept to herself, for luring Sir Lionel Mytchett away from her daughter. The greedy young fool was not hard to persuade that he was beloved by an older woman with a great deal of ready money. He had found her promises easy to believe. Relying on past experience, Esme had been convinced she could keep him in a state of anticipation for at least a week while she arranged with her bank for the release of the money she had once earned, which her generous husband had never drawn upon. It had accrued a quite considerable interest over the years. However, after the third attempt to negotiate a release, she was told that although the money was legally hers, she could not access it without her husband's permission, a serious hitch in her plans that upset Sir Lionel. Esme could hardly be surprised by his anger, but she had not expected anything like the terrible repercussions of his rage.

'You *what*?' he had snarled at her as she returned to their lodgings. 'What d'ye mean, couldn't get at it? Why not? It's yours, isn't it? Isn't that what you told me?'

Lady Benistone sighed. This was going to be difficult. They had been together less than a week, uncomfortable days during which she had used all her sexual allure to keep him sweet without actually letting him have what he thought would be his with very little effort. Now, she would have to bring her plan forwards. She was many years his senior and was not used to being snarled at. 'Lower your voice, if you please,' she said, coldly, removing her hat and pelisse. 'I told you we could use my funds, yes, but I was mistaken. We can't. Mr Treen at the bank was quite adamant that, without Lord Benistone's written permission, he cannot release the money. Somehow, we shall have to manage without it.' Even as she spoke the empty words, she knew the impossibility of managing, her intention from the very beginning having been to pay him off, then return to her family with what to her was a convincing reason for her uncharacteristic behaviour. And if Elmer had made time to listen to her concerns, none of this would have been necessary. He would have sent the deceitful creature packing as any father would and Annemarie could have begun again to rebuild her life with someone more worthy of her.

'Manage?' he yelled. 'How are we supposed to manage, your ladyship? I've been relying on you for this and now you tell me… God's truth, woman! If I'd known…'

'Don't use such oaths to me, Sir Lionel. I'll not hear it. You have no idea how foolish you look when you're in a childish temper. I've put up with you in this dreadful little place for almost a week now and I think that's probably as much as I can take. And, yes, if you'd known my funds were tied up, you'd not have been interested, would you? You'd have kept to safer ground with my daughter. You have sold my jewellery and chosen to gamble with the proceeds when we might have been safely in France by now. Well, your luck runs out rather too fast for my comfort.'

Anyone could have understood the ease with which Annemarie had fallen for Mytchett's suave good looks, his perfect manners and easy charm, his stylish dress, his talk of possessions and connections. Lord Benistone had been too

preoccupied to make thorough investigations
that would have verified, or not, his claims. In
a rage, however, Sir Lionel was frighteningly
unattractive, noisy and threatening, and Esme
Benistone realised too late that she had just revealed her intentions as she had not meant to do.
She could have slipped away while he was out.
But not now.

She saw the understanding dawn behind his
eyes, at first a blankness like an abacus before
the beads start to count, before the payment
takes shape, before the final reckoning. Even
then, she did not guess what form this would
take. Not once had she anticipated the danger
in which she had placed herself. As Lady Benistone, an aristocrat, she was due every respect.
This time, she had miscalculated.

She had tried many times since then to forget
what happened during the next half-hour, but
without success. Physical violence was quite outside her experience and, although fear lent her
an extra strength, it was not enough to prevent
his determined and brutal assault from reaching
its appalling conclusion. With a hand clamped
over her mouth she could make no one hear her
and she was forced into a helplessness so painful
that, when he released her, her stomach revolted
too. Before he left, his words were intended to
be as wounding and as insulting as his attack,
hurled at her as revenge for misfired plans, un-

lined pockets and the exposure of his baseness. He would make sure, he told her, that she paid the full price for finding him out, if not with money, then with shame.

Left alone at last, it took her some time to gather herself together sufficiently to stand, in a daze of pain, and to look for some way of washing herself. To go upstairs was impossible and she must get away quickly before his return so, still trembling and sobbing, she covered her torn clothing with her pelisse, tucked her hair inside her hat and pulled down the veil. With painful slowness, she left the house unnoticed and staggered to the end of the street from where, eventually, she was able to summon a hansom cab. 'Manchester Square,' she called up to the cabbie.

'You alright, ma'am?' he said, kindly. 'Nasty headache?'

'No,' she whispered, 'but drive carefully.'

'Right-ho, ma'am. Just leave it to me. Climb inside.'

Managing the steps into the cab was almost beyond her, but the kind man waited before clucking to his horse and, on arrival at Manchester Square, was concerned enough to climb down from his perch and help her out. It was then that Esme fainted in his arms, attracting the attention of a primly dressed lady's maid who was about to turn into the basement gate of the nearest mansion. 'Why, that's Lady Benistone, isn't it?' she said.

'Dunno, miss. She said to bring her here. But this looks like the Marquess of Hertford's place, if I'm not mistaken.'

'It is,' said the young lady. 'Be so good as to carry her ladyship in, will you?'

Annemarie told herself that Verne's kiss had meant nothing, really, except the annoyance of a thwarted man. Yes, that was what it was about. Annoyance and to pay her back for her rudeness as a hostess when she ought to have shown more courtesy to her father's guest. As for that non-sense of pursuing what he wanted...well...that was soldier's talk. Too many years in the army and too little opposition from women. That was the problem with his sort. Hardly worth getting upset about.

She threw her slippers into one of the leather trunks, but Evie gave a sigh and patiently took them out again. 'You'll be wearing these, m'lady, not packing them,' she said. 'Why not just leave the packing to me? Shall I bring you a nice warm drink?'

Regarding the piles of linens and silks, the shoes and chemisettes, the velvet pelisses and muslin day-dresses, Annemarie was unable to assemble any of the outfits while her mind still seethed with indignation. 'Yes,' she said. 'It's getting late and I'm not helping, am I?' Throwing herself on to the *chaise-longue*, she made use of Evie's absence to hear again his crisp, 'No. This', and to feel his hard demanding fingers pressing into her arm and neck, taking her too much by surprise to escape as fast as she could have done. As she *ought* to have done. Words like 'churl' and 'lout' faded against the sensation of the kiss and once again she was making comparisons like a silly untutored schoolgirl while pressing a cushion against her breast.

During the six hours it took to reach Brighton, it would be less than the truth to say that she had banished the incident from her mind, having little else to occupy her. But her father need not have feared her being alone when she had her maid, two coachmen, grooms and footmen with her, some of whom would take the coaches back to London. A few stops to change horses, to take a light luncheon, and by evening they were amongst the wheeling, yelping seagulls, by which time she had examined the incident from every angle and at every tollgate and inn. Knowing how her father was quite capable of arranging an escort whether she wanted one or not, her eyes had surreptitiously searched for a physique that might resemble Lord Verne's, but thankfully, she need not have bothered.

The sight of her own pretty house lifted her

spirits even more than the blustering wind and the grey-blue expanse of sea. This was the place bought for her and Richard by Lord Benistone to use as a retreat, which she had decided to keep as a useful second home. Too close to the Steyne for her taste, it had been perfect for Richard who liked to be in the centre of things and, situated on the corner of South Parade, there were good views from the large windows.

Annemarie was right about Brighton being deserted during the London celebrations—the area of open lawn between the house and the Marine Pavilion was only thinly scattered with the summer colours of muslin gowns and bright uniforms. A few doors away, Raggett's Men's Club seemed strangely quiet, and Donaldson's Library across the road was almost forsaken. It suited her well enough. She decided to pay a visit there tomorrow.

The cook, housekeeper and maids had been at the house for three days already to remove dust covers, make beds and prepare food, so the rooms were welcoming and well aired, flowers in bowls, hot water, the lingering scent of polish and scrubbed floors. After the heavy clutter of Montague Street, the pale prettiness of her patterned walls, the delicacy of the furniture and the fabrics reflecting sunshine and sea were like a breath of fresh air filling her lungs with a new freedom. She went from room to room to greet

all the familiar feminine things that her father
would certainly not have looked at twice. Nor
would Richard, had he ever seen them.

She realised at once that the new bureau would
be too large to fit comfortably in her cosy bedroom, but after some rearrangement, a space was
made for it in an alcove by the chimney-breast as
she experienced an unaccountable wave of pos-
sessiveness that recalled Lord Benistone's blunder about Lord Verne having to get to her first.
Until the bureau arrived, there would be plenty
to keep her occupied, things she had stopped
doing in London in case she met someone who
knew her. It was their sympathy she could not
bear. Revenge was what she wanted, not pity.
Any kind of revenge would do as long as it hurt.

On the next day, sooner than expected, the bureau arrived and, after hours of tipping and tilting, trapped fingers, muffled oaths and doubts,
the heavy piece was fitted into the space she had
made for it. Lady Hamilton's rooms at Merton
Place, she thought, must have been vast to ac-
commodate two of these easily. But that evening, all alone, she took the brass key from her
toilette case and inserted it into the beautifully
decorated keyhole on the long drawer above the
knee-space, imagining how Lady Hamilton and
her lover, Lord Nelson, would have stood to look
at themselves in the mirror under the lid that

now stood upright. At each side of the mirror were the sections that had intrigued her most in Christie's saleroom, a maze of polished compartments holding ceramic pots and cut-glass bottles with silver tops, ivory-and-tortoiseshell brushes and combs, hand mirrors and silver scissors, ornately inlaid trinket boxes, slender perfume bottles with the fragrances still clinging to the glass. The Prince Regent had its twin and, in most respects, the two were identical except that this was the one made for a lady, which is why she had chosen it.

The mania for Lord Nelson memorabilia had gripped the country in the years since his death at Trafalgar in 1805, and even after nine years there were collectors who would pay well for any of his personal possessions, even a shaving brush. Perhaps, she wondered, that was why the Prince Regent was so keen to acquire his furniture. Or was it more to do with Lady Hamilton, with whom he'd once been infatuated, even while her husband and her lover both lived? Neither of the men had approved of the royal obsession, although since their deaths, Lady Hamilton had found it necessary to keep well in with the royal family in the hope of financial help that never came. The Prince's disloyalty to his friends was as notorious as his appalling fashion sense.

In the fading light, Annemarie sat before her newest acquisition to unscrew tops and guess at the contents and marvel at the craftsmanship, the details, the coloured inlays, swags and festoons, gilded handles and key-plates. At one side of the centre was a neat hole where a long brass pin could be inserted to hold the lower drawer in place when the lid was locked. Having taken a cursory look into the drawer only to find an odd glove and a few empty silk reels for mending, she tried to close it before replacing the pin in its hole. Obviously she had disturbed some other fragment, for it refused to close.

Bending to look inside, she slid her fingers deep into the recess at the back of the drawer, easing it out further and discovering that the back panel was hinged to lie flat, concealing an extra compartment. Then, lowering her head to the same level, she caught sight of shadowy bundles tied with ribbon like miniature piles of laundered sheets in the linen cupboard, so flat and uniform that she knew they must be letters. She pressed one pile, releasing the one that had snagged on the woodwork above.

Her first instinct was to leave them where they were, for she had no right to read what Lord Nelson had written to the woman he loved. No one had. But curiosity lured her hand reluctantly inside to draw out first one bundle, then the next, until there were eight of them balancing on top of the silver stoppers, releasing an aroma of old paper and the acrid smell of attar of roses. Instantly, she was reminded of a visit to Carlton House with Richard to meet the Prince of Wales at his inauguration as Regent, where the cloying perfume had made her head reel. Richard had told her later that it was the prince's snuff. 'No taste,' he had remarked. 'Not even in snuff.'

Even then, she failed to connect him with these letters, being so certain of Lord Nelson's involvement, especially after the furor of a few weeks ago, in April to be exact, when his personal letters to Lady Hamilton had been published in book form by the *Herald*, causing the most embarrassing scandal. Few people would have missed the storm that followed, the mass gorging upon every salacious detail of their passion and the inevitable condemnation of the woman who, it was assumed, had sold them to pay off her enormous debts. Few believed her insistence that they had been stolen from her by a so-called friend who was writing a life of Nelson, at her request. Those who knew her better were sure of her innocence, although few had rushed to her defence, and certainly not the influential Prince Regent who professed to adore her and regularly took advantage of her generous hospitality. If these letters were more of the same, Lady Hamilton had kept them well away from ill-intentioned servants and had then forgotten about them in one of her removals to temporary addresses and the sale rooms. Poor unfortunate woman indeed, she thought, turning over one of the bundles to look at the back. It was sealed with a coronet, as aristocrats did. Delivered by hand. No postmark or address. Only the name, Lady Emma Hamilton.

Flipping a thumb across the crisp folded edges, Annemarie reminded herself that, for all she knew, they could be perfectly innocent and not worth returning, though the stale perfume warned her of a different explanation. So she slid off the faded ribbon and unfolded the first letter with a crackle, turning it round to find the greeting, once so personal, then the foot of the page, whispering words never meant to be heard out loud. *Your ever devoted and loving.... Prinny.*

Her hand flew to cover the words on her lips, hardly daring to believe what she was reading. *Prinny* was what the Prince Regent's closest friends called him.

These were *his* letters to *Emma Hamilton.*

Private. Scandalous. Priceless.

The significance of the discovery was both frightening and exciting as, one by one, Annemarie slipped off the ribbons to release the dozens of intimate love letters, all the same size, paper, ink and handwriting with the flourishing signature of effusive endearments: beloved, eternal friend, adoring servant, always your own, Prinny. The greetings were equally extravagant. Dearest Muse. My Own Persephone. Most Heavenly Spirit, and so on. Repetitive, unoriginal and maudlin, sentiments that roused her fury that here again was a lover whose flowery words failed to match his actions, whose promises were empty and worthless. Lady Hamilton must by now have realised that her letters were lost, that someone somewhere would find and read them, and could use them to blacken her name further, and that if they were indeed made public like the Nelson letters, she could expect to be cut out of the royals' lives for ever without any hope of help.

She began to refold them, tying them back into bundles. And yet, she thought, surely it would be the Prince Regent himself who would look like the villain if ever these were made public. Despite his protestations of enduring love and friendship, it was common knowledge that he'd refused to offer any help since the death of Lord Nelson, even refusing to petition Parliament to grant her a pension, using the excuse that she had not lawfully been Nelson's wife. Having abused her friendship and ignored her vulnerability without a protector, he had offered nothing in return. More than likely he would become a laughing-stock to the whole nation just as he was acting host to all the European heads of state, all through the summer. With letters like these in the public domain, what would be his chances of getting Parliament to vote him more funds for his building projects, his banquets and lavish entertainments? Virtually none. No small wonder he'd sent a trusted friend to retrieve the bureau where his letters were kept which, for all he knew, might still be undiscovered by the purchaser. Herself.

It was not difficult to understand how the Prince could know where Lady Hamilton kept her correspondence. The *Herald* had often reported with some malice how, at her wild parties lasting for days, her guests had access to all her rooms at any time. She and the Prince had not been lovers, by all accounts, but he would have known her bedroom as intimately as all her other friends, to talk, watch her at her *toilette*, flirt and drink. He would know of her famed carelessness, her disorganisation, her hoarding of gifts and her generosity. Why else would he have dispatched Lord Verne so quickly to find the other bureau and to buy it at any price once he'd discovered that its twin was not the one he wanted? And why else would Lord Verne have attached himself to Lord Benistone like a leech until he could find a way to worm himself into his daughter's favour? That was the plan. She was sure of it. The only way of saving dear Prinny from utter disgrace. He had already made a start and Annemarie had unobligingly removed herself by some sixty miles. Yet another reason for his annoyance.

The feeling of power that washed over her in those moments of discovery was difficult to convey. The almost sensual realisation that revenge was, literally, in her hands. At any time, she could do enormous damage to that irresponsible, immature fifty-two-year-old heir to the throne without morals or principles, who could turn his back on a woman he professed to adore and refuse to help. Epitomising everything she had learned to despise about men, he would be the perfect target for her retribution. At the same time, she could give what she got for the letters to Lady Hamilton to lend some dignity to her retirement, to help her and her young daughter find a new life away from her predatory family. How ironic would that be, she thought, to refund her in money what the prince had withdrawn in support? She fell back upon her bed, breathless with euphoric laughter and the heady feeling of control, wishing she had made the discovery in London instead of here, for then she could have taken them straight to a publisher to broker a deal without delay.

Later, in the peace of the night when she had listened to the distant swish of the incoming tide, she rose and, wrapping a shawl around her shoulders, sat before the bureau where the stacks of letters made a shockingly silent threat until she could choose a moment to let the cat among the pigeons. The full moon washed across the silk damask-covered walls, its white stillness somehow commending a safer and less contentious option that would place the responsibility where by rights it ought to be, with Lady Hamilton herself. Annemarie ought to take them to her, as the owner, and explain. Let her do with them whatever she pleased, for if the blame from the previous scandal could be heaped on Lady Hamilton, as it had been, then surely this could be, too, if the letters were published. Some of the blame would certainly damage his Royal Highness, but there would be others only too ready to ruin Lady Hamilton even further, and to what purpose? The likelihood of her ever being freed from scandal would be small. Annemarie's own selfish motives must be put aside. The choice could not be hers.

Pulling out her old leather portmanteau, only recently emptied, she stashed the bundles inside and fastened the catch, deciding to take them back to London as soon she could. Mr Parke at Christie's would know of Lady Hamilton's whereabouts. She climbed back into bed, shaking her head in amusement at her father's absurdly unthinking gaffe about having to get at Annemarie first, and wondering how long it would be before she could expect to see Lord Verne here in Brighton about his master's sordid business. For some reason, the challenge disturbed her rest and the first crying of the seagulls had begun before her imaginings were laid to rest.

Annemarie's last visit to Brighton had been in the preceding autumn, since when spring had struggled out of a protracted winter worse than most people could remember. Even in June, the gardens surrounding the Steyne were only just recovering and the continuing alterations to the Prince's Marine Pavilion were nowhere near complete, mainly through lack of funds and because he changed his mind every time he saw it. Sprouting the same scaffolding and heaps of building materials, it was attended by the same unhurried workmen with time to stare at every passable female who came close enough. Behind the Pavilion, the Indian-style dome that had received her sharp criticism sat like a glittering half-onion on top of the Prince's stables, the palatial building designed to house his riding, carriage and race horses at a cost that would have fed London's starving and homeless for the rest of their lives. Not to mention his disgruntled unpaid workforce.

Strolling past toiling gardeners and arguing foremen, Annemarie explored new pathways across the grass towards the great dome set behind pinnacles and fancy fretwork, torn between admiration for its perfect proportions and the fantastic mixture of Gothic with Oriental. Such was the extravagance of the man, she thought, who would one day be king, the same man whose extravagant sentiments had poured into letters to a woman he now ignored. Like a wound still aching, the need to inflict a similar hurt welled up again before she could hold it back and force herself to be rational. She had never knowingly hurt anyone. Could she begin now and truly enjoy the experience?

Yes, I can. All I need is half a chance. Just show me how.

A speckled thrush hauled at a worm only a few feet away from her red kid shoes, flapping away in alarm at a deep shout from behind her. 'Hey! No right of way here, my lady. Private property, this.' A burly man waving a plan from one hand approached her so fast that it looked as if he might pick her up and carry her off over his shoulder.

'It was not private property last September,' Annemarie replied, standing her ground. 'So how is anyone to know? Who's bought it?'

'Prince o' Wales,' the man said. 'That's who. Fer 'is gardens. An' you'll 'ave ter go back the way you came.' He pointed, belligerently.

'I shall do no such thing. I'll go out *that* way.' Annemarie turned back towards the stable block. But she was no longer making a lone stand against authority, for hastening towards her with

long strides was a tall figure she instantly recognised. He was emerging from the central arch
of the building, as though her impulsive plea
was about to show her the half-chance she had
requested. By his tan breeches and looped-up
whip, she saw that he had been riding and, even
though his eyes were shaded by the rim of his
beaver, they glared like cold pewter at the offi-
cious foreman.

'M'lord…' the man began, 'this woman…'

Verne came to a halt beside Annemarie. 'Lady
Golding is my guest,' he said. 'Return to your
work, Mr Beamish.'

'Yes, m'lord. Beg pardon, m'lady.' Mr
Beamish nodded and walked back the way he
had come, shaking the plan into submission,
leaving Annemarie to face the man who, since
last night, she had known must appear.

Now he had, she was unsure whether to be
satisfied by her prediction or annoyed that, yet
again, she would have to try to get rid of him,
somehow. Which, when she was the trespasser,
might have its problems. In the circumstances, it
seemed rather superfluous to snap at Lord Verne
with the first thing that tripped off her tongue.
'What are *you* doing here?' She knew before it
was out that thanks would have been more polite.

He showed not the slightest surprise, as if
she'd been a terrier whose snappishness came
with the breed. 'If you care to walk with me, my

lady, I will tell you what I'm doing here,' he said, unable to conceal the admiration in his eyes at her elegant beauty, the silk three-quarter-length pelisse of forest-green piped with red in a military style worn over a frothy spotted muslin daydress, the hem of which made it look as if she walked in sea foam. Her bonnet was of ruched red silk piped with green, with a large artificial white peony perched at the back where green and red ribbons fluttered down like streamers. Red gloves, red shoes and a green-kid reticule showed him that, even when by herself in all other respects, fashionable dress was still important to her. Compared to other women, he put her in a class of her own.

Annemarie did not comply at once, though it would have been the obvious thing to do. 'I do not think I want to walk with you, my lord, I thank you. I only came to...' She paused. Why should she tell him?

But as if she had, he turned to look at the exotic stable building. 'Yes, it's a fine-looking place, isn't it? That dome is all glass. A miracle of engineering. The inside is even better. Come, I'll show you.'

'The public are not allowed.'

'I'm not public. And neither are you.' The way he said it brought a breathlessness to her lungs and an extra meaning to the words.

'Lord Verne,' she said, pulling herself together, 'the last time we met, you were...'

'I was less than gentlemanly. Yes, I know. Shall we start again? And this time, sartorially correct, I shall not put a foot wrong. You have my word.'

'I was not referring to your *dress*, my lord.' She wanted to say, *Go away and leave me alone, I don't know how to deal with this kind of danger because I know why you're here and this meeting is not as accidental as it looks. You want what I've got and we're both pretending to know nothing of it.*

'Then I can only beg for a chance to redeem myself, Lady Golding. Allow me one chance, at least. I keep my curricle in there. We're both at your service, if you would do me the honour.'

'What *are* you doing here? I don't remember you saying anything about a visit to Brighton. If it has something to do with me, then I think you should understand that I came to be alone with my memories. Having to make myself agreeable to comparative strangers with whom I have nothing in common is likely to have the opposite effect from what *you* have in mind. Please don't let our meeting prevent you from doing whatever you came here to do. I'm sure the Prince Regent will need you by his side at this busy time.'

'What *do* I have in mind, Lady Golding?' he said, softly.

He would know, of course, how she had glanced more than once at his beautifully formed mouth as she talked, watching for reminders of how it felt upon her own lips, wondering what she was missing by such a determined rejection of his offer of friendship. He would *not* know whether she had found what he was looking for, nor was he likely to take no for an answer before he knew, one way or the other. He would have to convince her of his interest in *her* and she would be obliged to pretend that it was for her own sake, not for the sake of his mission. She was anything but flattered. Why make it easy for him?

Her reply had an acid sting. 'Why, my lord, what the rest of the Prince's 10th Hussars have in mind, I suppose. Everybody knows what's on *their* list and I've seen nothing yet to suggest that you are any different.'

His wide, white smile did little to allay her fears in that direction, for it showed her that their thoughts had reached dangerous ground that ladies were usually careful to avoid. 'Well, for one thing,' he said, struggling with his smile, 'the 10th and I parted company some months ago and, for another thing, there are always some exceptions to the rule, you know.'

'I suppose you are one of the exceptions.'

'Most certainly, or I'd not be in the Prince's employment now.'

'And the Prince is employing you to purchase a piece of furniture the owner has no intention of selling. Are you not rather wasting your time, Lord Verne?'

Mrs Cardew had warned him that he would need to be patient.

'Lady Golding,' he said, gently, 'I am standing in a garden in the sunshine in front of a fabulous building, with the call of seagulls and the distant sound of the sea in my ears, while talking to the loveliest woman I've ever seen in my life, and you ask me if I'm wasting my time. Well, if this is wasting my time, all I can say is that I wish I'd wasted it years ago. Now, shall we just forget his Highness's pressing need for expensive furniture and take a look at more interesting things? Then, if you wish, we can go across to Donaldson's Library and take a cup of coffee, followed by a drive round town in a curricle. Do you drive?'

'I used to.'

'Good. Then we'll find something in here for you to practice on, shall we?' He offered her his arm and, because he had just said something to her that scalded her heart with suppressed tears, she placed her fingertips on the blue sleeve, feeling both the softness of the fabric and the rock-hard support beneath. It was as if, she thought, he knew what he had done and that his subdued flow of talk about the decoration, the materials, and the fittings inside the building was his way of buying time until she could find her voice again.

It would have been a pity to miss seeing such a place, just to make a point about not wanting to be in his company. And in spite of her reservations, and not knowing how best to handle the awkward situation, Annemarie could find nothing in his manner that made matters worse. Not once did they mention the bureau or the real reason for his being in Brighton, for it began to look as if Lord Verne had several good reasons for being there, one of which was to check on the paintings and ornaments being added to the Prince's collection at the Marine Pavilion. He had been allowed to use a suite of rooms there, he told her, usually occupied by the Prince's Private Secretary, so his acquaintance with the palace and stables staff meant that he had access to all the amenities, including the Prince's cooks.

No one could have helped being impressed by the accommodation for the Prince's horses. It resembled a Moorish palace, Annemarie remarked, more than a stable. Above them, the glass rotunda filled the circular space with pure daylight that sparkled on to a central fountain where grooms filled their pails. Carriage and riding horses, some still rugged-up in the pale royal colours, were led in and out through the fan-shaped arches while, on the balcony above, were the grooms' cubicles behind a gilded façade. 'And through here,' said Verne, smiling at her awed expression, 'is the riding-house. The horses are trained and exercised in here, and we have competitions too. The Prince is an excellent horseman. Always has been.'

'You admire him, then?'

'There's much in him to admire, but he's as human as the rest of us.'

Annemarie thought that the future monarch had no business trying to be as human as the rest of 'us', but she held her peace on the subject, at least for the time being. In a different way, the riding-house was as impressive as the stables, even more spacious, but lined and vaulted with timber to muffle the sounds. A thick layer of sawdust thudded beneath pounding hooves and the occasional bark of an order brought an instant response from the riders, many of whom were wearing Hussar uniform. There was no doubt that Lord Verne knew them, and the instructors, for hands touched foreheads as they passed, and nods reached him across the vast space. Obviously, Annemarie thought, Lord Verne had the Prince's favour.

'This is where *you* trained?' she said.

'No, this place went up while I was in Portugal with Wellington.'

'So you'd have known my late husband.' It was an unnecessary question dropped into the conversation, she knew, to remind him again of her background.

'I knew *of* him,' he replied. 'Everybody did. He was well regarded.'

'Yes.'

Another little barrier put in place, he thought. Well, I can deal with that, Lady Golding. I've managed difficult horses and I can manage you, too.

One of the uniformed instructors trotted across to greet them on a sleek and obedient grey gelding, patently pleased to see Verne there, but equally interested in his lovely stylish companion. Verne introduced him to her. 'Lady Golding, allow me to introduce an old friend of mine, Lord Bockington.'

The pleasant-faced fair-haired officer made a bow from the saddle with a smile of approval and a grin at his friend, and she suspected that he was receiving a coded message to suppress what he might have said, had she not been the widow of Sir Richard Golding. 'I am honoured, my lady. We always try to perform better when we have a special audience.'

'Then I shall watch even more carefully,' she replied, smiling back at him.

'Watch this, then,' he said. 'See if you can see the difference since last week, Verne. This young lad learns fast. Brilliant potential.' He trotted away to the side of the arena, reining back slowly before setting off to dance diagonally across the space. Annemarie had not seen this being practised before.

'You were here last week?' she said, without taking her eyes off the grey.

'And the week before. *And* the week before that too,' Verne answered, also watching. 'A big improvement. Nearly fell over himself last week.'

'Oh. I see.'

'Good,' he said, quietly, without indicating exactly what he meant. 'Now, would you care to see the driving carriages while we're here? He has some dashing phaetons and my own curricle is—'

'Lord Verne,' Annemarie said, stopping just inside the coach-house, a cool, spotlessly clean place lined with black-panelled coaches, shining brass and silver, and padded upholstery. The idea of driving again was more than appealing, in Brighton where she would not be remarked. But not with this man, not while she was being used so flagrantly to help him achieve his purpose. She had had enough of being used and now she was not so innocent that she couldn't tell when it was happening again. Even if he *did* come to Brighton on weekly visits, that was no reason why she should be obliged to play this cat-and-mouse game with him. He had kissed her and today paid her an outlandish compliment and sought her company. She had better beware, for these were the first signs of something she must avoid at all costs. And she was one step ahead of him, which he must be aware of by now.

'My lady?' he said, stopping with her.

'Lord Verne, I believe our scores are equal now.'

'Enlighten me, if you will?' He removed his beaver hat and, pulling off his gloves, stuffed them into the crown and placed it on the seat of the nearest vehicle. 'What scores are we talking about?'

'I showed you my bad manners when I was angry and you retaliated by showing me yours when *you* were angry. Now we have both redeemed ourselves, as you said you wished to do. You can go and get on with whatever you have to do here and I can do the same. *Alone.* Thank you so much for the tour of the stables. Do these doors lead to North Street?' She had already seen the questions forming in his eyes. Angry? Me? When?

'When was I angry with you, my lady? Do remind me.'

She ought to have kept quiet. She had set out the premise of a debate and now would have to refuse to elaborate. 'Never mind,' she whispered. 'If you don't recall it, then why should I? Please, which way is the exit?'

Shaking his head, he tried to hide his smile

behind a knuckle as he came to stand four-square in front of her, lifting her chin to see beneath the bonnet into her deep violet eyes rimmed with black lashes long enough to sweep up moonbeams. 'You thought I was angry when I kissed you?' he said. 'Really?'

She tried to move away, mortified that she had shown him so clearly what was in her mind. Secret thoughts, not to be shared. But now her back was against the cool wall, held there by his hands braced on either side of her, and she feared he meant to repeat it, after all her denials and disapprovals.

'Since you ask, yes! Why else but to…?'

She saw his eyes widen. 'To what? Humiliate you?'

'Yes,' she whispered. 'It was unforgivable, my lord. I am not to be used so.'

'If that's what you believed, then it was indeed unforgivable of me and not at all what I meant. I would never use such means to humiliate a woman.'

'Then if that is the case, please don't say any more. We shall forget about it.'

'I hope not,' he murmured.

'I would like to return home, if you please.'

'Steady, my lady. I shall take you home, but there's no need to go galloping off like a spooked filly.' His head lowered to hers and she was compelled to watch his mouth, to hear the softly spo-

ken words, few of which she could remember
later, that sounded like those he might have used
to a nervous horse about to bolt. Gentling. Calming. Words of admiration about breeding and
class and exclusiveness, elegance and loftiness
that needed a man's hand, not an old man's, nor
a boy's. She might have shown irritation at that
too-personal opinion, but she did not, for something deep within her kept her still and listening, as though at last she was hearing the truth
for the first time.

'Come on, my beauty,' he whispered, holding
out his arm for her to take.

Placing her fingers again on the blue sleeve,
she walked with him to the door, blinking at
the sunlight.

Chapter Three

Giving oneself a good talking-to, Annemarie decided, was all very well if there was one talker and one listener. But now, besieged by voices of both reason and unreason, the pearls of wisdom fell on deaf ears. Added to these were other deep beguiling words that echoed round her memory, all the more potent for their lack of finesse: earthy, provocative words that men used about thoroughbred horses and, privately, about women. She ought to have been insulted, disgusted, but she was not. He had not kissed her again, but she felt as if he had. And more.

Impertinently, she thought, trying her best to malign him, he had referred to her late husband. Verne had said she needed a man's hand, not an old man's or a boy's, a risky opinion only a man like him would dare to venture to the widow of Lieutenant General Sir Richard Golding. As he apparently anticipated, she had not reacted at all except that, in her mind, something was released like a moth from a chest of old clothes, silent words thought of but never used. Now, with a cup of tea and a warm scone, her feet up on the *chaise-longue* and the sound of rain lashing at the windows, she glanced across to the side of the white fireplace where hung the painting of her late husband.

To a stranger, he might have been taken for her father. As Lady Benistone had married a man many years older than herself, by coincidence so had Annemarie done the same, believing what she'd been told that wealth, security and a position in society was all a woman had any right to expect. She had been more easily influenced then. As a wedding present, Richard had given her a portrait of himself, a gilt-framed oval showing a silver-haired, black-browed soldier whose imperious gaze was levelled at something over to the left, his mouth unsmiling. Silver side-whiskers encroached like sabres on to his cheeks and covering his red coat were black cords and bright gold buttons, braids and badges, ribbons and stars. He'd told Annemarie exactly what they were, often enough: the army had been his life as well as his death and, innocently, she had seen herself as yet another decoration, another conquest to be prized and shown off like his medals. In the ten months of their marriage, she had accepted that that's what army wives were for, apart from bearing the next heir.

After less than a year as Lady Golding, a whole year of deep mourning had seemed excessive when they had had so little time to get to know each other, several months of which had been spent apart. Ever one for priorities, Richard had told her all about himself and his astounding achievements, his position in Viscount Wellington's trust and the high esteem of his own men, but as for getting to know his young wife, he had assumed that there was nothing much to know, even in bed. Since she knew so little about herself either, in that department, her indefinable feelings of disappointment became a guilty relief when that part of her wifely duties was discontinued, the nightly grunting and groping, squeezing and heaving, the rough irritable directions that made her feel foolishly inadequate. Craving appreciation and tenderness, she had sometimes thought that, if he could have worn his spurs in bed, he would have used them.

So, as a young widow, when she was made much of by a handsome young rake, flattered and soothed with fine words as soft as a perfumed breeze, Annemarie had soaked up the comforts of his attentions like a dry sponge waiting for the tide, not caring which direction it came from or what it brought with it. Warnings from her mother and Cecily went unheeded.

All she cared for was to hear words of esteem and praise and, ultimately, of seduction, words never spoken by Richard, but which tripped off Sir Lionel's tongue like honey. With uncomfortable memories still haunting her, Annemarie had never allowed much in the way of intimacies and, to be fair, Sir Lionel never persisted, saying that there'd be time enough for that. They had kissed, just a little, and she believed she might get used to it, given more practice and the right conditions, and several other provisos that, since she'd been kissed by a man rather than a boy, she now saw as being completely irrelevant.

Looking back, she realised it was not so much Sir Lionel and his clever wiles that seduced her, but the contrast. Youth versus age. Fun versus pomposity. Irreverence versus rules and an interest in her for her own sake rather than the obsessive requirements of a soldier-husband that infiltrated every waking hour. Since having the Brighton house to herself, she had changed almost everything: wallpaper and carpets, curtains and furniture. The portrait was kept as a reminder never again to allow any man to control her life, that nothing was half as satisfying as being able to direct one's own affairs.

Thoughtfully, Annemarie sipped her tea and finished off the crumbly scone and strawberry jam while hearing those words again that were neither harsh nor conventionally seductive. *A man's hand, not an old man's or a boy's.* What could be more exciting from one who must have known Sir Richard Golding better than he pretended to? And how much did he know about Sir Lionel Mytchett? Ringing the bell, she thought it was time to set things moving before the situation got out of hand. The letters must be taken up to London immediately and, in one stroke, get them out of her life for ever. The letters *and* the man.

Perhaps because more people than usual were leaving Brighton for the London celebrations, Mr Ash, the housekeeper's handyman husband, had a hard time of it obtaining a post-chaise with postilions who were willing to drive all that way in torrential rain.

'But it may not be raining tomorrow, Ash,' Annemarie said, hopefully.

Dripping pools on to the hall floor, he was adamant. 'It will, m'lady. They know it will, too. I tried all four posting-stables and only one had anything to offer and that's an old clapped-out thing with only a pair of 'orses.'

This was not going to be the quick there-and-back trip she had hoped for. No wonder the Ashes were puzzled by her determination to spend six or seven hours on roads pitted with rain-filled potholes, but there was little choice and she could not afford to wait, not knowing how long it would take to find Lady Hamilton either. Nor did she particularly want her father to know of her mission. Lord Verne had taken her straight home without the slightest direction and she knew that their first meeting in Brighton would not be the last. Next time they met, she would be able to put a stop to his presumed interest by telling him she no longer had what the Prince Regent wanted.

With the first lurch of the post-chaise through inches of muddy water, her optimism was tested to its limits as the rain thundered down on the flimsy canvas roof that had already sprouted a leak down one corner. Through the front window they had a clear view of the two horses and the postilion riding one of them, huddled in a drenched greatcoat, his black shiny hat throwing off water with each bounce. The horses looked decidedly unhappy, but it was the state of the coach that concerned Annemarie most, groaning unsteadily over roads now awash with hours of heavy rain, one of the doors flying open as they dipped into a rut, then a window that would not stay up until it was jammed with a glove. The two portmanteaux were pressed against their feet, otherwise they might have fallen off before the coach came to grief on the long slow haul up to Reigate.

Some coachmen preferred a different route to

this long punishing climb, so it was no particular surprise to the passengers when the coach slowed to a standstill, tilted dangerously, then swerved backwards into the hedge with a ripping crash, dragging the exhausted horses with it. The tilt immediately worsened, throwing them back into a corner of the seat with the floor angled like a wall and the inside waterspout spraying their heads with perfect precision.

The unflappable maid went to the heart of the matter. 'Back axle gone,' she said, readjusting her bonnet and brushing water out of her eyes. 'Lost a wheel, too. We shan't reach Reigate, never mind London.'

The postilion's first duty was to his horses, which had suddenly found the energy to plunge about dangerously and to kick over the traces which he could not unhook from the chaise. But as the two passengers watched, helping hands came to hold the horses' heads until they were released. Now they found that the door that would not stay closed would not open, despite all outside efforts to budge it. For such an immediate response, it was obvious that help must have been very close behind.

It may have seemed uncharitable to allow suspicion to take the place of thanks at that critical point, but how else could Annemarie have viewed the appearance of the very person she was hoping to cheat out of the prize they had both set their hearts on, the one in her portmanteau, the one they pretended did not exist? This was something she had not expected and which, in hindsight, she ought to have done. So much for taking control. Angrily, she kicked at the door just as a hand pulled from outside.

'Lord Verne,' she said, 'are you making a habit of helping me out of difficult situations? Or is this truly a coincidence?' Even with water running down his face, he was breathtakingly good looking. His buff-coloured fifteen-caped greatcoat was dark with rain and it was obvious he had been in the saddle, not inside.

'We'll discuss that later, if you please,' he shouted against the roar of the rain and the thumping and neighing of horses. 'This thing's going to tip over any minute. Be quick and get out, then make a run for the carriage behind. Come on, woman! Don't let's get into an argument about it. Give me your hand.' Grabbing the precious baggage with one hand, she gave him the other while preparing for his objection. 'Leave that!' he commanded. 'I'll bring the bags. Let your lass get out.'

If she had thought in her wildest dreams that this might happen, she might have done as smugglers' wives do and stuffed the valuables into pockets around her bodice. As it was, she was determined not to let go, thereby making it clear to him as if it had been spoken out loud that here were the infamous letters and that she was taking them to London, even in a ramshackle coach with the heavens opening above them. His stare at the portmanteau in her hand, then at her grim expression, left her in no doubt that he understood what she was about. Even he could not hide the realisation in his eyes.

'Valuables,' she said, clambering up the sloping floor with the bulky thing under one arm. 'Taking them to Christie's. I can manage it, thank you.' As an excuse not to allow the Prince Regent's most trusted aide to hold a battered old bag, it was bound to sound ludicrous, but it was the best she could do, though it hampered her exit from the shattered vehicle and must have tested Verne's patience sorely. He said nothing, handing her out through the narrow door, lifting her and the extra bulk on to the saturated grass verge where the soft mud almost pulled off one half-boot. Thrown off balance, she pitched forwards and would have fallen flat on her face but for his arms across her body, keeping her upright, but as helpless as a child.

'Here, give it to me while you get your boot back on,' he said with noticeable tolerance. 'Come on. I'm not going to run off with it.'

'I'm sorry,' she muttered, passing it to him. 'I didn't mean…'

Unable to tell whether he squinted at the rain running into his eyes or from laughter, her heart flipped at that moment and the sneaking thought that she might even be glad to see him was pushed firmly back where it belonged, in cold storage. He was the very last person she wanted to see, of course. Wasn't he?

The beautifully appointed travelling coach to which Annemarie and her maid were consigned like two shipwreck survivors could hardly have been more different from the rickety post-chaise and its unroadworthy livestock. At once it was obvious that it was one of those from the Prince Regent's carriage-house that Annemarie had seen the day before, every detail indicating quality and comfort, from the soft green-velvet upholstery inside to the team of four matched bays outside, steaming in the downpour. Twice as roomy, the carpeted interior was like a sumptuous cocoon in which they could hear themselves speak without having to shout. When the carriage moved off, bouncing gently over the verge which set the tassels swinging, Annemarie peered out of the window to catch a glimpse of Lord Verne mounting his horse. 'So who did he bring this carriage for?' she said. 'And, for that matter, what is he doing here?'

Their baggage was now stored safely in a rack above their heads, leaving the last mile to Reigate to provide Annemarie with a revised plan of action, for now she had lost not only her private conveyance but also the secrecy that was paramount to the success of her mission. Whatever plan she could come up with would have to include Lord Verne, whether she liked it or not.

The Swan at Reigate had accommodated the Prince Regent's guests many times before and the businesslike host who might have assigned the occupants of a clapped-out post-chaise to a back room had no hesitation whatever in showing Lord Verne's lady, however bedraggled, to the best bedroom where a boy was even then lighting a fire in the cast-iron grate. Annemarie's whispered objection to Lord Verne as they entered the Swan's portals had received a terse reply. 'This is not what I had planned, my lord,' she told him, holding the portmanteau away from her damp pelisse. 'I intended to go straight on after changing horses. I cannot delay, you see.'

Travellers off the stagecoach were stomping in, damp, stiff, crumpled and hungry, and wishing their plans were more flexible. The passageway smelled of wet wool and leather, and Lord Verne's only response was to place an arm across her back to move her on and to say, 'Yes, we'll discuss it when we've dried off, shall we? Have you eaten since you left home?'

'No, I intended—'

'Then come down to my private parlour when you're ready. I've ordered a meal. You can lock

your room. Your valuables will be quite safe
while we eat.'

Following the landlord up the polished staircase, there was no chance for her to argue before
she and Evie were ushered into the best chamber,
low-beamed and pine-scented, cosily furnished
and creaky-floored. Assured of the Swan's very
best service, however slight, the two were left
alone to recover from their ordeal.

In his chamber next door, Lord Verne's air
of quiet satisfaction was picked up by his valet
who had now seen the latest object of his master's interest, after much speculation. 'So far so
good, m'lord,' he ventured, holding a clean shirt
in front of the fire. 'Like clockwork, I'd say.'

Verne made no reply. Luck had played a part.
The weather, for one thing. One of the coachmen from the royal stables had been present at
the posting-house when Ash, who had had several jobs in Brighton before being employed by
Lady Golding's late husband, had tried to hire
a post-chaise. The coachman had commiserated
with him about the lack of choice, had heard
him hire it on his mistress's behalf for the next
morning and then, because he had seen her with
Lord Verne that same day, had gone to tell him,
thus receiving a nice little warmer for his pocket
along with his lordship's thanks. From that, it
needed little more than common sense to see

that the lady's impetuosity, of which he had been warned, was at work either to distance herself from him or to pay a flying visit to the capital on some important matter. And since the post-chaise had been hired for two to three days, it had looked as if the latter was the case, verified only an hour ago by the portmanteau full of 'valuables' and her determination not to be parted from it. To Verne, no other explanation was likely but that the Prince Regent's private correspondence of a highly controversial nature had been discovered, bundled into a battered old leather bag and was now intended for any publisher with the courage to make it public. He remembered well Lady Golding's passionate criticism of the Prince's excessive spending habits and how unfair it was that Lady Hamilton was having to sell her effects to make ends meet. It would be just like her, Verne thought, to turn the letters over for some exorbitant sum to give to Lady Hamilton, for she herself would not wish to benefit from their sale. Not at all.

Not at all? 'Except…' he said, breathing the word out loud.

'M'lord?' Samson said, eyebrows raised.

Lady Golding's thinly veiled dislike of the Prince Regent was surely another good reason why she would not think twice about discrediting him, making him a laughing-stock and the butt of coarse jests about his latest passions and short-lived *amours*. According to Mrs Cardew, the prince had even thrown out lures to Lady Benistone. That would be good enough reason for Lady Golding to sell the letters, make some money for the destitute recipient and bring his Highness down in the eyes of all Europe who, this summer, thronged the capital at his expense. She would see it as a justification, a kind of retribution for the hurts she had suffered at men's hands.

Verne had refrained from telling her what he'd heard about her late husband, how the high regard of his superiors did not accord with the opinions of those lower down the pecking order concerning his appalling harshness and bullying ways. If his manner as the older husband of a beautiful and sensitive young woman was anything like his reputation as a lieutenant-general, then she must have had a hard time of it, he thought, and no wonder she was wary and standoffish. Especially after the brief but devastating episode with Mytchett, of all the pernicious little toads. Why had somebody not warned her? What had Lord Benistone been thinking of?

He waited until Samson had arranged his cravat to both their satisfactions and then requested his valet's unwavering attention. He was to make the acquaintance of Evie, Lady Golding's maid. An attractive young lady, yes?

'Indeed she is, m'lord. You want me to get...
er...friendly?'

'I don't want you to ravish her, lad. No. I know
your kind of friendly.'

'M'lord!' Samson sounded hurt.

'Never mind "m'lord!" Just listen. This is
what you do.'

Then followed detailed instructions, with allowances for some variations, that made good
use of Samson's youthful experiences at the
more disreputable end of London from which
Verne had once rescued him.

Ash's warning about the timing of the journey was, as it turned out, not far off the mark,
for now it was late afternoon, the sky darkening
with ominous intent, and Annemarie ought to
have been glad of comfort and shelter when so
many other travellers had no choice but to carry
on. Not expecting to influence Lord Verne's
plans in the slightest, she was nevertheless determined to try, for the longer she remained here
with the letters, which she was convinced he
knew of, the more difficult it would be to ensure
their safety. After all, she would have to leave
the room occasionally and could hardly carry
the portmanteau with her wherever she went.
Not being of a particularly wily nature, she had
not considered removing the letters from the bag
and putting them somewhere else, which anyone

more used to that kind of thing would have done. As long as they were there, locked up, not even Evie would stumble upon them, she thought.

'You must go down and bring some food back on a tray as soon as I've gone,' she told Evie, 'but lock the door after you and again when you return.'

'Yes, m'lady,' Evie said, frowning at the muddied half-boot on the end of her arm. 'Is there bad company, then?'

'You never know,' said Annemarie, glancing in the mirror and preferring not to elaborate on the bad company that awaited her downstairs, thinking that he would be as unimpressed by her inappropriate dress for dinner as she'd been by his.

Downstairs, she sought out the obliging landlord to ask about the availability of a post-chaise to take her on to London that evening. The news was catastrophic. There had been a landslide on Reigate Hill that had washed the road clean away, which was why the stagecoach passengers were still there instead of moving on. No one and nothing would be able to use the road until it was cleared, he said. Much better to stay put, for the time being. 'Ah, m'lord…I was just telling—'

'Indeed, Hitchcock,' said Lord Verne, appearing through the milling guests. 'I've just heard the news. Bad for travellers, good for landlords, eh? Lady Golding and I will have our supper as soon as it's convenient, if you please.'

'It'll be with you in a matter of moments, m'lord. M'lady.' He bowed himself away, wondering why Lady Golding was so anxious to leave by herself in the middle of a thunderstorm.

Far from being unimpressed by Annemarie's appearance, Verne could hardly take his eyes off her, for the mulberry-coloured pelisse had given no hint of the pale mauve creation beneath: long, lace-frilled sleeves, low neckline and tiny bodice which she had tried to conceal with a lilac-patterned shawl of finest cashmere. Faint mud-stains still clung to the hem, but these hardly showed in the shadowy candle-lit parlour, and now her hair was piled high in thick tumbling waves only just held up by a gauzy scarf shot with silver threads. As when he'd first seen her, the effect was sensationally negligent due in part, he thought, to her extraordinary beauty and the way she moved, like a gazelle. He also assumed that she must have brought little with her in the way of clothes.

This was the first time Annemarie had seen him in evening dress and the sharp opening salvo she had prepared evaporated in the genteel atmosphere of the cosy parlour, the blazing fire, the well-laid table and his amazing elegance. 'Lord Verne,' she began, 'I really must thank you for—'

'Will you be seated, my lady? A glass of sherry, or madeira?'

'Yes, thank you. As I was saying—'

'Your room? Will you be comfortable there? Have you stayed here before?'

She took the glass from him with a sigh. 'You're not going to allow me to thank you, are you? So let me try another angle, my lord. Why did you follow me from Brighton with an empty carriage belonging to his Royal Highness?'

His white knee-breeches glowed pink in the firelight as he settled himself opposite her in a high winged chair, like her own. Placing his glass on the small side-table, he smiled at her indulgently. 'You are convinced that I followed you, are you not? Well, in a sense, I did, but only because I happened to set off when you did. I'm returning the Prince's carriage, you see, and this is the day I would normally leave Brighton. I do this most weeks. I thought I'd told you.' In the circumstances, he thought, there was no harm in stretching the truth just a little further than usual.

'So you prefer to get soaked rather than ride *in* the carriage?'

'I need my horse for the return journey and I've no intention of taking my curricle out on roads like river-beds. It was just fortunate that we caught up with you when we did, other- wise...'

'Yes. Otherwise. And now I'm stuck here until the road is cleared, which is not at all what I'd planned. I need to reach London as a matter of some urgency.' His explanation about returning the carriage was not convincing. The horse could easily have been led behind while he stayed dry.

'As we all do,' he said, 'but at least you now have a place to stay until tomorrow. Then I'll convey you through the side roads and we can be there before mid-day if we set off early enough. Will that suit you? The coachman knows all the alternative routes like the back of his hand.'

'Thank you. Yes.'

'But…?' he whispered, catching the note of doubt in her thanks.

Tipping the amber-coloured liquid in her glass to catch the reflections, she shook her head, accepting the inevitable with obvious reluctance. 'But…it seems to me, my lord, that each of our chance meetings has so far resulted in *me* being obliged to do something I don't particularly want to do. It's all getting rather predictable, isn't it? Perhaps, once we reach London, we might try harder to avoid each other. I shall *certainly* do so.'

'Not a chance,' he said. 'I cannot agree to that. What an absurd suggestion.'

Until you get what you want, my lord. Then you'll disappear fast enough.

'Ah, yes, the bureau. Of course. I'd almost

forgotten the bureau. Do give his Highness my apologies, won't you, and tell him how well it looks in my room?'

His smile at her sarcasm was lazily understanding, sending shivers through her in spite of the warm fire. She need not have tried to rile him or sail so close to the wind with her reference to the bureau, but some devil in her told her to tease him, tempt him and pull back safely, playing the arrogant creature at his own game. The devil had not reminded her, however, that the arrogant creature was a past master at this kind of thing, whereas she had no expertise at all.

'You may be sure that I will convey your message to him, word for word,' he said. 'And is your business with Christie's so urgent, my lady?'

'Private,' she said. 'Nothing anyone need know about.'

'I only ask because I could take you either straight there or to Montague Street. Whichever you prefer.'

'Neither. I shall stay on Park Lane with Mrs Cardew. I have my own good reasons for not wanting my father to know I'm in town. He'd want to know what I'm selling, who to, how much for, that kind of thing. It's best if he doesn't know.'

'Exactly. Parents can be over-curious and well meaning, can't they?'

Annemarie stared at him. 'You have parents, too?' she said.

The sherry in his glass slopped dangerously before he managed to anchor it to the table. Then, with a cough and a thump upon his shirtfront, he was able to answer, 'Oh…indeed…I think so…somewhere.'

'Oh, dear. I beg your pardon. Of course you do. I only meant…' Placing a hand to her forehead, Annemarie could only blame the day, the warmth, the sherry and the anxiety of the moment for her lapse of good manners. She was saved from having to explain her train of thought by the arrival of dinner borne by white-aproned waiters who soon covered the table with dish after dish, releasing succulent aromas of steaming meats, pies and sauces as the silver domes were lifted off. She suddenly realised that her last meal had been a hurried breakfast, that she was desperately hungry and that, as Lord Verne's guest, she had an obligation to be civil. There was no need, she told herself, to fear the change of plan for she still had the letters and was on the way to returning them to their owner. This was merely a hitch. Nothing more. There was nothing Lord Verne could do about that.

He was a more amiable host than she had been those few evenings ago, helping her courteously to the best portions of roast pigeon, pork with apple sauce, baked trout and fresh vegetables

cooked to perfection, like the fried celery with
melted butter. Between morsels, she tried to redeem her blunder by asking him about his family on the basis that men love nothing more than
to talk about themselves. She soon discovered
that, unlike Sir Richard, this man was much less
forthcoming on the subject of his personal life,
and all she was at first able to glean, without
seeming to be over-curious, was that he was the
eldest son of the Marquis of Simonstoke, near
Salisbury, and that he had three siblings, one
of whom was the mother of three small children. She was surprised at how much more she
wanted to know. She wanted to keep him talking, to watch his face without seeming to stare.
*His hair sweeps over the tops of his ears. How
many women has he made love to? Does he have
mistresses?* She was silent, wondering how to
find out about his work for the Prince, which she
could easily have done a few nights ago, had she
not been so annoyed. He had placed his knife
and fork down and leaned back in his chair, one
tanned hand on the white tablecloth, his index
finger just touching the stem of his glass, stroking…slowly. *As if it was skin…mine…* 'And your
work with his Highness? I fear Sir Richard never
had a very high opinion of his taste.' She regretted it, instantly. To hide behind a dead man's
disapproval was cowardly, to say the least. She

should learn to form her own opinions about such things.

Unsmiling, he countered her clumsy remark. 'And but for one remarkable exception, his Highness never rated your late husband's taste very highly either, my lady.' Before Annemarie could pick up on the remarkable exception, he went on in defence of his royal patron. 'Have you met him?'

'Once, at his inauguration as Regent at Carlton House three years ago. It was not a comfortable experience.'

'Well then, you saw a different man from the way he was in his youth. I met him first when I was a lad, and he could not have been kinder or more courteous to me, when he had far more important things to do. When he heard I was interested, he showed me his paintings and porcelain and told me how to recognise the makers, and I can tell you there's little wrong with his taste in fine things. If he dresses rather flamboyantly, that's his nature. He won't pretend to be what he isn't. You either like him, or you don't.'

'You said he was a fine horseman, too.'

'He is. One of the best and most knowledgeable. And before you tell me horses cost a fortune, I agree, they do. He wants only the best, but I can't dislike a man for that. So do I.'

'Which is why, I suppose, you profess to pursue what you want and make it yours. A fine sentiment, my lord, but quite unrealistic, apart from causing unnecessary heartache.'

'I'm glad you remembered my words. Keep them in mind.'

'I will. Your loyalty to his Highness is commendable, but I have never thought that a penchant for the finer things of life gives one the licence to ignore one's duty as a husband and father. Or as a future king, either.'

It was obvious to them both that, as the words slipped out, warmed on good food and wine, she had her own father in mind as well as the Prince Regent. Verne's silence allowed her judgement to go unchallenged while her eyes flickered away from his and she made a play of pulling her shawl more closely around her shoulders to hide the peachy skin from his sight. The conversation had swung round to herself, the very thing she had wished to avoid. Perhaps she ought not to have mentioned his royal employer when she had so recently discovered material that could damage him beyond repair.

'I take it, then, my lady, that you would derive some satisfaction from seeing erring husbands dealt with harshly. Do you have anything particular in mind?'

Deep waters. Too deep to wade into at this time of night. Any further and she would have verified what he already suspected. 'It was *your* work I meant to ask about, my lord, not the Prince Regent's qualities, or lack of them.'

Accepting her retreat with a nod of his head and what Annemarie thought was a barely disguised grin of satisfaction, he passed her a plate of fruit tartlets. 'Will you try one?' he said. 'I can recommend them.'

'Thank you. Your approval of fruit tarts must be reliable, at least.'

Concentrating on the first sweet mouthful, she did not see his reaction, though she heard the deep laughter at her riposte, and the rest of the meal was conducted in an atmosphere of amicable stalemate.

Some time before the table was cleared and glasses of wine taken back to their fireside chairs, Annemarie felt herself succumbing to the appeal of Verne's company. If only their motives had not diverged so acutely. He had the kind of intelligence she admired, but what would he be making of *her* limited knowledge and experience? His manners, apart from one aberration, were faultless, but how could one overlook the immoral behaviour that epitomised his old regiment, The Prince of Wales's Own? Was he the exception he claimed to be? He was loyal, but was his loyalty misplaced? Or did it show that he preferred to see strengths rather than weaknesses, even when these were serious? His personal magnetism went without saying, but what was his record with women? To her bewilderment, he had tried his charm on her, with some success. Obviously, he was well practised and sure of himself, sure of getting what he wanted and of walking away afterwards without a backward glance, but how she would love to call his bluff, for what had been that question on dealing harshly with erring husbands if not about what she intended to do with the letters? He was probing, of course, and she could keep him guessing even after the return of the letters to Lady Hamilton.

Seated once again in the comfortable fireside chair, waves of exhaustion threatened to extinguish the hostility hovering over their conversation, none of which was lost upon her host when words with more than two syllables began to suffer noticeably and stifled yawns kept her black-lashed eyelids weighed down with tiredness.

In different circumstances, he would never have taken advantage of a woman's weakness. But Verne had concluded some time ago that this situation called for something altogether more dramatic, something that would make an impression on her other than the rescue, the accommodation, the food, wine and company, something that would shake the foundations of the contempt for men upon which she was building her opinions. She might well be fighting fatigue, but he was a reasonably good judge of women and, although her particular problems were new to him, he knew that it would not be her memory that would suffer in the morning, but her conscience, and therefore her attitude towards himself. That had to change, for he had not been deceived by her attempts at politeness in between the embittered remarks, nor did he believe she was as unaffected by him as she pretended to be. There was an interest there that she would like to have kept hidden, which Mrs Cardew herself had noticed, as he had. It was time for her to be stirred out of her complications.

'How long do you intend to stay in London?' he asked.

Blinking, she summoned back the wariness with an effort. Was it something she should be telling him? 'Not long,' she said, blearily. 'I have to find someone first.' She did not notice his sudden alertness, nor her own indiscretion.

'Lady Benistone?' he ventured.

A sad frown clouded her eyes as she tried to focus on him, nodding her head as if he'd uncovered a secret thought. 'What do *you* know about Lady Benistone?' she asked. 'You were out of the country.'

Smoothly, he replied. 'Yes, and now I'm back.'

'It's time I was going.' With astonishing speed, she was out of the chair and swivelling towards the door with one foot treading upon the long shawl that her other foot was holding down. Her legs, usually so agile, refused to compensate.

He caught her as she fell, knocking over the small table and sending the empty glass bouncing across the floor, holding her hard against him until she could untangle her feet. But although she clung to him for support, she was tired and needled by his mention of a painful subject, by her feet being stuck in folds of cashmere and by trying to hold back the guilty stirrings of a physical attraction she had sworn never again to release. Her usual composure deserted her along with the last remains of her energy as she tried to twist herself out of his restraint, pushing instead of clinging. Too tired even to plead for release, she felt the predictable tightening of his arms and the pressure of his hard thighs and, without knowing quite how it happened, the warm searching invasion of his mouth over hers, silencing even the thoughts that waited there.

Warnings evaporated. Resistance became compliance and, with her rock-solid objections wavering in the deepest corners of her mind she was carried helplessly on a wave of bliss that her body craved, but had never experienced. No kiss she had known or imagined compared to those few moments when nothing was required of her except to bathe in his exciting closeness and to let him show her what he had meant by 'a man's hand'. A man's kiss, not an old man's or a boy's. Exhausted as she was, untutored and still nagged by latent hostility, she could tell the difference.

He had known that, for the first few moments at least, she would lack the energy and motivation to protest, but he could not have predicted her unexpected eagerness that went way beyond his hopes. Nor had he quite foreseen how his first taste of her lips threatened to drive from his usually cool head any thought of restraint or regard for her inexperience. A widow she might be, but of lovemaking she probably knew little beyond what two short disastrous encounters had taught her. Yet in his arms she was softened by tiredness and pent-up desire that neither of them had managed to hide. What hot-blooded male would resist the temptation to prolong the experience for the sake of tomorrow's recriminations?

He felt the sinuous bending of her body and the reach of one hand towards his ear, effectively permitting him to drink deeply at the lips he had watched all evening, even while remaining aware of how, at any moment, she might take flight as she had almost done moments before. Carefully, expertly, his mouth moved over the silken skin of her throat, his hand deep in her hair to hold her entranced and yielding to the butterfly touch that travelled erratically so that she could not anticipate its course towards the skimpy bodice, shoulder and neck, then to the beautiful rising mounds of her breasts.

She gasped and held his jaw to stop the journey, telling him by her signal that here lurked a spectre dark enough to break the spell. He closed her startled eyes with his whispers and soft kisses. 'Hush, my beauty. Stand still.' Lapping at her lips one last time, he drew away just far enough to keep her there, half-expecting an explosion of outrage, once her awareness had returned to berate her conscience.

But there was no explosion, only breathless words of reproach, clearly linking his desires to more material matters. 'This is not the way, my lord,' she said. 'There is really…no need…'

'No need to what?'

'To go to these lengths to get what you want. Following me to London. Dining with me. Now…this. I am not to be bought…this way.'

'You think that I arranged for the rain and a landslide? You credit me with more influence than I deserve, my lady. This was not planned any more than your stumble against me was, but if I take advantage of the situation, who would blame me?'

'I would. Most people would. It is not the conduct of a gentleman towards a lady, nor is it the way to get at the bureau.'

'To hell with the bureau,' he said, brusquely.

'That's the last thing on my mind while I'm standing here with you in my arms, believe me.'

His plain speaking made her blush and she looked away angrily. 'I wish I could believe that,' she whispered.

'Do you? You still think this is all about persuasion? You think I have no more regard for your intelligence than to think you'd fall for that kind of low trick? That I would use coercion of this kind to change your mind about a piece of *furniture*? Saints alive, woman! What kind of man do you take me for, a rogue, like Mytchett?'

'Leave him out of it, if you please.'

'Gladly. But answer my question.'

'I cannot!' she cried, squirming against him. 'All I know is that you have your orders and that's why you're here, isn't it? How should I know what kind of a man you are, my lord? You must have heard how skilfully I form opinions in *that* direction.'

'Yes, I have. Stop struggling and listen to me.'

'Let me go!'

'No. Listen. This is not what you believe.'

'You will never convince me of that, my lord. If I did not own something you'd been told to get hold of at any cost, you would show no more interest in Lord Benistone's scandalous daughter than in any other widow. I suggest you return to one of your mistresses in London…or wherever…and let her take your mind off things. I'm not such a hen-brain that I can't see when I am being used. I've learned a thing or two in one year.'

'Wrong on two counts,' he said, keeping her pressed against the wall, though now he held her face in one warm hand while his thumb stroked softly across her chin and lips, his other hand clasping her wrist against his shoulder. 'Shall I tell you?'

'No.'

'One is that, having discovered the existence last weekend of Lord Benistone's scandalous daughter, owning her has become more important to me than anything she owns. When I said that I pursue what I want and make it mine, you knew then that I meant you. Didn't you?'

'No.'

He smiled, moving the soft pad of his thumb again. 'Little liar. That kiss, by the way, was not meant to make you angry, but to show you that I was serious. I want *you*, Lady Annemarie Golding.'

'That's *ridiculous*!' she said. 'Utterly—'

The thumb pressed softly, stopping the protest. 'On the second count, I don't have a mistress in London or anywhere else and, even if I did, she would not manage to take my mind off *things*, as you call them. My mind has been on you since we met, my scandalous, damaged, re-

clusive beauty, and I intend to take you back into
society and show you what you've been missing.'

'I *know* what I've been missing,' she retorted.

'No, you don't.' The way he said it, looking
deeply into her eyes with such intensity, left her
in no doubt of what he meant.

'Lord Verne, just because my parents had an
unorthodox relationship before their marriage,
you should not assume that they would approve
of their daughters doing the same. Besides, I
want no more to do with men. I have decided to
take full control of my life. Alone. You think I
need help. Well, I don't. I can manage.'

'As you did today, you mean?'

'I would have managed, one way or another.'

'So was it better to do it my way? Or yours?'

'Safer, and possibly more comfortable,' she
said, ignoring the ambiguity.

'Safer,' he echoed, softly. 'So you're going to
play safe for the rest of your life, my lady, and
let a bad experience colour your views of mankind in general. A woman of your calibre should
not be hiding herself away from the world, in
case—'

'I see! So I'm a coward! That's what you're
saying? Let *go* of me!'

Having been quite prepared for her fury at his
accusation of faint-heartedness, his hard body
and arms closed like a vice around her, tilting
her head back against his deep-blue coat for an-

other kiss that gave her a glimpse of what she *had* been missing, whether she would admit it or not. From beneath his searching lips, a mewing cry emerged as she felt his hand pass down her body from breast to thigh, lingering over each undulation with a gentle pressure that spanned her like an octave before the return journey. Yet this most intimate and indecent caress held her spellbound with a confusion of guilty pleasures. While she knew that any well-brought-up woman would have resisted it to her utmost, she let it happen, abandoning her lips to his in a sweet distraction of senses. Thoughts of outrage scattered in all directions, leaving nothing except the deep rapture of desire, of being made to feel rare and precious, not for a man's pleasure alone, which had always sullied her previous experiences. She felt herself become still again under his touch, waiting for the next caress, for the direction of his kisses, for the intoxicating male scent of him, the taste of his skin and the softness of his hair on her fingertips, his support of her wilting body.

It had gone too far. Her fine words about controlling her life were meaningless. He must have known, even then, how he could change all that. He also knew how to be gracious as the victor. 'I shall not let you go,' he whispered against her cheek. 'But no more decisions now. We'll talk again tomorrow. You need to sleep.'

'I shall not sleep.'

'You will. I'll take you up. Come, can you stand? Take my arm.'

'Lord Verne,' she said, pressing her lips with the back of her hand.

'My lady?' he said, smiling at the gesture.

'You have compromised me. It was most unfair of you.'

'My lady, only you and I know what has passed between us. To the rest of the world, we met on the road and dined together. That's all. We sleep in different rooms and tomorrow I shall be offering you a lift in my carriage while I ride outside. Now what could be more correct than that? Whatever agreement we reach in the morning will be the result of an amicable discussion taken over breakfast, although I should warn you that my mind is already made up. I dare say yours might take a little longer.'

Exactly what this so-called discussion would be about Annemarie was not sure, for he had not proposed anything more specific than wanting her, which she dismissed as meaning wanting what she had, in spite of his denials. The need for sleep, however, was greater than her need to understand, so she allowed him to draw her hand through his arm as he opened the door, walking out into the passageway to the distant sound of laughter coming from the taproom.

But as he walked back to his room, Verne recalled Mrs Cardew's advice that, if he wanted to make headway with Annemarie, he must first find the mother. Better than that, he thought, would be to help Annemarie to find her, and to do that, she must venture out into society, with him. What better reason than that did he need to stay close to her, as he'd told her he would?

Chapter Four

$\infty\!\!\!\bigotimes\!\!\!\infty$

B y dawn, the Swan at Reigate was already preparing for the day. Annemarie's room faced east,
the rain had stopped and the clouds had scattered
to allow a watery sun to brighten by the minute.
Creeping back into the warm bed, she watched
Evie move quietly round the room while she pon-
dered over the events of last evening, hauling
back for examination each word, gesture, look
and touch. Clinging desperately to her original
plan to get rid of the letters and return to Brighton without any more interference, she refused
at first to contemplate an alternative, telling herself that what had happened was no more nor
less than a man taking advantage of the situation. What made Lord Verne any different from
the rest in that respect?

Perhaps she ought not to have asked herself a
question that was so easy to answer. The differ-
ences were impossible to ignore and the more

she thought about them, the louder the warning voices became. Remember what happened a year ago, they said. Don't allow it to happen again. Revenge is what you seek, not beguiling words about wanting and pursuing and possession, however sweet the accompanying kisses that melted your knees. Stay in control, the voices told her. If it's too pleasurable to let go of so soon, why not use it to your own advantage instead of his? Lure him on. Let's see what he means by his persuasive methods. Suggest some real commitment, something more serious than a flirtation that will tie up his time and his money. Make him work hard to reach his goal. The letters.

The temptation became more and more irresistible, not to shake him off so soon, but to keep him guessing as to whether, or when, where or how she had passed the letters on, to whom, for how much, and for what purpose. He would think, naturally, that her intention would be to discredit the Prince Regent. So let him think so. After all, there was some truth in it. He would have deduced by now that the silly slip about visiting Christie's was to find out where Lady Hamilton lived so that she could be given the money when the letters were sold. So let him think what he liked. Make him hang on, turn his pretence of desire into reality and then stop all

contact. Tell him the letters had gone. Damage
his pride, just as hers had been. Make him suffer.

Of course, she assured herself, she was not in
the least influenced by that flutter in her throat
she'd begun to feel when she thought about him.
Not at all. The sweet melting of her body in his
arms last night had nothing whatever to do with
any longing to repeat the experience, or even
to go further, eventually. She could control all
that. True, she had not done so far, but she could,
once her strategy was in place. After all, if her
mama and papa had been lovers, then so could
she take a lover, and if she had suggested last
night that her parents might not approve of an
unorthodox relationship, she was also reasonably certain that her father would not judge her
and that Lady Benistone would probably never
know. Less certain about the reaction of the others—Cecily, Oriel and her fiancé, and Marguerite, too—she decided she could not be expected
to mould her life around their concerns when she
was being offered a chance like this. She would
take it. She'd be a fool not to.

Smiling, she rolled out of bed and sent Evie for
some hot water. When she was gone, Annemarie pulled out the portmanteau from under the
washstand, took a quick peep at the lock, then
toed it back again. Today she would be taking
his Highness's letters to London in one of his
own most comfortable carriages. And now, with

good reason, she was about to suggest a liaison with a man who, only yesterday, she had asked to leave her alone. The contradiction of messages gave her butterflies.

The butterflies were still performing their dance when Annemarie entered the breakfast parlour an hour later to find Lord Verne already taking a cup of coffee before the food arrived. He was dressed immaculately in a snuff-brown cutaway coat, pale doeskin riding breeches and a crisp white shirt under a creamy-striped waistcoat with a gold seal and fob-watch hanging below. She thought she had rarely seen any man so well set-up at this early hour when most men of his sort would have been abed. Her father would have been up hours ago, but he was in every sense an exception.

She took the hand extended to her, accepting the touch of his lips upon her knuckles that afforded her a closer look at the thick brushed-back waves of dark hair and the tan on his lean cheeks that had not yet worn off. As he stood erect, she could not help wondering how much she would enjoy deceiving a man like him while preventing him from doing what he'd been sent to do. Would he accept her sudden change of attitude without question? Would he believe that his lovemaking had made her biddable and pliant? She would have to tread carefully to convince him that she was sincere.

'Good morning, my lord. You were right. I *did* sleep.' This was going to be the most bizarre conversation of her life, she thought. 'I think I was halfway there before…er, before…'

'Before you closed your eyes. Yes, at least halfway,' he said, laughing. 'I hope your memory is unimpaired, however. It would be a great pity if our conversation was all for nothing. Will you take coffee?'

'Thank you. Is breakfast ordered?'

'Yes, it's best to get one's order in early. Those stagecoach passengers had to stay overnight, you know. Heaven only knows where they all slept.' He pulled out a chair for her, then poured the coffee into her cup and, as she watched his strong hands on the handle and lid, she recalled their shocking explorations last evening and the way she had not stopped them.

Outside the window, rooftops shone with sunlight and rain. 'We'll be there in no time,' he said, cheerfully. 'They may have cleared a track through the landslide by now, but we'll go round to the west. Are you sure you want to go to Park Lane, not to Montague Street?'

A line of starlings strutted along the roofridge, jostling for position. 'Yes, but I've been thinking,' she said.

'About our conversation?'

Before she could continue, the breakfast was brought in and laid upon the white tablecloth, dish after dish. Yet as Lord Verne helped himself to the eggs, bacon and hunks of warm bread, she knew that as soon as there was a lull in proceedings, he would expect an answer and now there was no time to backtrack. 'About something you said.'

He waited, knife and fork poised. She was not finding this easy. 'Good,' he said. 'So you *did* remember.'

'About…oh, dear…this is *so* indelicate…about wanting me.'

'Ah.'

'Could you…perhaps…elaborate? Did you have something particular in mind? Or was it simply how you felt at that moment? You will not shock me, my lord, by explaining. I am not an innocent girl.'

The knife and fork were laid down as Verne gave her his full attention. 'Believe me,' he said, softly, 'it was not said lightly, on the spur of the moment. I did not expand on the notion because I didn't want to alarm you. Did you think I might have been insincere?'

'It had occurred to me,' she said, lifting the cover off a jam pot to look inside. 'It's difficult to know, isn't it?'

'I can see why you would think so. Did *you* have something specific in mind?'

Yes, I have it in mind to be your mistress, my lord. No, she couldn't say that. He would immediately suspect something. Hostility one day, a close relationship the next. No, it was inconceivable.

'You expressed a desire to help me back into society, my lord,' she said, speaking to her plate. 'And I suppose…well, I've been thinking it may not be such a bad thing to have someone like you to…be…er, to be seen with. Which, of course, would set tongues wagging. So…well… then I thought that, if I were to go one step further, I might suggest becoming…er…something closer?'

'Closer than a friend, you mean? More like a mistress?'

There, the word was out in the open, like a weight falling from her shoulders. Piling a spoonful of golden honey on to her plate, she scooped it on to the corner of her toast and took a bite, nodding in agreement. 'Mmm,' she said.

The bacon and eggs remained untouched as he supported his lower lip with his knuckle, weighing up what it had cost her to make the suggestion after such recent antagonism. Whatever deep game she was playing, it had little to do with a desire to take her place in society once more, of that he was certain. It had even less to do with a sudden reversal of her feelings towards him, despite her participation in their lovemaking, for Lady Golding's antipathy towards men would not be dispelled by a few hours of overnight reasoning. There had to be more to it than that, something that concerned him personally. Or the Prince Regent personally. Or those damned letters. Or all three.

'I'm sorry,' she whispered. 'Say no more about it. I thought you would—'

His hand reached out across the table to stop the retraction. 'No, please! I was a little...well... surprised, that's all, and delighted, of course. I have no problems whatever with that. None at all. I can see many advantages, one of which would mean that you would be free of duties at Montague Street and this would give you the chance to do the things you used to do. In my company. Protected. I've never been one to think that a man's mistress should be kept hidden away and ignored in public as if there was some shame in the connection. I have my own good reasons for wanting an alliance of the kind you suggest, too, you see.'

'Other than the usual one, you mean?'

He smiled at that, sure that they were thinking along the same lines. 'Yes, other than that, although I won't deny the pleasure we'd both find there. It's all these social functions I'm duty-bound to attend. Like you, I want a regular partner of whom I can feel proud, a woman I can admire for more than one reason and who has a certain position in society already. A beautiful intelligent mistress would be ideal, even if our agreement lasts no longer than this Season.'

'Well, thank you for admiring me for more than one reason. That's very gratifying, my lord. And for making it sound as if such an arrangement might benefit yourself as much as me. I would have thought you could have your choice of any single woman in the country, especially as an escort in such close contact with the Prince Regent, able to guarantee a place at all the best functions. But I have little experience at this kind of thing. Being a mistress, I mean. I imagine one is expected to set out certain…er…requirements? To avoid misunderstandings? Is that what one does?'

By the sound of things, he thought, she had already given the idea some detailed consideration, for she was coldly matter of fact about it, meant to convince him that he'd had no effect on her feelings and that it was a business arrangement devised to serve her some particular purpose, not necessarily one of those she had mentioned earlier. He was therefore prepared for a very precise list of benefits meant to test both his dedication and his pocket. She was a wealthy woman: she would expect him to match her standard of living, or to exceed it.

'My lady, I do not expect there to be anything you could ask of me that I would balk at, unless of course you wished to use a team of white mules to draw your carriage, or bathe in asses' milk twice daily. With all these foreigners in town, that could be a bit difficult to acquire. You will need a house in London, naturally. That goes without saying. With stabling for your horses. A place in Mayfair, perhaps?'

'Mayfair…yes…would be perfect. Near enough to Father and my sisters, and to Mrs Cardew.'

'And to me.'

'Yes, to you, too. I would wish to live there permanently, you see, not to use the address only for…for assignations. That would not serve my purpose at all.'

And what exactly *is* your purpose? he wanted to say. But she had outlined a perfectly acceptable reason that would have to suffice until he could discover more, and he was not about to look a gift horse in the mouth when she had offered him more than he could ever have expected so soon. If there was an ulterior motive, he would have to wait for it to be revealed. 'I can understand that,' he said. 'A London home of your own would be much more convenient for you, wouldn't it? I would not like to deprive your father of you altogether, but you would be glad to have more space, I'm sure.'

'Nevertheless, I feel a little selfish leaving my sisters to manage without my help. You have not met my older sister, have you? She's engaged to be married to Colonel Harrow. Your breakfast is getting cold.'

'Harrow? Fourteenth Light Dragoons? Is she indeed? Well then,' he said, picking up his knife and fork, 'perhaps we're both urgently in need of some socialising. I'm sadly out of date, it seems. We shall do well together, my lady.'

Annemarie could feel nothing but relief, now that her proposition was understood without the dreaded need to explain herself. For one thing, she could not have explained herself any better without revealing something of the artifice, the year-old pain, the lacerated pride and the loss, especially of her beloved and treacherous mother, about whom he need be told no more than he already knew. And now, for the first time, it began to occur to her that, once more in contact with the *beau monde*, she might hear something of Lady Benistone's whereabouts, some clue that her sisters hadn't been able to discover. If Oriel and Marguerite required a convincing explanation of her uncharacteristic behaviour, that would be as good as any. It would not be far from the truth, either, for if Papa would not bestir himself to search for her, then she would. Whether Lady Benistone had resorted to her former way of life, had fallen on hard times, or was happily settled with her lover Annemarie had no way of knowing until she could make enquiries.

Memories of her mama's beautiful face formed into the folds of the white napkin on her lap, sad violet eyes filled with regret, the lovely mouth trembling with wretchedness, the soft bloom of her cheeks streaked with tears. Like a sudden premonition, and without warning, Annemarie's breath was drawn up into a sob too noisy to prevent it being heard. Raggedly, it fell out again as her hand flew to hold her forehead, but by that time Verne was beside her, lifting her bodily out of her chair to hold her against him as if he knew what the matter was without being told.

'I know,' he whispered into her hair. 'I know. It's all right. It goes against the grain to put yourself in my hands, doesn't it? Hush, don't try to deny it, my beauty. I know how it is with you, but whatever your reasons, I shall keep my side of the bargain. I shall not be unreasonable, or unfaithful, or anything less than careful. And I shall dress for dinner every evening.'

She inhaled the fresh scent of his skin. 'I told you my reasons,' she said.

'Some of them, yes. But when a woman like you offers herself to a man she's been trying to get rid of since they first met, he would have to be a serious ninnyhammer not to suspect some ulterior motive, wouldn't he? And my reputation is not for being queer in my attic.'

'No, I know that. I'm sorry. It's too complicated. Too many issues.'

'Hardly surprising. A lot has happened to you,
so I believe. Well, we may not see eye to eye on
everything, but however much you disapprove
of me, there is at least one area where our tastes
combine. Which you have obviously appreciated,
or you'd not have suggested a liaison with me.
Not in a million years. Would you, my beauty?'

'No, I suppose not,' she whispered.

His kiss was soft and undemanding, more like
a reward for everything she had offered him and
for what he'd won from her. Neither of them
could have failed to see the direction of their
shared interest, nor did they see any reason to
pretend otherwise when there were so many at-
tendant advantages. But Annemarie had already
begun to notice that the revenge at the back-
bone of her scheme tended to weaken at times
of physical contact with this amazing man. That
problem would have to be addressed, or disaster would strike again, for he had implied a certain impermanence when he'd said '…even if
our agreement lasts no longer than this Season'.
He could not have made it plainer if he'd said
'even if it lasts no longer than it takes to get hold
of those letters'. Withdrawing herself from his
arms, she wondered which of them was the de-
ceiver and which the deceived.

'Your breakfast will be quite cold, my lord.'

'Nothing to worry about,' he said, helping her back into her chair. 'Only a few months ago I was glad to get any breakfast at all. You should eat a little more than a slice of toast, too, although we can stop for a bite along the way. Are you in a hurry to get back?'

'Not any more. In such a comfortable carriage, I shall enjoy the rest of the journey.'

'Glad to hear it. But we have a lot to discuss, and I don't want to give you time to change your mind.'

'I shall not change my mind, except about telling Father I'm in town. He'll have to be told now, won't he?'

By the time she returned to her room after breakfast, Annemarie's butterflies were doing a different kind of dance that reached her legs and made her sit rather suddenly on the bed to think it through. Rarely had she made such an impulsive decision of that magnitude, the enormity of which astounded even her. Did she share this trait with her mama? Had impulsiveness led Lady Benistone into a situation from which she could not extricate herself? Would it do the same to her? Would she regret this to the end of her days? Was her bitterness still such a potent force that she would enjoy the eventual humiliation of a man who was doing no more than his royal employer's bidding? Was that really what it was all about, or was she being influenced by other factors, too? The idea of living in her own London house and being seen on the arm of this particular nobleman would signal that the earlier scandal attached to Sir Richard Golding's widow was hardly worth a mention and that the next tasty bit of gossip would cause envy rather than pity. She could expect some resistance from her loved ones, but that would have to be overcome. Had they not tried to persuade her for months to restart her life?

'Yes, but not *this* way, surely?' said Cecily later that same day.

'His *mistress*?' said Oriel, trying to keep the horror of it from showing. 'Did you have to go that far? Couldn't you just…well…be *friends*?'

Dear Oriel. So conventional. Foes would have been a more appropriate word. 'No, love,' Annemarie said, preparing for a sustained argument. 'Why do you think I preferred to stay here in Park Lane rather than home? I couldn't possibly have invited Lord Verne there as a friend of *mine*, knowing that Father would catch him by the lapels and drag him off to see his latest things. I wouldn't get a look in, would I? A place of my own is what I need. Lord Verne understands that.'

He was, she had discovered, a very understanding kind of man. She had hardly needed to explain how desperate was her desire to separate herself from the set-up at Montague Street that had such bad memories for her. Thinking back on their conversation over lunch while the horses were being rested, he himself had been the one to enumerate what she would require by the way of servants: a cook, a butler and a housekeeper as well as the usual underlings. It would need rooms large enough for her to entertain, he said, to have friends to stay, and empty enough at the start for her to make choices about furnishings which they would have the pleasure of finding together. She would be able to polish her driving skills in town and the nearby Hyde Park, and she would be his companion at functions he was expected to attend. That, it seemed, was to be a part of the deal and Annemarie saw no reason to object since it would serve her purpose too. Quite willingly, she also agreed to accompany him on his art-collecting trips and to Brighton, too, and to entertain those collectors from whom he wished to purchase. As the daughter of Lord Benistone, one of the British Museum's greatest benefactors, she would be an asset, he told her.

The discussion of allowances for housekeeping and personal expenditure had been postponed, but since the financial aspect of the arrangement was not of prime importance to her, she was content not to press for details. There was, after all, a limit to her new-found ill intentions that she preferred not to explore until later.

'I'm glad to hear it,' Cecily said. 'It was just as well he came to visit, isn't it?'

Annemarie was relieved to think that Cecily was more perplexed than scandalised, though in fact Cecily was taken aback more by the phenomenal speed than by the contract itself. Had Annemarie considered how this would affect Oriel's situation? she wanted to know.

Before Annemarie could answer, Oriel spoke up in her sister's defence. 'Oh, no, Cecily. That's unfair. Of course she's thought about it, but one cannot always be using excuses of that kind to remain stuck for ever in a situation. I'm glad Annemarie has accepted Lord Verne's offer. It may be rather sudden, but it couldn't have come at a better time, and it won't affect William and me in the slightest, not until he leaves the army, and he says that might not be for another year. I cannot wait to meet the brave man who's managed to prise Annemarie out of her shell. I'm sure I shall like him, if she likes him well enough to agree to be his mistress.'

'Thank you, dearest,' said Annemarie, noting the mistaken change of roles. 'I hoped you'd understand.' She did not dare correct Oriel's assumption that it was Verne himself who had suggested it.

'I understand, too,' said Cecily. 'Of course I

do. Wouldn't anyone prefer to live in their own place with a lover, rather than...tch! Oh dear! How clumsy of me.'

'It's all right,' said Annemarie, taking Cecily in her arms and soothing the *faux pas* with a stroking hand over the gaily striped satin shoulder. 'Say no more. This sounds a bit like history repeating itself, doesn't it? But it's not. There's more to it than meets the eye.'

'Oh?' they said, in unison. 'More to it? Tell.'

What a fool to let secrets slip. That's what sympathy does.

As upright as penguins, they sat down again on the pale-grey brocade sofa, smoothing their knees in anticipation of whatever it was they ought to be knowing.

What did it matter? They won't approve, but I cannot keep this to myself for ever. 'I don't want Marguerite to know,' she said. 'Or Father.'

'About you being Lord Verne's mistress? How...?'

'I don't mean that. They'll have to know about *that*. I mean...this.' She pushed forwards the battered portmanteau that had stood beside her chair, half-hidden under the padded arm and the claw foot as if it had no business to be in such a tastefully furnished room.

'I wondered why you insisted on bringing that in here,' said Cecily. 'What does it have to do with…the other thing?' She glanced at it, ac-cusingly.

So, starting with the purchase of the bureau, the alarming visit of Lord Verne and his inten-tions, and then the discovery of the letters in Brighton, Annemarie told them as much as she thought they needed to know because by that time it had become clear that, without the as-sistance of someone trustworthy, getting rid of them was going to be fraught with too many complications. Lord Verne had made it clear, in the nicest possible way, that he meant to spend quite a lot of his time in her company. Her mar-gin of opportunity was already shrinking.

The portmanteau quickly became an ob-ject of fascination. 'In *there*?' said Cecily. 'So that's why you can't let go of it. Good gracious, Annemarie, that's *dynamite*. What are you going to do with them? Give them back? Is that why you've rushed back to London?'

Courteously, they listened to her options that stopped well short of the less-than-creditable scheme that would end it all, which she knew would find no favour in their eyes and might indeed antagonise them enough to refuse their help. With only a few unrealistic alternatives to offer, both Cecily and Oriel agreed that the let-ters should be returned, as quickly and as se-cretly as possible, to Lady Hamilton to whom they rightly belonged, fully understanding that

to keep Lord Verne guessing would add to the
fun, until she felt like telling him. Besides, they
said, it would do no harm at all to frighten his
Royal Highness to death—no, not literally—
over something as potentially calamitous as a
batch of intimate letters to a forlorn woman on
whose friendship he had preyed. Could they read
one? Just one?

Annemarie frowned at this. 'No, dear,' she
said. 'They're private and very personal. We
must not pry.'

'Didn't *you*?' Cecily wheedled.

'Only a few, just to see if they were all the
same. They're utterly ridiculous, from a man of
his supposed intelligence.'

'I'll take them to her for you,' Cecily said. 'I
know where she is.'

'You do? I intended to ask Mr Parke at Christie's, where I bought the bureau.'

'No need. She's been living under the Rule
of the King's Bench, on and off, for over a year
now.'

'Debtors' prison?' said Oriel. 'Oh, the poor
woman.'

'With her daughter Horatia. I doubt she'll ever
be freed.' Cecily's matter-of-fact tone grated
harshly on Annemarie's tender heart. A forsaken
woman and her twelve-year-old child confined to
a debtors' prison, losing not only her lover and
her friends, but all hope, too, while she herself

was debating the neatest way to feather her own
comfortable nest, to nurse her temporary hurts,
to settle old scores upon a man who was not even
remotely involved except that she distrusted his
motives, as she would have distrusted any man's.

'*Would* you?' said Annemarie. 'Would you
really go to a place like that?'

'Number Twelve Temple Place. I can get in
there. Others do. Of course I'll go.'

'Thank you, Cecily. Remind me to give you
the key before you go.'

'Give it to me now, dear, then you can go
up and change. You must be tired. I'm so glad
you came here. When does your house-hunting
begin?'

Delving into the depths of her velvet reticule,
Annemarie found the tiny key and handed it to
Cecily. 'Tomorrow. It was kind of you, dear one,
to let me stay. I shall now have time to go shopping for clothes. I left most of my things behind
in Brighton.'

'I'll go with you,' said Oriel, heading for the
door. 'You know there's nothing I like more than
that. After breakfast?'

'Yes. But what about Marguerite? Is she at
home?'

'Staying at the Sindleshams. They're taking
her to see the firework display in the Park. Come
and have dinner with Father and William and
me. It'll be a good opportunity to tell him what's

happening without little sister to stir things up.
We'll expect you both for seven, shall we?'

'We'll come,' said Annemarie, embracing her.

But when Oriel had taken her leave, the perceptive Cecily appeared to need clarification on a few more points. With a hand on her waist, she propelled Annemarie towards the abandoned portmanteau, poking at it with the point of her toe. 'So Lord Verne thinks these are still in your bureau, does he?' she said.

'I…. Why do you ask?'

'Because, you little goose, any woman who insists on carrying her own luggage, as you did, from a carriage like that one is telling the world that no one else can be trusted with it. If he's not worked it out for himself, he's not the man I took him for.'

'I told him I had valuables to take to Christie's.'

'Yes, dear. He deals with valuables most days of the week, I expect. Did you know he's Simonstoke's eldest son? There's more wealth in that family than in the Prince Regent's. Property scattered everywhere.'

'Cecily, you may be right about him thinking I must have discovered them. That's why I want them off my hands as soon as possible and I want you to take her some money, too. I cannot bear to think of her being penniless in a place like that. She deserves better. Although, of course, she took another woman's husband, didn't she?'

With a flicker of her eyebrows, Cecily agreed. 'And you still intend, do you, even after they're back where they belong, to let Verne believe *you* have them? Is that *really* just to keep his Royal Highness from sleeping at night, or is there more to *that*, too, than meets the eye?'

'Oh dear. Have I not managed to convince you, Cecily?'

'You have not quite managed, my love, to pull the wool down far enough over my eyes. And somehow I doubt that Verne will be as gullible either.'

'The shoe is on the other foot. His interest in me goes only as far as those letters. After that, I shall cease to be of the slightest concern to him and I'm not in the least flattered that he thinks I don't know it.'

'So you intend to take him for a ride. Is that it?'

'Yes, if you must know, it is.'

The uncompromising words cut no ice with Cecily, being no stranger to the confused emotions of young women, or to the conflicts that tear apart otherwise loving families. 'Mmm,' she said. 'You wouldn't want any advice from me, then, concerning the dangers.'

'I've thought of the dangers, love. I know

what I'm doing. How soon can you visit Lady Hamilton?'

'I'll go tomorrow while you're out with Oriel. Will that do?'

Annemarie pulled out a handful of banknotes from her reticule. 'This is what I was going to use for the journey,' she said, handing it to Cecily. 'Will you give it to her with my regards?'

'That's a lot,' Cecily said, taking it with obvious reluctance.

'It won't be a lot to her. Now, shall I go up? Keep a close eye on the bag, won't you? Put it somewhere *very* safe while we're out this evening.'

'You can be sure I will, m'dear. You'll find everything you need in the Chinese Room. I'll order the carriage for just before seven, shall I?'

Well done, my lord, she said to herself as Annemarie disappeared upstairs. You certainly don't let the grass grow under *your* feet, do you? Opening her hand, she smiled at the key upon her palm before closing her fingers gently round it.

Upon her return to Montague Street, Oriel discovered that her fiancé was with her father, deep into a discussion about a collection of antiquities that the British Museum had bought in 1805, which was now thought to be less valuable than the £20,000 they had paid for it. 'Mine is far superior, in fact,' Lord Benistone was saying in a voice that bounced off the statue-lined corridor. 'Ah...Oriel, m'dear,' he said, catching sight of his eldest daughter, 'we should ask Colonel Harrow to have dinner with us.'

'We already have done, Father,' she said, smiling sideways at her handsome William. 'And I have a surprise for you. Annemarie and Cecily will be dining with us, too.'

Lord Benistone's pale eyes wrinkled tightly round the edges like an old envelope, fixing his eldest daughter with a look of deep suspicion that she found more amusing than alarming. 'Why isn't she at Brighton? What's going on?'

'Lord Verne brought her back. There's been a...a development.' Oriel drew off her gloves and pulled at the ribbons of her poke bonnet, still smiling.

'Oh! Has there indeed? Well, come along, miss. Are you going to tell me what this is all about?'

'No, Father. We should allow Annemarie to do that herself, I think.'

'In which case, Verne ought to be here when she does it, since I expect it concerns him, too. Invite him to dine, then we'll get the story from both sides.'

The smile wavered, finding no support in William's mischievous silence. 'Wouldn't it be better if she could tell you without—?'

'No. If this is another of Annemarie's impulsive decisions, I'd better be knowing about it before it's too late.'

'Too late to what, Father?'

'To stop it. Where is she?'

'Staying with Cecily. She thought—'

'Hah! She thought I'd ask too many questions. She's right. I shall.'

'Father, Annemarie is a widow, you know.'

'Exactly! Ought to know better.' Crooking a finger at the footman who stood discreetly at one end of the hall, he scribbled a hasty message on one of the cards from the table and placed it in the man's white-gloved hand. 'Lord Verne. Bedford Square,' he said.

'Do you think you might find time to dress, Father, since we shall be having guests?' Oriel enquired, with little hope of agreement.

Lord Benistone peered over the top of his spectacles with a frown. Catching the merest hint of a nod from his future son-in-law, he gave a non-commital grunt. 'If there's time,' he said.

'I'm glad Verne's coming to dine,' said Colonel Harrow. 'I met him a few times. Quite a reputation he had in Spain. Remarkable chap, you know. It'll be good to see him again.'

'If he's managed to interest Annemarie, he certainly is,' she said. 'I'd better go and talk to cook, dearest. I'll join you in the conservatory.'

* * *

Knowing Lord Benistone as well as they did, Annemarie, Oriel and Cecily were not entirely taken in by his assumed concern about the new arrangement which, although it must have come as a surprise to him, he appeared to accept after some close questioning to which he must already have known the answers. Or most of them, anyway. There was no one else, he admitted rather grudgingly, he would have considered for the role as Annemarie's escort, although he did not explain how he might have prevented it when her last one had been such a disaster. If he had any reservations about the unconventional nature of the relationship, he supposed they were both old enough to know what they were doing, by which he meant, they all understood, that he was hardly the one to protest when he had done the same himself.

But the ladies' scepticism remained; Father would have shown less interest in the details had not Colonel Harrow been there as an interested observer. The answer he gave to the question of how much help Annemarie would be expected to give to showing his visitors round the collection, however, surprised them all.

'Oh, no need to bother about that,' he said, airily. 'That's been attended to.'

Cecily looked up, sharply. 'Has it, Elmer?' she said. 'How?'

'I've enlisted some help, dear,' he said with an impish grin. 'And before you ask where from, they're from across the road. British Museum. They're sending in three men on each of our open days to help with the extra visitors and with the cataloguing. I've had visitors here in droves, lately.' Beaming mildly at his two daughters, he continued, 'So you won't be needed, either of you. Oriel dear, you're free of duties. I've got some of their cleaners, too. How does that sound?'

It sounded, after a moment of stunned silence, too good to be true. 'Are you expanding then, Papa?' Oriel wanted to know, thinking of the new head.

'Mmm, not exactly, m'dear. Now, isn't it time for pudding?'

Unable to elicit anything more on the subject, their natural assumption was that, partly through their own devices and partly through his, they were being squeezed out of Number Fourteen Montague Street in favour of the collection. And while Annemarie was relieved by her father's acceptance of her own plan to begin socialising, her feelings about being relieved of duties at home were ambivalent, to put it mildly.

'It's not that I *wanted* to be here three times a week,' she told Lord Verne as he prepared to escort her and Cecily back to Park Lane, 'but it does begin to look as if he was just waiting for me to disappear before getting in all this help. Why could he not have done it sooner? Why the sudden cataloguing? And cleaning. What would have happened if I'd not decided to…to live… somewhere else?'

'To be my mistress? You'd have come back from Brighton to find a life-size marble statue of Adonis in your bed,' he said, taking her hand in his. 'Or worse, one of those leery centaurs. Just as a hint to move out.'

She struggled not to laugh, but failed. 'Now you're being vulgar,' she said.

He grinned. 'So you know about centaurs, do you? Ah!'

'Enough, thank you. It was good of you to come at such short notice. Papa wanted you to meet Colonel Harrow again. He was glad to see you.'

Verne had been a few minutes late, delayed by his visit to his Royal Highness at Carlton House, but quite unaware that, while they waited, his exploits with Wellington's army in Spain last year were being revealed in detail. Colonel Harrow's 14th Light Dragoons and the 10th Hussars had joined forces for the Battle of Vitoria exactly one year ago when Jacques Verne's bravery and daring had been the talk of the officers' tents for months. Viscount Wellington himself had visited him in the field hospital and had commended his fierce attempts to save a crowd of French women who were fleeing with the Emperor Joseph from certain atrocities by uncontrollable men from his own side. The Emperor's wagon train of over three thousand carriages had been over twelve miles long, full of priceless art and antiquities, taken from Valladolid by Napoleon's brother, the Spanish king, accompanied by families, court officials and terrified women. Once intercepted, the carnage was indescribable, the looting a disgrace to the British army, the loss of the five-and-a-half million gold francs, countless treasures, jewellery, furniture and libraries, grabbed, torn, destroyed and stolen. Badly wounded, Verne had personally fought off the rampaging foot soldiers of his own side to protect the women dragged from the carriages. Ultimately, Vitoria had been a success, but at a terrible cost, including Wellington's fury. Verne had been sent home to recover, returning to the capital only after months of nursing at his parents' country home.

Sitting open-mouthed with astonishment, Annemarie had noted the admiration dawn upon the faces of her family as Colonel Harrow praised the courage of the man she was planning to bring to his knees. He had protected a crowd of helpless women, French, not English, from a howling mob of soldiers who would have torn them apart to get at the valuables they wore, a mob for whom a single jewel represented more than they could earn in a lifetime. Unlike her late husband, whose death had been his only injury, Verne had said not one word to her about his exploits, while she had casually labelled him with the usual anecdotal misconducts attached to his elite regiment. Apart from suggesting that he might be an exception, which she had chosen not to believe, he was allowing her to find out for herself what kind of man he was. The discovery did nothing to commend her programme of revenge and, when he eventually arrived with profuse apologies for lateness, Annemarie had already begun to see him more as a protector than a predator.

'I was glad to see Harrow, too,' he said. 'He's a good man. Perfect for your sister. They should be our first guests, with Mrs Cardew. D'ye think?'

'We'll give a dinner party. All your friends and mine.'

His white smile broadened into a laugh. 'That's my girl,' he whispered. 'Already you're entering into the spirit of the thing. Shall we invite your father?'

'If he dresses as he did tonight, then certainly,' she said. Lord Benistone had risen to the occasion, giving his valet more to do than he'd had for years, as well as a shock that earned him a brandy after his master's departure from the untidy clothes-scattered bedroom.

'Last time I kissed you goodnight in this hall,' Verne said, looking around him, 'we were watched by a row of erotic nymphs on pedestals. Do you think we might have some more privacy, this time, before the others appear?'

Earlier that day, Annemarie would have made excuses not to, but with his hand pressing hers and a whole evening of his closeness, his talk and graceful mannerisms, his staggering good looks, the cold core of hardness in her heart, so long nurtured, had begun to soften round the edges enough to let him in. To her own surprise as well as his, she drew him towards the door of the morning room where they had first talked at cross-purposes and, once in the dark overcrowded space, turned to him as he closed the door softly.

'No David's hand this time,' he said.

'So mind the priceless Attic vase,' she replied, lifting her arms to enclose him.

For a woman whose interest was flawed, Annemarie's surrender to his kisses must surely have been convincing to anyone less astute than Verne. He had noticed the difference in her demeanour during the evening which, although by no means effusive, had been warmer than that first chilling experience, but not for one moment did he believe that the change had come about naturally. Not in a woman of her sort. Not so fast. Not so easy. So when her body bowed into his, her arms linked around his neck, he felt the apprehension as well as the curiosity and would liked to have known more about the change and the reasons for it. So hurt and vulnerable, yet prepared to sell herself for some cause or other.

This time, she was neither exhausted nor mellowed by wine, but fully aware of every part of him pressing against her from knee to nose, the strong hands across her back and grasping her shoulder, the intoxicating taste of his lips covering hers, warm and persuasive, enticing her to stay and respond. She could easily have pulled away when he took her head between his hands, holding her for a soft shower of kisses falling upon her eyelids, cheeks, chin and mouth. But she did not, smiling instead at the tender caress of a man who, with his sabre, could put to flight a rabble of blood-lusting men. That, while he was wounded.

'That's new to you, isn't it, my beauty?' he whispered, still holding her.

Huffing with laughter, she agreed, 'Mmm. Everything is.'

'Then I shall have the pleasure of teaching you.'

'Have you had a great deal of experience, my lord?' she said, holding his wrists.

'That is a question mistresses and wives may not ask. If one says no, that implies a certain restraint which may not be entirely true. And if one says yes…'

'That implies a certain intemperance that may not…'

'Quite. Does it matter much to you?'

'No, my lord. I knew the answer before I asked.'

She could not see his smile before his next kiss, but felt the sudden surge of energy behind it, as if her answer had pleased him. But instead of thinking him arrogant, her thoughts veered towards the lessons that awaited her in his arms and the pleasure she would have in learning from him. For how long they remained locked together in the darkness she could never remember, only that by the time they emerged into the hall, her legs had turned to water and a strange unfamiliar ache of longing had begun to suffuse her thighs, making her gasp at its sweetness.

Chapter Five

From the very beginning, Cecily had not entirely approved of Annemarie's unconcealed hostility towards Lord Verne. Now, when she had been told of the reason for the abrupt change, she could not approve of that either. Being resentful and distrustful of men was one thing, but this was a dangerous game to play with a man of his calibre and deceitful, too, given his proven gallantry towards women. She had watched with some consternation how Annemarie had responded to him during the evening and wondered how much of that was due to Colonel Harrow's glowing account and how much to whatever had happened in Brighton. Was Annemarie as good an actress as that, or was her heart being softened, despite her protestations? Cecily knew her very well and did not believe she had it in her to persist in any attempt to break a man's heart, thinking it would mend hers in the process. Annemarie had never been in the least spiteful. She would not be able to do it and, what was more, Verne did not deserve it.

With these worrying thoughts in her mind as she prepared for bed, the idea of a further collaboration with Verne seemed like a natural progression. Perhaps to let him know where the letters had been taken? Just to keep him one step ahead instead of one step behind? He would know how to handle the information, what to do next, whether to proceed with this unsound domestic relationship that was intended to lead nowhere, or not.

She decided to take a look, to reassure herself.

Placing the portmanteau beside her feet, she unlocked the catch and flicked the leather tab back, pulling the sides apart wide enough to allow one hand inside. But instead of contacting the firm edges of folded papers, her fingertips encountered something soft. She gave a yelp, withdrew her hand and opened the bag wider, staring in disbelief at the corded upper edge of a cushion.

'Of course,' she whispered. 'I should have known. He doesn't need my help, does he? Clever devil. He's already got them. One step behind, indeed. Was it ever likely, Cecily my girl?' She pulled the cushion out, a pretty thing, a blue-velvet border round a silk patchwork, neatly made with tassels at each corner. But for whom?

Would the owner be missing it? Of the letters there was no sign. She placed the cushion beside her on the bed as a tap on the door made her start, guiltily. 'Who is it?' she said, kicking the portmanteau under her legs.

'Me, ma'am. Evie.' The door opened enough to allow Evie to peer round. 'Sorry to disturb you, ma'am, but m'lady wonders if—?'

'Come inside and close the door.' The very person who would know.

'Yes, ma'am.'

Cecily rarely beat about the bush to no purpose. Patting the cushion, she directed Evie's attention, observing with some satisfaction how the pretty eyes latched onto the contrast of pale blue on the bright pink silk of her bedspread. 'Where did this come from?' she said. 'You appear to recognise it, Evie.'

At Cecily's beckoning finger, Evie approached and took the cushion for a closer look, turning it over and over as if to make sure. 'Yes, ma'am. There were two of them on the window-seat.'

'Where?'

Evie's eyes opened wide as they met Cecily's. 'Er…at the Swan, ma'am. In Lady Golding's room. Last night. Where we stayed.'

'Yes? And who else was in the room? With you, I mean.'

'No…er…no one, er…' Her gaze dropped back to the cushion as if it might contradict her.

'Ee...vee?'

The young maid stroked the cushion as a deep pink blush flooded her face, deeper than her pale curls, and the blue eyes filled with tears at being so soon discovered in a lie she could not maintain.

'For heaven's sake, don't weep,' Cecily said, 'or your mistress will want to know why. What is it you came for?'

'A pearl button, ma'am, to replace one that's missing.'

'Over there in the drawer. Needle and thread, too. Go and stitch the button, then before you go to your own room, come back here to me. We have to talk. And don't look like that, lass. I'm not about to have you dismissed.'

'Yes, ma'am. Thank you, ma'am.' Evie fled.

Twenty minutes later she was back with the rest of the story. 'It was Lord Verne's valet, ma'am. Samson. He came to the room to ask if I needed to go down for some supper. His lordship had told him there were valuables to be watched and he offered to stay with them while I went to get a tray. He's a very superior kind of young man, ma'am. Quite top-lofty he is.'

'I'm sure he is, Evie. So you went down and left him in the room.'

Evie nodded, glancing again at the offending cushion. 'I didn't think,' she said.

'Didn't think what? That he couldn't pick the lock of a portmanteau? Most lordship's valets can pick locks as easy as breathing, girl. And much else besides. They'd not be much use to them if they couldn't.'

'Oh dear, ma'am, this is terrible. What's her ladyship going to say when she discovers her valuables are missing?'

'Leave that to me. I take it you had supper together, then, you and Mr Samson?'

'Yes, ma'am, I took supper up for us both. It took ages for me to get it, what with all the stage-coach passengers staying overnight. He took the tray back down when we'd finished. Very polite he was. I'd never have thought he was a thief. Such a correct young man, ma'am.'

'Very nimble-fingered he was, too, Evie. Listen to me. I don't suppose for a moment he'll have told Lord Verne that he took anything from the portmanteau, so you must not say anything either. Lady Golding has left it for me to deal with and I shall. So now you need take no action, except to beware of presentable polite young men who offer to do you a favour. Was it only supper you had together, Evie?'

Evie did not pretend to misunderstand, for by then she was quite capable of believing the worst of Samson, despite their pleasant hour together. 'It was only supper, ma'am. Nothing else. I know when to draw the line.'

'Good. Now, this should be taken back to where it belongs, or they'll be thinking at the Swan that Lady Golding is a real rum touch, nicking their best room cushions.'

Cecily's slang brought a weak smile to Evie's face. 'I'll take it. Lady Golding would not have noticed it, so I can always slip it back if we call there again. Goodnight, and thank you, ma'am,' she said, tucking it under her arm. 'I'm so sorry about this. I shall not be so trusting again.'

'Goodnight, Evie.' Cecily's eyes rolled heavenwards as the door closed. 'Tch!' she said. 'Now what?' So much for Verne wanting no more to do with Annemarie once he had the letters. He had taken them and then decided to take her as his mistress. The Prince Regent would now be breathing a huge sigh of relief and no wonder Verne had been late for dinner. Mission accomplished.

Cecily was not the only one to have reservations about Annemarie's newest plans. Since that morning, when Annemarie had first suggested it, there had been time enough, as the countryside passed her by, for her to ponder on the wisdom of becoming the mistress of a man she scarcely knew. Such a position was fraught with danger even if it had been arrived at after a lengthy consideration, which it had not. But now she felt as if she'd been manoeuvred into it without being able to blame anyone but herself. Mistresses were not in the least uncommon, nor were they particularly ostracised except by the envious, but it had never been an ambition of hers to live the life of a *demi-rep* rather than a wife. What would be her chances of marriage when this *affaire* came to an end? Was she effectively devaluing herself by this? Would it be worth the effort? Or the risk?

Later, after returning to Park Lane, she saw the chances of a change of mind becoming even more remote after her father's approval, which she suspected would not have been so forthcoming if he'd not already seen Lord Verne as a fellow antiquarian and collector. He had not even suggested she should give it more thought. Were fathers not supposed to be a little more protective? Resistant? Suggesting alternatives? Nor had Verne's lengthy goodnight been calculated to give her time to think again. For the second time, and without the excuse of fatigue, she had put up no resistance to his kisses. Worse, she had been thinking about the earlier ones all through dinner. No wonder he was suspicious of her swift change of heart when she herself was unsure how much was pretence and how much was genuine. Was it all moving too fast for comfort?

The problem of how to rid herself of the letters, however, was virtually solved, the only consequence now being to keep Verne from knowing whether she had them and what she had done with them. Obviously, his attempts to stay close to her in order to find out would be his main concern, and so when he arrived after breakfast to escort the two sisters on their shopping expedition, with a smart two-horse barouche waiting outside, that was seen as a game to be played out by them both.

They were back on Park Lane in time for a late luncheon after several productive hours of shopping, finishing off at Gunter's in Berkeley Square for refreshing ices. 'Oh, Cecily, you never saw such fabrics. And the lace. And furs. The *glacé* silks and grenadines. I purchased striped *barège* enough for a skirt, with a violet silk to make a matching jacket,' said Annemarie, searching through the parcels, 'a shilling and threepence a yard, and satins at four shillings. But I need something for this afternoon. Perhaps I could borrow your maid to go with Evie to Montague Street to bring a few of my other clothes back here. It'll be a few days before my new things are ready.'

'Of course. You cannot continue to borrow Marguerite's evening dresses as you did last night.'

'I bought her a pair of satin shoes, to say thank you. And this, dear Cecily, is for you.' The hatbox was deep with layers of tissue to protect a white-lace and silk-flower creation for Cecily's fair curls, exclusive, expensive, and utterly extravagant. 'For you to wear at the theatre with your Chantilly lace shawl,' said Annemarie.

'Oh, my dear child, there's really no need to thank me. You know you're always welcome here, love.'

'Not just that,' said Annemarie. 'This morning, too. Did you see her?'

In view of the shopping spree, Cecily thought she had forgotten about Lady Hamilton. 'Yes, I saw her,' she said, trying on the lace cap before the mirror.

'And? Was she pleased?'

Cecily came to sit beside her. 'Tie it for me. Should the bow be to this side? Yes, she was surprised *and* pleased. She wants you to know how immensely grateful she is for your thoughtfulness. In fact, she sent you a note. Here you are. She apologises for its hastiness, but I got the impression she was preparing to move again. Rather quickly.'

'They're letting her out, then?'

'That's how it looks. She didn't say, and I didn't like to ask, but she nearly wept when I gave her the money. She could hardly believe it.'

'Poor lady. Well then, that's all out of the way, isn't it?'

'Indeed it is. Now you can forget about it at last.'

The note was brief and made no mention of

the letters, but that, Annemarie thought, was probably not surprising if she was in a hurry to leave. For another thing, it was safest to leave such matters unspoken. Her relief to have the letters returned would surely be as great as Annemarie's.

For a few moments, the thought kept her still and pensive. She had so much enjoyed her morning's shopping with Oriel and Lord Verne, who seemed to know what she would like without being told. She had felt completely at ease each time his friends had waved and saluted him, or her acquaintances had nodded and smiled to see her in town again, and it had taken some effort to remind herself that she needed no man in her life when his company had made such a vast difference to her enjoyment.

So now, just as she was about to agree with Cecily that she could forget about the controversial matter at last, the darker side of her memory prompted her to recall her wounds, to keep them open and not to allow a morning's pleasure to soothe them.

Cecily was quick to notice the hesitation before the reply. 'You *are* going to forget about it, love, aren't you?' she said, rising to take another look in the mirror. 'You're not going to pursue this revenge thing, are you? Verne's interest is quite unfeigned, you know. Can you not tell?'

'Cecily, pursuing the revenge thing, as you

call it, is what it's all about. That's why I've agreed to become his mistress, isn't it? The deeper he commits himself, the better. And the longer his Royal Highness is made to squirm, the more I shall think it all worthwhile.'

'That's not like you, Annemarie. Not like you at all,' Cecily said. 'I've put the empty portmanteau in your room. You'll need it again before long.'

'I shall, my dear. Verne is taking me to see a house this very afternoon.'

'So soon? Where? Did he say?'

'He wouldn't tell me, but I hope it's not too far away from you.'

Layers of tissue and ribbon spilled from bed to floor, soft fabrics, printed and plain, silky and sheer, their colours mingling like pools of paint on an artist's palette. And there was another treat, she thought. She would ride with him in the park. The days ahead seemed all at once filled with new possibilities, with colour, and promise, and purpose.

Mrs Cecily Cardew, however, did not share Annemarie's optimism, seeing this vengeful side of her intended specifically to hurt the man who least deserved it. Convinced that Annemarie would not have agreed to become Verne's mistress unless she felt something for him, how could she now intend to use him so badly, a man she herself could have fallen for thirty years ago?

Ought she to warn him? Or would he already have suspected some ulterior motive? Of course he would. The man was no fool to be taken for a ride by a bruised-hearted beauty like Annemarie Golding.

The house on Curzon Street could easily have been reached on foot had it not been more fun to arrive in the handsome curricle Lord Verne had brought from Bedford Square. At the Park Lane end of the street that ran almost parallel to Piccadilly, the white-fronted house was elegant and discreet, rising in four storeys behind black-and-gold cast-iron railings, white stone steps and polished wall-lamps. Nothing, Annemarie thought, could be more fitting than this for a house of one's own, not even the house he'd mentioned on the very superior Upper Brook Street.

She was even more convinced of its rightness when they entered the hallway; the graceful classic lines were in the latest style, spacious and beautifully decorated in pale apricot and white with a winding staircase as delicate as a spider's web. The narrow frontage was misleading, for the rooms leading off the hall were large, high-ceilinged and airy, the salon at one side having tall windows at both ends, one of which overlooked a private garden filled with the afternoon sun.

'Stables beyond,' said Verne, watching her

face for signs of pleasure. 'Large enough for three horses and a phaeton. The house has only just become available, recently redecorated.'

'I can smell the paint,' she whispered. 'I like the flock wallpaper. And the oak floor, too. It would be a pity to cover it. Perhaps a small Turkish carpet in the centre.'

'Want to see the other rooms? Through here. Dining room and breakfast parlour. A small study where you can do your accounts and letters. Kitchens are below.'

Their feet echoed in the unfurnished rooms, yet in Annemarie's vivid imagination each one took on the aspect of the private and personal London space that had so far only existed in her dreams, near enough to Cecily and within easy distance of her father, where she could either be alone or with those old friends she had avoided for so long. Here she could be mistress of her own home, as she was at Brighton, but with all the other amenities she had done without for a year and with the freedom from marble intruders in the form of dust-collecting clutter. Being the mistress of this man at the same time would be a small price to pay for such benefits. She might have to compromise. She might have to make it last longer than planned.

Upstairs, the wide landing led to several bedrooms and dressing rooms equipped with the latest facilities, marble-topped, gold-plated and mirrored. 'It's a little palace,' she said, smiling at one of their many reflections.

'Like it? Will it do? Would you like to see the other place I found?'

'No. I mean…yes, I *do* like it. I don't need to see anywhere else. This has all I need. Thank you. Is it expensive?' She knew it must be.

'I've told you,' he said. 'I choose only the best.'

She did not expect him to tell her. The question was indelicate.

Two pigeons alighted on the windowsill outside, the female looking distinctly unimpressed by the male's strutting and bobbing. 'Silly things,' she whispered.

'He's trying to make himself agreeable,' Verne said.

'Beware of men who try to make themselves too agreeable.'

Verne took hold of her shoulders as the female flew off, his hands sliding down to her elbows, along her forearms to take the gloved hands that rested beneath her high bodice. 'I know,' he said. 'You've enjoyed our sparring as much as I have, my beauty. I expect there'll be more. But just remember that I hold the reins.'

'No white mules, then.'

'No white mules. I shall not be made a laughing-stock.'

'I was not serious, my lord.'

'I am,' he said, turning her round, deftly.

She knew then by the glint of steel in his eyes that he had begun to understand some of her motives. Her question about the cost of the house had been a mistake, revealing what was on her mind. Except that it had now begun to matter rather less than it had at the beginning. His unsmiling mouth was close to hers. 'Perhaps we *should* take a look at the other house,' she said. 'Perhaps this is a little too large. Really...I wouldn't mind.'

He kissed her before answering, to reassure her. It was softly comforting, meant to ease her awakening conscience. The variety of his kisses astonished her. One for every mood and occasion. 'Too late,' he said, touching the tip of her nose with his lips. 'You and your sisters have been uncomfortable for far too long. I can offer one of them some space. Leave it at that.' He kissed her again, hungrily, as if kissing was easier than explanations. 'Now, at risk of being thought too agreeable, how about that drive in Hyde Park? It's about time for the Prince's Military Review.'

She took his arm. 'It's been a long time,' she said, studying the tassel on her reticule. 'A whole year.'

'And society has a remarkably short memory,' he said. 'There are no questions to be answered. Just smile, that's all you need to do. Everyone

will be watching the soldiers and the Prince's
guests.'

'Yes, of course.' She heard the sound of her
own too-easy acceptance and knew she ought
to have been making things more difficult for
him, to test his resolve as she'd planned from
the start. Once she was installed here, he would
believe his access to the letters would be rela-
tively simple, and she would have to keep him
thinking so until she could choose a moment to
tell him that, this time, he really *was* wasting
his time, money and effort. For some reason,
the thought did not give her the same pleasure
it had only days ago.

I shall not be made a laughing-stock, he'd
said, words that challenged all Annemarie's no-
tions of revenge and sent a cold shiver along her
arms. By now, he would have understood more
of the scandal involving Lord Benistone's beautiful wife and, by implication, their daughter and
he would be thinking, as such men often did,
that he would be the one to come to the rescue.
He would think, no doubt, that with a little persuasion she would gratefully open up her heart
and let him in, that all would be well, wounds
healed, pride mended.

But that was not how it would be as long as
Mama was still missing and sorely needed by
them all. For Annemarie's heart to heal, she
would have to know that Mama was safe and

happy, and the way to find out was to throw
herself back into society and search. Papa was
too proud to try. It was entirely up to her. A year
was too long for both of them and Lord Verne's
intervention had opened up a way to solve several problems all at the same time. She rubbed
the hair along her arms back into place, hoping
that the price of revenge would not be beyond
her means and that Verne's interest in the precious letters would not wane too soon. Had it
already begun to wane? He had asked no questions about her proposed visit to Christie's with
the portmanteau since their arrival. Ought she
to stir his memory, just to find out?

By the time Verne's curricle arrived at the
park through a sea of coaches, carriages and pedestrians, the Military Review was well under
way and every open space was occupied by
smartly uniformed troops and their mounted
leaders, kings, czars and princes, generals and
officers of state. To Annemarie, it looked as if
the whole of London had turned out to see the
colourful occasion in all its splendour, to cheer
everyone in uniform except the Prince Regent
himself, whose unpopularity must by now have
been glaringly obvious to his royal guests. Hiss-
ing and booing, cat-calls and insults followed his
every move, and although Annemarie understood the reasons for this as well as anyone, it

made her sad and uncomfortable to see the poor man publicly reviled on what was intended to be a day of rejoicing. He had been forbidden, both by his father and by Parliament, from taking an active part in the offensive against Napoleon. Now, in his bid to thank the generals who had organised the victorious armies, the only thanks he personally received were grumbles about the too-lavish hospitality and gripes about the general discomforts of being on daily and nightly display in London.

Verne glanced at the gloved hand covering her lips and the frowning eyes above. 'You are shocked, my lady?' he said. 'I thought you'd—'

'I'd what?' she replied, glaring at the hands holding the reins. 'Be happy to see him so insulted, in public, and unable to stop it? Why doesn't someone take his part? He's putting on a good show for them. What more could he do?'

In fact, to entertain Londoners, the Prince Regent could have done little more when every park was busy with booths and fanciful structures from bridges to pagodas, temples and towers, mock battles and firework displays. Every blade of grass was worn away, the air reeked of smoke and food, and the noise had sent even the cows running away to greener pastures, depriving ordinary folk of their milk. The loud critics complained that laundry-women were neglecting their duties and that the expense of daily extravagances on this scale were not being met by his Royal Highness any more than his massive banquets were.

'But you're one of his sternest critics, surely? Are you not?' he said.

'I am, yes. But I cannot agree that humiliating the poor man in front of his guests is the thing to do. Making one's displeasure known is allowed, but this is altogether different. Let's go. I've seen enough.'

He did not at once turn the horses but, from a distance of several carriages, watched how the Prince, his friend, tried to ignore the hostility of the crowd and to pretend that the cheers were as much for him as for General Blücher, everyone's favourite. The fixed smile on the Prince's florid face was pitiful to watch, for Verne knew that he dared not venture anywhere in public on his own for fear of being attacked by mobs. 'Would you care to meet him again?' he said.

Her reply came after only a moment's hesitation. 'Yes. Yes, I would. This is unbearable. You knew how it would be, didn't you?'

'It's always like this. He knows what to expect.'

'Yet he's arranged for weeks of celebrations. He must be hating it.'

'He does. Every minute of it, but he has courage, I'll say that for him.'

Annemarie could have countered this with

some less praiseworthy attributes, but feelings of
sympathy for the Prince and disgust at the rude
behaviour of the crowds suspended any words
of censure which, until now, had been the only
ones to spring to mind.

Before she herself could question this unexpected compassion, the Prince's eyes, which had
been searching the carriages for the sight of a
more friendly face, suddenly found Verne's curricle. She noticed how Verne touched the brim
of his grey beaver in salute and saw the Prince
take in his partner, herself, reverting to a smile
so explicit in its hope of an exchange that she
found herself responding, in spite of all her earlier reservations. The merest dip of her bonnet
and the smile cost her nothing, but the relief on
the Prince's face made her feel that, to him, it
had been beyond price.

The royal cavalcade moved on, prancing and
wheeling, and Verne turned the horses' heads
away through the crowds with only inches to
spare. 'That was well done, my lady,' he murmured. 'He won't forget.'

'From what I've heard,' she replied, returning a wave from a surprised acquaintance, 'his
Highness forgets such things quite easily, but
remembers insults for years. I hope you're prepared to be dropped like a hot brick when your
usefulness comes to an end.'

He smiled at her cynicism. 'I'll try to remember your caution, my lady. Do you predict my usefulness ending any time soon?'

'No,' she said. 'I would not be so foolhardy. I'm sure you'll know as soon as I do.'

They could have been talking about their own relationship rather than the royal patronage, but now she had already begun to see matters in a different light and did not want his usefulness to end in the foreseeable future, let alone any time soon. She had hidden away for so long that the memory of being driven in flashy curricles by handsome blades had been stifled in favour of her bitterness and it had taken only one morning of shopping, a look at a new house and a drive past nodding and waving acquaintances to lift her spirits well beyond her memories of darker things. Not only that, but she had surprised herself as well as her escort by an unforeseen softening of her attitude towards one who, although still a sad character, was being given no credit whatever for trying to please. No matter how many times Annemarie would like to have given the man a good dressing-down, she still could not find it in her heart to rejoice at the public indignities the prince was suffering. She had not expected to care.

Whatever thoughts Verne harboured about Annemarie's pity for the beleaguered Prince, which he believed was as unexpected to her as it was to himself, he understood instinctively

that it would be best not to press for an explanation. So he manoeuvred the curricle beyond
the crowds to where she might take the ribbons
more safely and there relinquished the matched
pair of bay geldings into her hands with only
the slightest of misgivings, taking into account
the lapse of a whole year. He need not have been
concerned about her proficiency for he could
see that, as soon as she arranged the reins between her fingers and flicked the whip, catching
its tail-end deftly, that everything she had ever
learned about driving came back in one moment.
Without feeling the need to offer any advice except, once, the word 'steady' on a bend, he sat
back with no more to do than admire yet another
of this complex woman's capabilities.

As she had suspected, he had known many
women, but loved none of them, having grown
quickly tired of their predictability and of the
ease of the chase, which to a man like him was
more than half the excitement. This lovely creature had allowed herself to be caught, almost,
with the intention of wreaking some mischief,
and he was under no illusions who it was she intended to hurt most. Not after the betrayal she
had suffered. His plan now was to play the same
game, but to make her enjoy it too much to end
it. The sooner he could show her how much more
she had to learn, the better his chances of changing her mind, as she had just demonstrated was

by no means impossible. What he must find out without delay was whether she had in fact discovered the theft of the letters, or whether she was pretending not to have done. And for this, he decided that Mrs Cardew would be the one to help.

'Stop at the end, if you please,' he said. 'Did you have your own curricle and pair, my lady? Or did you hire?'

'I had a phaeton and pair,' she replied, drawing the horses to a gradual halt. 'I've never driven a curricle before.'

'Never driven…? Are you serious?'

She had surprised him yet again. Sitting there in her cool grey-and-white riding habit with a white fur pill-box pinned to her glossy black hair and a black feather boa flung over one shoulder, she looked for all the world as if tooling a high sporting curricle round the park called for no great skill, which he knew was not the case at all.

Turning her laughing eyes to his, she caught the blend of admiration and concern before he was able to conceal it. 'Quite serious,' she said. 'Now nothing will do but for me to have a curricle, too. Or a perch-phaeton, perhaps. One can see so much more from this height.'

If she had expected him to demur at the cost, she had certainly not expected that he would jump at the chance of spending hundreds of pounds on a vehicle such as his, at least one-hundred-and-fifty pounds a year on the cost of keeping a horse, not including the groom's salary and his livery. A horse for her to ride would be an additional expenditure, twice as much as a curricle with extra for fodder, care and tack. The mercenary sound of her casually delivered requirements sat ill on her conscience, so it was all she could do not to contradict herself when he took the reins without betraying the slightest alarm and said, 'Of course you must. I've seen a rather nice pair of dapple-greys that might suit you well. I'll take you to see them, now I've satisfied myself you'll be able to handle them. As for a sporting phaeton, I think that more suitable for a lady than a curricle. We'll go and see my coachmaker.'

'Whatever you wish,' she said, handing him the whip. 'But there's no particular hurry. Perhaps I may be allowed to drive yours until then.'

'Certainly, as long as I'm with you.'

He was too engrossed in navigating the bouncing vehicle between two groups of pedestrians to notice the slight smile that lit her eyes and twitched at her lips. Only a few days ago, she reflected, his proprietorial reply would have set her back up. Now, she felt that things were going according to plan and that Jacques Verne's presence beside her was not nearly as disagreeable as it had been at first.

* * *

If tensions appeared to be lessening as a result of their accord over material matters, neither of them had forgotten the underlying motives behind this new understanding. Each of them had something the other wanted: in his case, the letters, in her case, his adoration and all the trappings that went with it. Nevertheless, none of the theatre-goers at Covent Garden that evening would have suspected anything from the handsome couple except the wish to enjoy each other's company.

Annemarie's maid, Evie, taken on for her skills in dressmaking, had that afternoon brought an armful of gowns from Montague Street to Park Lane to be restyled using the trimmings bought only that morning. By evening, she had turned a white-silk overgown of satin and sheer stripes into a watery vision of flowing ripples by constructing a new undergown of cerulean silver-threaded blue, layering the lower part with deep ruffles that just skirted the new blue-satin slippers. The neckline echoed the hem with soft ruffles tied on the shoulders with narrow silk roulette-cords, leaving Annemarie's upper arms exposed. Her long gloves of finest white lace looked as if she'd dipped her arms in foam. The foamy look was one she rather cared for. Her hair was so luxurious as to need no covering except silver ribbons tied *à la Grecque,* piled high on top of her head from which a profusion of tendrils escaped from the edges. Her only jewellery was a pair of long diamond-and-pearl earrings that accentuated her swan neck. Verne could hardly keep his eyes off her—nor in spite of the other attractions around them, could many of the audience.

Verne had a box in the theatre to which he had invited Mrs Cardew, Oriel and Colonel Harrow. Escaping from the noisy throng downstairs in the saloon where Annemarie had been recognised and welcomed by polite friends as if nothing in particular had happened, the small party arranged themselves without quite appreciating the extent of the interest they were causing to those down below. From their own level, heads craned forwards to look and wave, shouting things that could not be heard over the din and, from below, eye-glasses were raised to inspect every detail of the group with blatant curiosity. Annemarie herself might have wished for less attention, but could hardly complain when to be seen with her new and influential lover, a companion of the Prince Regent, no less, was exactly what this was all about. Back in the *beau monde* once more, she was parading her recovery as though what had happened a year ago had had no lasting effect. Outwardly. Inwardly, matters were rather different, but who was to know that except, perhaps, dear Cecily?

'Look over there,' said Oriel, in her ear. 'To the left.' Several boxes further along, young faces peered over the balcony, their pale gowns softened by fluttering fans and the deeper tones of more mature figures and a bevy of young men crowding behind them. The small space seemed to be overflowing. 'That's Marguerite, isn't it? With the Sindleshams?'

'So it is,' Annemarie said, catching the shriek of recognition over the din as Marguerite spotted her sisters. Her wave was anything but discreet. 'She's coming over.' An uncomfortable quiver of alarm and annoyance pulsed through the older sisters, though not Cecily, who swayed aside as the sudden onrush of female bodies swept like a tidal wave into the confined space of their box.

The three Sindlesham daughters had been brought, apparently, not so much to see the rare appearance of Lady Golding, but to gaze at close quarters with nothing short of veneration at the undeniably handsome figure of Lord Verne. He towered over them, meeting their awed upturned faces with an avuncular amusement although, at Marguerite's effusive greeting to her sisters, he quickly realised that this excess of joy was meant to impress him, in a roundabout manner. His heart sank, however, when Marguerite lost not a moment in recalling their last meeting, as if her friends needed reminding.

'Such a fine dance it was,' she gushed to

Annemarie and Oriel. 'I swear Lord Verne and I quite outshone every couple on the floor. Just as if we'd danced together for years. Where? Why, at Lady Sindlesham's ball,' she went on, unstoppable, bouncing her brown curls. 'You should have been there, Annemarie. We had no idea you were ready to socialise again after—'

'Thank you, Marguerite,' Cecily said, laying a hand on the girl's arm. 'But look! The curtains are parting. You should return to your box now. We'll catch up with you in the interval, shall we?'

'Oh, yes. I shall be coming home with you afterwards.'

'Really? Well, thank you for letting me know, dear.'

'I would have, Cecily, but I haven't had a moment to think.'

'Sounds to me,' said Cecily to the swarm of departing muslins, 'as if you've had plenty of time to think. Little minx.' Glancing sideways at Annemarie, she saw something of the damage Marguerite's boast had done, wishing with all her heart that she, Cecily, had found a quiet moment to impart the information before the garrulous mischief-making sister. But it was too late. Annemarie's expression, usually so unrevealing, sent goose-bumps along Cecily's arms.

Even Annemarie herself could not have explained exactly how or why the tidings just foisted upon her at the end of a very satisfying day should have affected her so adversely, so severely, so unreasonably. In a random heap, it seemed as if every insecure thought, every white-hot jealousy and all the heartbreaking pain of loss came crashing through a barrier behind which they'd been lurking, waiting for just such a moment to revisit her despite her conviction that, this time, she was in control. In one resounding crash, she saw her plans disintegrate and, much worse, the feelings for Verne that were growing, heedless of her permission, deep in the vulnerable regions of her heart, exposed, torn and tangled.

Yes, it was a monstrous over-reaction, but such was the delicacy of this new situation, well planned and sure to work, that even the slightest impediment was enough to tear the inconsistent and fragile ties that had begun to form, ties that only she would break when the time came. So, he had danced with Marguerite after spending the evening at Montague Place, after kissing her. And Cecily must have known too, for she'd been at the Sindleshams' ball and had said nothing of it. If that was not a conspiracy, then what was?

Watching the damage sink into Annemarie's imaginings, Verne cursed himself for not seeing it coming, for not quelling Marguerite's babble of girlish excitement, not being able to explain that the dance had been no more than a kind-

ness to Mrs Cardew for her assistance. As the
play began, still to an ill-mannered chatter from
the audience, he took Annemarie's hand in his,
to comfort her. But she withdrew it and, taking
his wrist, would have slammed his hand heavily upon his knee had he not resisted in time. He
knew then that he would have his work cut out
to smooth things over.

Chapter Six

Stunned by the pain of undiluted jealousy, Annemarie gave no thought to how it would look for her to leave, just as the play was beginning. Uppermost in her mind, apart from being alone, was the thought of having to meet Marguerite at Park Lane and either to suffer more details of their evening together, or strangle her.

A hand held her arm as she stood. 'No, dear,' said Cecily. 'You mustn't. Stay. It's nothing. I can explain.'

'I'm leaving. Let go. I cannot stay.'

'I'll take her back,' Lord Verne said, recognising the determination in her voice. 'It would be best. I'll send the carriage back for you, ma'am.'

'I don't *want* you to take me back,' Annemarie retorted, 'I prefer to be alone.' But Verne's arm was across her shoulders and, as their exit was already being noticed, Annemarie saved her tirade until the curtains closed behind them, with only a few latecomers to overhear.

'Not now,' said Verne. 'Not here. Come. You must hold your peace a while.'

'For pity's sake, leave me alone,' she said, furiously striding ahead of him. 'I want nothing to do with you, my lord.'

'Too late,' he muttered.

But without making a scene, she was obliged to suffer Verne's company all the way back to Park Lane in his barouche where she sat trembling in silence in one corner, her lovely eyes brimming with tears that caught the moving reflections from outside. He could see how she shook with the effort of containing her distress, yet felt certain he could explain, once they were able to speak freely and at length.

He was mistaken. Annemarie turned on him, white-faced, her voice breaking with emotion. 'You waste your time, my lord. I don't want to hear what you say and I have nothing to say to you except that I wish we had never met. If you want to flirt with my young sister, go ahead. I ought to have seen that you would try that angle, too, to get what you want. What a pity the elder Miss Benistone is out of bounds, or you might have tried your luck there. Don't follow me. I'm going to my room.'

'Annemarie, listen to me…please? It was not like that at all.'

She refused to listen. Before he had said no more than a few words, she was almost at the top of the stairs and there was nothing to be done but for him to go into the library and await the return of the others. In his own home, he would have pursued her. In hers, he might have done the same. But here where they were guests in Mrs Cardew's house, he was not prepared to risk the gross impropriety of it.

Knowing better than to ask what the matter was, Evie fielded the clothes that flew across the bed, but felt helpless to do anything more to help her mistress when she crumpled into a velvet chair, head in hands, and gave way to loud rasping sobs that Evie had heard before, a year ago. It was then that the maid had suspected the depth of Annemarie's heartache and the intense desire that had come too soon and unexpectedly, taking her unawares. More than anyone, she had seen the change in her mistress, the bloom in her cheeks that was not only for the return to London life but also for the man at her side, demanding her attention. Evie was now sure that Lady Golding was deeply in love and that Lord Verne was somehow responsible for this latest torment. Did it, she wondered, have something to do with the theft of the portmanteau contents?

It had not taken Evie long to come to the

conclusion that, since none of Lady Golding's valuables were missing from her collection of jewellery, and that the portmanteau would have been much heavier if it had indeed contained such items, something else had been stolen by that silver-tongued valet that Lady Golding could not speak of, even to her trusted maid. Faced with Mrs Cardew's instructions to say nothing about it, Evie decided that now was not the time to ask. Not until she could get a quiet word with Mr Samson, who had probably never suffered the humiliating experience of being savaged by an irate lady's maid. Not yet.

Verne's wait in the library was not as prolonged as he'd expected, none of the party having enjoyed the highly charged melodramatics of Mr Keane in the title role of *The Merchant of Venice*, especially after Annemarie's abrupt departure. Nor was Marguerite sorry to make her excuses to her long-suffering hostess either, since she'd nursed hopes of being taken to a masquerade party rather than the theatre. Her poorly timed request to be taken there by Cecily, however, had resulted in the sharpest set-down she had received in many a month. From both Oriel and Cecily.

'Sit down, miss! And don't say another word till we reach Park Lane.'

'And even then, you may find you've said too much!'

In the library, Verne stood as they entered. 'Ma'am, I hope you don't mind...'

'Not at all, my lord. This is a sad business. Where is she? Upstairs?'

'Wouldn't discuss it. I'm afraid she has badly misconstrued the situation.'

'Thanks to Marguerite,' said Oriel, angrily. 'Yes, dear,' she said to her betrothed, acknowledging the gentle hand on her arm, 'I know it's bad form to rake one's sister down in company, but I think it's time she began to understand how her behaviour is affecting other people's feelings. *Your* discomfiture at this moment,' she said, turning to her sister, 'is nothing compared to the distress you've just caused Annemarie by your silly boasting. Have you *no* discretion?'

'I didn't know...' Marguerite faltered, blushing, turning a beseeching glance upon Lord Verne.

'So why did you think we were all sitting in Lord Verne's box? Didn't that tell you something? No, don't answer that. Clearly, it didn't.'

'I'm...I'm sorry, my lord. I'll go up to her and explain.'

'You'll do no such—' Oriel began, ready for the next salvo.

Hastily, Cecily intervened. 'Not now, Marguerite. Tomorrow. Go upstairs.'

Marguerite's lower lip trembled as she made her escape. 'Yes. Thank you.'

The colonel had never seen his gentle Oriel so furious and was inclined to think that this was an interesting side of her character. Opening his mouth to speak, however, was no guarantee that he would be listened to. 'That little *madam,*' Oriel said to the closing door, 'needs taking in hand. Her silly behaviour is becoming an embarrassment to us all.'

'Perhaps you're being a little harsh, dear,' Cecily said. 'I'm sure if she'd known how things stand between Annemarie and Lord Verne, she'd not have—'

'She knows how vulnerable Annemarie is,' said Oriel, uncompromising. 'If she bothered to think about anyone at all other than herself, of course.'

'Mrs Cardew,' said Verne, 'I wonder if I might have your permission to go up to Annemarie? If she'll allow me to explain, I may be able to repair the damage.'

'In the circumstances, my lord, I can hardly refuse. But you've seen for yourself how fragile her emotions are and, knowing her as I do, I'd be surprised if she'll see you. You may try, though.'

Oriel was also doubtful, but still held out some hope. 'She won't,' she said to Verne, 'but don't be put off, my lord. Cecily and I will work on her when she's calmer. She's not seeing things too clearly at the moment, you understand.'

'Thank you, Miss Benistone. I shall not give up, I can assure you.'

Verne's attempt to gain access to Annemarie's room met with the refusal Oriel and Cecily had predicted. The door remained locked against him in spite of prolonged entreaties to let him explain.

When he at last returned to the library, Cecily was alone and waiting to comfort the one who had hoped to be the comforter. 'Come and sit down, my lord. A little brandy? Don't despair,' she said, noting the tension in his face. 'We might even use this moment profitably to share what we know about the letters, do you think? It's sure to prevent more misunderstandings, isn't it?' Secretly, she took some pleasure from watching for that spark of alarm in his eyes and equally from finding out how well he hid it from her.

His hand was perfectly steady as he accepted the brandy glass, his first sip leisured and appreciative. 'Ah!' he said, studying the amber swirls. 'So they've been discovered. I wondered, of course. That might help to explain matters.'

'Well, yes and no,' said Cecily. So, with one wary eye on the door, she gave Verne the information he required while assuring him that

Annemarie's extreme reaction to her sister's boast had nothing to do with the letters directly, but to her distrust of his motives where she was concerned. 'She still believes, you see, that all *you* want is the letters.'

'Then she's mistaken, isn't she? I don't want the letters. I have them.'

'Yes. Quite. So might it be best, do you think, if she was told?'

Verne disagreed. 'No, I think not,' he said. 'I think it's best if Lady Golding continues to believe that they're safely where *she* wants them to be, with Lady Hamilton. I don't mind at all if she wants to think I'm still waiting for her to dispose of them. This is a game she's chosen to play for her own good reasons and I don't propose to end it for her yet. She must attempt to do that in her own way, in her own time.'

Cecily was sorely tempted to tell him more, particularly about the exact nature of the game her beloved Annemarie was playing. A wicked game of revenge in which he would be hurt, but Annemarie even more so. But this was a confidence she could not disclose. Rather she would have to hope that Verne had enough wit to work it out and extricate himself before the damage was done. It was a pity. She liked and admired the man. 'You don't see it as ended already, then?' she said.

'Good heavens, ma'am, not at all. Much as

I hate to see her upset and angry, it gives me a good indication of where I stand in the scheme of things.'

'Somewhere at the bottom, I'd say.'

He smiled at her pessimism with a flash of white teeth. 'On the contrary. When the game *does* end, I dare say we shall all be too old to remember what it was.'

'Really? As long as that?'

'As long as that, ma'am. Now, may I trespass on your wisdom further by asking what you predict Lady Golding will do in the immediate future?'

Cecily stood up in a billow of white lace. 'Wait here, if you will, my lord. I'll go and find out what I can.'

'She'll see you?'

'Oh, yes, she'll see me.' She paused at the door. 'By the way, my lord, something I found out only this morning. Lady Hamilton has left the security of the debtors' prison and disappeared with her daughter. Isn't that interesting?'

'Then Lady Golding's generosity came just in time.'

'Sure to have helped.'

Although not quite as luxurious as the Prince Regent's carriage, Cecily's well-equipped town coach served the same purpose in every respect, which was to convey Annemarie and her maid

safely and comfortably to Brighton. Any attempt
to persuade her not to flee London at quite such
an early hour had met with an obduracy typical
of a broken-hearted young woman who could
see nothing but her own dark unhappiness. She
had accepted, up to a point, Cecily's reason to
keep the news of the vexatious dance with Marguerite to herself, since the appearance of Lord
Verne there that night had been only to speak
to the Prince Regent, whom he'd known would
be there. Naturally, he'd had no option but to
change into evening dress for that, but he had
been ready to leave immediately had not Cecily *pleaded* with him to stand up with Marguerite. If she'd suspected how the silly child would
embroider the facts, she would never have done
so. As for there being any more to it than that,
Annemarie was much mistaken.

In her present state of mind, Annemarie could
hear the sense of it, but did not want to find it
a place in *her* view of events. He had danced
with Marguerite. He had partnered her, been
seen with her, smiled at her, softened her stupid little heart, pandered to her self-centredness
and given her a weapon with which to damage
Annemarie's new confidence. So easy to inflict
and so effective. And the only way to nurse the
pain was to return to obscurity. Why had she
ever thought any different?

Forget the town house on Curzon Street.

Forget the imaginary bed, his arms, his kisses.

Forget the tender way he'd talked to her, wooing her with sounds.

Forget it all.

By this time, the tears had changed to a cold numb fury that disturbed Evie as much as the tempestuous sobbing of last night had done. 'Coming into Reigate,' she said. 'Here, m'lady, let me pull your veil down. There, no one will notice. I'll go in and secure a private parlour while they change the horses and we can have breakfast. Just leave it to me. Ready?' Having heard no word since leaving Park Lane, Evie did not expect one now, though it seemed that her plan met with some approval when she was allowed to take charge, accepting without a moment's hesitation that the parlour had been prepared for them as arranged.

'Arranged by whom?' Annemarie said, frowning at Evie.

'I don't know, m'lady. Mrs Cardew, perhaps?'

Not wishing to argue the point, they followed the landlord into the cosy room that, flooded with bright daylight, appeared quite different from their last eventful visit. But before Evie could request a tray of food to be brought, the bowing Mr Hitchcock had taken his leave with an ingratiating 'm'lady...m'lord' that caused m'lady to twirl round on one heel to face the tall man who, while not exactly lurking, had not

until then done anything to make his presence
obvious.

'*You!* This is *intolerable!*'

Annemarie made a quick stride towards the
door, but Verne was there first, too large and
too determined to be pushed aside, booted feet
planted firmly apart and not a crease in either
buckskin breeches or dark-grey cutaway tailcoat to suggest that he had travelled at all that
morning. Although he had. 'Yes, I know. But
could you tolerate it long enough to listen to
me?' he said.

'I'm heading for Brighton, my lord, with
the express intention of avoiding exactly that,'
she said, her voice unsteady with past hours of
weeping. 'Now stand away from the door, if you
please, and let me pass. I told you last night I
have no wish to be in your company, and nothing has changed.'

'M'lady,' Evie whispered, 'ought I to…?'

'Yes, go and see if the horses are put to. We
need to be away from here immediately.'

Bobbing a curtsy, Evie was allowed to slip
through a gap in the door that Annemarie knew
she herself would not be permitted to use. Yet
even then, after running the gamut of every emotion concerning his duplicity, his untrustwor-
thiness and disloyalty, Annemarie experienced
a sneaking surge of desire as they faced each
other, equally resolute but totally unequal in the

stamina needed to win an argument. She had hardly slept. Now the unexpected appearance of the one who had drifted and woven himself through her dark hours seemed almost like a taunt, reminding her of what she stood to lose. Every handsome inch of him. She was to have used him, mercilessly, to salve her pride. He might have helped to find her mama. And already, damn him, he'd taken hold of her heartstrings. She would have to snatch them back before it was too late.

'Lord Verne,' she said, forcing an energy into her voice, 'I can guess who informed you of my intention to make this journey, but I can assure you that, whatever *your* plans are, they won't affect *mine*. Nothing you can say will prevent me from going on to Brighton.'

'Good. So when we've had breakfast, we'll proceed, shall we?'

'Proceed?'

'Yes, to Brighton. That is what you said, isn't it?'

'I did, my lord. But *alone*. I shall be going nowhere with *you*.'

'That point,' he said, gravely, 'is one upon which we may disagree. You are, remember, my mistress and mistresses always try to please their lovers. Did you not know that? We shall go on to Brighton together.'

'Wrong. Allow me to mention another small

point, my lord. I am *not* your mistress and you have no control over my movements. It was a mistake. We shall not suit. Indeed, we never *did* suit. What's more, since Mrs Cardew and you appear to be in cahoots, she will no doubt have told you that your ridiculous pursuit of what was in my portmanteau can now be called off. The contents have been safely returned to their owner, as you probably know, so they can be of no more concern either to you or the Prince Regent. So, having got that out of the way, you can see that there is no reason at all for you to pretend any interest in my affairs. You need keep secret from me no longer your flirtation with my younger sister, either. What a pity I had not learned of your strategy sooner. It would have saved…' She turned away from him to hide the crumpling of her face and the pain in her eyes caused more by her imaginings than by the facts. Cecily had explained. To continue doubting was a way of justifying her own excessive reaction and to disbelieve *him* would mean dismantling every esteem and approval he had won from her so far.

A tap on the door introduced trays of food borne by straight-faced servants who might have been able to sense the tensions that quivered like bowstrings between the tall powerful man stopped in mid-stride and the willowy lady whose veil was still in place, even after several minutes. It was not the first time they had witnessed such anomalies, inn-parlours being what they were. Setting the table to rights, they withdrew smartly at the tip of the landlord's head, their ears straining to catch a word before the door-latch clicked.

There was no word. Instead, Verne came to take hold of her sleeveless pelisse by the shoulders and slip it down her arms without encountering the least resistance. 'Shall we sit, sweetheart, and discuss this over coffee?' he said, laying the garment aside. 'And your hat? One cannot eat breakfast through a veil, can one?' Before she could object, his fingers had deftly removed the hat pin that anchored the drum-shaped creation to her hair, revealing in one quick sweep the full extent of her ravaged face, the swollen eyelids, pale cheeks, pink nostrils, the lovely mouth distorted by misery. He felt the tiredness in her shoulders. 'Oh, my sweet girl,' he whispered. 'What on earth is all this about? Eh?'

She turned her head aside so as not to see the pity in his eyes which she knew would quite undo every one of her resolutions. 'Don't,' she replied. 'Don't try to talk me out of it. My mind is quite made up. Irrevocably.'

'Irrevocably,' he said, moving a tendril of her hair away from her eyes. 'So why not let it rest for a while, and sit down and eat. I don't suppose you had anything before you set out, did

you? Come. It's indecently early for arguments,
I agree.'

His conciliatory tone was hard for her to
fathom, though she was not deceived into thinking he would accept a word of her refusal. But
she could find no more to say as he steered
her bodily towards the table where the warm
aromas of bread, bacon, sausage and eggs reminded her that it was over twelve hours since
she had touched any food. Her weak protestations were gently ignored as, little by little, he
plied her with morsels of food and watched as
each mouthful disappeared. Not for years had
she experienced such personal and particular
tenderness. Not since her childhood, in fact. 'I
don't think,' she said, watching him cut up her
bacon, 'that this is what people do when they're
about to part company, is it?' At that point, she
was obliged to open her mouth as the forkful
was presented to her. 'Well,' she mumbled, 'not
in my experience, anyway.'

Returning his attentions to his own plate,
Verne also broke with good manners to reply
while he chewed. 'In *my* experience, sweetheart,
there has never been a single occasion,' he said,
dabbing at his mouth with his napkin, 'when I've
cared a damn about parting with any woman's
company, until now. And certainly not enough to
feed her at the expense of my breakfast getting
cold. No, I can safely say that you, Lady Gold-

ing, are an exception in every sense and I have
no intention of parting with you for any reason
you can offer me, and certainly not for the pa-
thetic reasons you've offered so far. Eat the fried
bread, it's delicious. You may pick it up in your
fingers, if you wish. Just this once.'

With a resignation that bordered on the verge
of laughter, she did as she was bidden, savour-
ing the bacony taste and crisp texture, and for
some moments it would have been hard to guess
that all was not right with their worlds. 'Well,
my lord,' she said at last, 'I suppose I must feel
honoured to be an exception in your life. But are
you truly telling me that you have never been
saddened to lose a woman's company?'

'Not for more than half an hour. Relieved,
usually. And before you refer to your younger
sister again, my lady, allow me to tell you that,
if Mrs Cardew had not particularly wanted it,
nothing in the world would have persuaded me
to stand up with her. Relief when the set was
over hardly does justice to my feelings, for I
was never so simpered at in all my life. And let
me tell you also, while I'm about it, that I had to
promise to line my friend Brummell's pockets to
get him to take my place while I escaped. Hand-
somely, I might add. Those are not the actions of
a man with a strategy, amorous *or* mercenary.'

Without actually saying so, she was bound
to agree that his flight from her simpering sis-

ter was totally at odds with the heroism towards
the French women at Vitoria. The comparison
made it all the more believable. And human. She
watched him mop his plate with the last of his
bread roll, place his knife and fork together and
sit back in his chair, satisfied in one department,
at least.

'Where's your maid got to?' he said. 'Won't
she want to eat?'

'She's being diplomatic,' Annemarie said.
'She'll find something.'

'I expect she will,' he agreed, thinking that
Evie might also find his valet in the process.

'Lord Verne, there is something you ought to
understand before we go any further.'

'I'm listening.'

'Yes. About——'

'About my intention not to part with you.'

'For any reason. Yes.'

'You've discovered another reason?'

'If you continue to interrupt me, I shall——'

'Lose the thread of your argument? Easily
done when the argument is unsound to begin
with. But do go on.'

'My argument is as strong as ever it was, my
lord, and although I thank you for your hospitality——'

'Not at all.'

'I am quite determined that our former agreement cannot continue.' There, she thought, now

I've said it. 'You will have to reconsider, I'm afraid.'

'Running away again. It really won't do, my lady. You cannot solve this kind of problem by running away from it, cancelling it, pulling the blinds across.'

'Coming from you, that's rich, isn't it? Haven't you just told me of your flight from Lady Sindlesham's ball?'

'Not the same at all. There was no agreement or commitment there. With you and me, there is. Listen to me, sweetheart,' he said, noting the quick frown of irritation cross her face. He leaned upon the table, forearms and hands projecting towards her like swords. 'I can sympathise with your change of heart. I expected it. You're like a nervous filly spooking at your own fancies, ready to bolt for home.'

'Not *fancies*!'' she flared. 'I've *seen* the obstacles.'

She could not tell him how, seeing him again so unexpectedly after an interminable night of longing, jealousy and despair, she could see an obstacle she had never anticipated, that the longer she allowed this relationship to continue, the more severely she herself would be wounded, much more than him. He could walk away, apparently, without a moment's regret, even though he'd quoted her as an exception, and she would be left without the bitter sweetness of revenge,

once again her heart in pieces. This would bear
no comparison to those other losses. Any affection she might have found for Richard had
quickly been smothered and the infatuation
for Mytchett's charm paled into insignificance
against the overwhelming mind-consuming
emotions she'd begun to feel for this man who
insisted he would not let her go. Had she not
heard that before somewhere? Was that not what
all men said, in hot pursuit? It would be best to
end it now, before they became lovers.

'If you're referring to our being seen together
yesterday,' he said, 'surely that lends credibility
to *my* argument rather than yours. True, society
will make its own assumptions about that and
about our exit from the theatre, too, but to part
company now would do nothing but give the
scandal-mongers a field day. They don't give a
hoot when a woman takes a lover, even when
it's unexpected, but you'll have to suffer some
very wounding remarks from your peers, once
they see you can't stay the course for more than
twenty-four hours. Are you prepared for that?
Will the elder Miss Benistone be? And your father—does he deserve another scandal?'

Until his last rhetorical questions, Annemarie had been of a mind to dismiss the socialite
gossip as something that would eventually die
down. Again. But now she heard a different tone
to his argument, a harder line, less to do with

wanting her, needing her, and more to do with how it would look to others. She had thought he would not care about that, of all things.

'And you too, my lord? Is that what concerns you?'

'For myself, you mean?' He smiled and shook his head. 'Not at all. Anyone who attaches himself, for whatever reason, to his Royal Highness had better not be too concerned about the possibility of scandal. It follows him everywhere. Few of his friends are left unscathed by it, even if only by association.' His hard line was intentional, meant to reveal another side to the discussion that might work on her pride more than her pain. She was still highly suspicious of his motives for wanting her, despite the letters that had ceased to be an issue, and she was not likely, he thought, to believe that *his* feelings matched her own. Her extraordinary fury at her sister's behaviour and of what she saw as his part in it had convinced him that she had begun at last to open up her heart. But to her, a man's heart was not to be trusted, especially not a man who had made no secret about his original quest.

'So if your pride is not at stake,' Annemarie said, 'and you cannot now have what the Prince Regent sent you for, why are you so concerned about what happens to me? I suppose by now you'll have earned yourself a reputation for getting any woman you want—indeed, you implied something very similar early on in our acquain-

tance—but you can hardly expect me to help you
out with that, can you? If your friends rib you
for failing, this once, that's hardly my concern.
I know that yesterday I showed my pleasure at
the idea of having a private house in London and
someone to escort me. It was no pretence. I *did*
enjoy it. But after what has just happened, you
can see for yourself that I'm a bad risk. I think
that, after all, I may not be ready for…er…a close
relationship with you, my lord.'

He leaned further forwards, speaking quietly
as if he did not want her to miss the implication
of what he was about to say. 'And I think, my
lady, that you are handing me an escape route
that I have no intention of using. I'm not about to
make it so easy for you. But I *shall* remind you of
something I said only yesterday. I hold the reins.
And I shall not be made a fool of. For a man to
lose a woman he's set his mind on because of a
misunderstanding as flimsy as this would suggest that her intentions were unkind from the
beginning. Is that how you want it to look?'

'So it *is* about how it would look, after all.
How can you deny it?'

'How it would look for *you*, sweetheart, not
for me. Could you survive it? Would it be worth
it, to lose the chance of finding Lady Benistone,
regaining lost friends, being mistress of your
own home, having a man…a real man…in your
bed to teach you what loving is like? I shall take

you in hand, Annemarie. I shall accept no more
of your reasons. You *are* my mistress, and we
shall spend our days and nights in each other's
company, as we agreed, because you need me
and I need you. That's all there is to it. The out-
come will take care of itself.'

She ought by now to have been prepared for
some plain speaking from him, but although his
words brought a fiery glow to her cheeks and
neck, she could hardly complain that he treated
her like a schoolroom miss. Like a skilled fencer
he had found her weaknesses, even the one she
thought was concealed from him: her longing for
his arms, his control, his companionship, which
she professed not to want. He had not believed
any of it. He knew exactly what she wanted.

Busy bustling noises from outside leaked
into the silence between them. While Annemarie scanned the table for just one more line to
her argument, Verne's eyes remained on her face
watching for the tired acceptance and the accompanying sigh of defeat. She had too much to lose,
he knew, to turn her back on the advantages he
offered. She was a passionate woman, damaged
and still vulnerable, and he'd known how little it
would take for her to react to the slightest doubt
of his sincerity. He did not suspect Marguerite
of malice, but the sooner the silly chit was found
a husband, the better it would be for all of them.
'Shall we go?' he whispered.

The sigh came, accompanied by a barely perceptible nod. 'To Brighton?'

'To Brighton, my lady. Two or three days, perhaps, just to show that we planned it, then a return to London. We have to be there for an event, I'm afraid, but you can be in the house by then. It's being prepared as we speak.'

Her eyes locked with his in surprise and indignation. 'Oh, you great...arrogant...overbearing...*fiend*!' she said, snapping the words out like a whiplash. 'It's being prepared, is it? Are you not running ahead of yourself, my lord? Did it not occur to you that I might change my mind?' She had half-risen from her chair, exasperated by his laughter and cocksureness, yet secretly flattered by his determination to keep her as his mistress and to suffer no setbacks.

Across the table, her wrist was caught in a tight grip that prevented her from flouncing away and, before she could utter another word of protest, she was being pulled towards him and into his arms. 'Steady, my beautiful filly,' he said, holding her wrists behind her back. 'Steady! Did you think I'd let you go so easily? I never believe a woman who says she'll never change her mind, as you did.'

'You will, eventually,' she growled. 'You'll be glad to, *brute*!'

If she had hoped he might argue the point, she was to be disappointed, for he only smiled at her helplessness. 'Then we'll deal with that when we come to it, shall we? Meanwhile, you deserve a reward,' he said, lowering his mouth to hers.

After all the hours of anguish in which she thought never again to be held in his arms, to taste his kisses and to feel the melting of her knees, the warmth of his mouth upon hers drew a comforting blanket over that intimate world where sensations soared beyond their reach in seconds. At their first touch, desire flared like a dry torch, its flames seeking higher and more fiercely until, with hands freed, they clung and searched as if to make up for time lost, showing by their instinctive path the places to which they desired access most urgently. She moaned as he held her breast, his strong but tender fingers stroking through the high bodice of silk as if it were her skin. 'Tonight,' he said, hoarsely, 'I shall come to your room. No excuses.'

There was no need for her to agree, but her heart leapt with excitement. 'My hat...pelisse... we should go. No, no more, my lord. My carriage will be ready.'

'Your carriage, sweetheart, is already on its way back to London.'

'What!'

'You'll be travelling with your maid in the Prince's coach, as before. That's the reward I spoke of.' His pretence of innocence was not entirely successful in the face of Annemarie's astonishment. 'Well, what did you *think* I meant?'

'You are insufferable, my lord. Where did you put my hatpin?'

Evie, trying to keep out of the way of shouting passengers, was relieved to see her mistress emerge in what appeared to be a calmer mood than her entry. Evie's own demeanour, however, caused Annemarie to take a second look at the very pink cheeks and flashing eyes that suggested either a fury or a fever.

'Are you all right?' she said. 'Did you manage to snatch a bite of something?'

'Yes, my lady.'

'Which?'

'Both, I thank you. But I don't know what's happened to the carriage. The ostler told me it had returned to London, so…'

'It has. We're to go on in the one Lord Verne brought. But were you not here to speak to Mrs Cardew's coachman before he left?'

'No, m'lady. I was…er…elsewhere.'

'Oh, I see. Well, no matter. Shall we go?'

For Annemarie, that small hiccup was explanation enough for Evie's high colour, though if she had taken a look at Samson, Lord Verne's valet who stood in shadow some distance away, she might have observed how *his* face was red only on one side with the distinct imprint of four fingers running from brow to chin.

'What happened to you?' said his master, un-sympathetically.

The direction of Samson's resentful glance to-wards the pert lady's maid spoke volumes. 'Tell you later, m'lord, if you wouldn't mind,' he said.

Verne nodded. 'You'll be riding on the box outside with Levens for the rest of the way. I shall be sitting with the coachman.'

The command appeared to do nothing for Samson's chagrin. There had never been any love lost between Verne's cheeky young groom with a high opinion of himself and the valet, whose services were just as indispensable and more select. 'Can't *he* sit with the coachman?' he said, grudgingly.

'Would you rather walk?'

'No, m'lord. Indeed I would not. But nor do I want that young fly-by-night asking me 'perti-nent questions either.'

'Then you should have ducked, shouldn't you?'

'I told you there'd be trouble, m'lord,' Samson said, holding his cheek.

'So you did. I can't imagine how I ever man-aged without your vast store of advice. If you sit him on your right, he won't see. Come on, lad, we don't have all day.'

Feeling both piqued and relieved at Verne's understanding of women's minds, Annemarie gave in to the inevitable and tried to enjoy the rest of the journey as she was meant to do. Contemplating her earlier insistence that she was committed to being his mistress, she forgave herself for being forced into an about-face because, for one thing, she'd had good reason and, for another, because it had resulted in a very satisfying airing of views. It had also moved things in a different direction to place their first night together as lovers well away from the curious speculation of friends and family. That was something she was pleased to do without.

Mrs Ash, the housekeeper, and the aptly named Mrs Cookson were not overly surprised by their mistress's return, since she had expected to be away for two or three days, which she had been. What astonished them was the handsome coach with the Prince Regent's cypher on the panels and the resplendent coachman perched on a tasselled velvet-covered box. Mrs Ash was equally taken aback that Lady Golding's acquaintanceship with Lord Verne had developed in so short a time enough to allow immediate arrangements to be made for that evening. Together.

'And Lord Verne will be having dinner here,' Annemarie told her. 'At seven. The two of us. Inform Mrs Cookson, if you please.'

'Oh,' said Mrs Ash. 'Just the two.'

Annemarie watched the questions pile up behind the pale enquiring eyes. 'Yes. It's all right, Mrs Ash. I know what I'm doing.'

'Oh…oh, of *course*, m'lady. I didn't mean to suggest…'

'And Lord Verne likes to have a cooked breakfast, too.'

'Certainly, m'lady.' Mrs Ash was beginning to understand, making a mental note to place extra towels in the mistress's room and to find a few large coathangers. 'Will Lord Verne's valet be staying, m'lady?'

'Probably not, Mrs Ash. Evie doesn't like him much.'

'Oh, I see. Well then.' More baffled by this information than the rest, Mrs Ash hurried off to share the news with her husband and the cook while Annemarie went up to change into a walking-dress. She had asked to be shown round the Royal Pavilion after lunch, for which a more stylish gown would be appropriate.

But whether as a result of her release from the anguish of the last hours or whether because of Lord Verne's outspoken intentions concerning the evening, Annemarie was quite unable to give the Royal Pavilion the attention it deserved. At any other time she would have reacted to its magnificence with due amazement. Taking her by the hand, Verne drew her to a halt in a deserted saloon, noting the remaining shadows of suffering still etched around her eyes. 'Shall we go somewhere more comfortable?' he said. 'I can think of better things to do than this, sweetheart.'

She thought he meant to take her home. 'I'm sorry. I did want to see the improvements. But another time, perhaps.' The crazy red-and-gold ornament crowded in on every side, tiring her eyes and making her yawn behind her hand.

'This way.' Through a maze of bare passageways and anterooms littered with decorators' ladders and rows of firebuckets, Verne led her towards the west-facing wing and the opulent royal chambers where soft carpets muffled the sound of their footsteps. 'The Prince's private suite,' he said. 'His study. And here is where his Private Secretary stays when they're in residence. I use it when they're in London.' Opening an adjoining door, he showed her into a green, gold and white room with windows on three sides draped with green velvet, reflecting the light from the garden beyond. 'This is one of the tower rooms, like the one upstairs,' he said, closing the door. 'Would you care to see it, my lady?'

She ought to have shown some reluctance at the invitation to visit a gentleman's bedroom, but being unchaperoned in his living room was a venture only a mistress would risk and fatigue was quickly taking the place of argument. Too tired to bother with explanations, she leaned against the cool wall and closed her eyes. 'No, thank you,' she whispered, enigmatically.

Nevertheless, some kind of explanation was what Verne required if more misunderstandings were to be avoided. He thought he knew, but he also wanted the problem, if that's what it was, to be aired. Knowing better than to be flippant, he took her gently round the waist and eased her towards him, sliding a hand towards her neck. 'What is it?' he said. 'What is it you don't want to see, sweetheart? Can you tell me?' Untying the ribbons of her bonnet, he eased it away from her head.

'I used to keep my eyes closed,' she whispered. 'I didn't want to see…anything. I didn't want to feel anything either. But I did.'

'He hurt you?' Verne was well able to imagine how her late husband's legendary impatience and unkind manipulative hands would have been enough to turn her against lovemaking for ever. Sir Richard's known preferences were for the experienced whores who followed the army, rather than innocents like his wife. Yet Verne had discovered for himself how, in the right hands, her smouldering fires of passion still waited to be rekindled.

In a corner of her eye a glittering tear lingered. 'I never learned to enjoy it with him. He was always in a hurry. He didn't even take time to undress.'

'You? Or himself?'

'Oh, he never undressed me,' she said. 'I was usually asleep when he came to bed, hoping to be left alone. He would throw off his coat and boots, that's all. I've never seen a naked man. Not even him. I think I must have been out of my mind to suggest that you and I might be lovers, my lord, yet I still think I may be able to do it with you, somehow. I've never been kissed the way you do it. I'm willing to try again if only… you will…perhaps…'

'I know. We'll take it slowly, sweetheart. What happened before is not how it should be. I shall never do anything to alarm you. Just tell me what you want.'

'I don't really know what I want. I was never given any choices. You will have to show me.' At last the beautiful black-lashed eyes opened, spiked with repressed tears, and she was able to see the concern in his, as well as the desire. She had not intended to confide in him to this extent, wanting him to believe in her confidence rather than her fears.

'From what I've seen,' he said, 'there's little you don't already know. It's all here, waiting for the right moment. But I want our first time to be special for you and I don't think one of these narrow sofas is the best place to begin. Let me take you to my bed. No one will disturb us there.'

As he lifted her into his arms, Annemarie

knew that she had revealed too much of herself
and that compliance was not a part of her plan.
Her seduction ought to have been lengthier than
this, in her time, her place, at her choosing, when
she gave the word. Now, after the drama of the
last twenty-four hours, he would have little doubt
that her feelings for him had intensified. And
after this...what then?

The bedroom was partly shaded against the
sunlight, though Annemarie saw few details as
she was laid gently on the blue quilted coverlet
to sink gratefully into its softness, her fingers
searching for the sleek silky coolness as if for a
last link with reality. She wondered if she ought
to undress herself, but Verne had already decided what to do about that by sitting beside her
feet to slip off her shoes, then to caress her ankles, calves and knees so gently that, before she
knew it, her silken stockings were released from
their garters into his hand. It did not stop there,
for the delicious surprise of watching his dark
head bend to kiss the inside of her thigh made
her catch her breath in an audible gasp as the
sweetness of it stole upwards into her body. Her
other leg received the same attention, but with
an even greater boldness, his warm hands ven-
turing well beyond the remaining garter. Before
this, legs had been no more important than an
appendage to be shoved roughly out of the way.

Under Verne's attention, they became the source of a yearning she had never known before.

He sat up to observe the progress of his hands smoothing over the slender thighs and shapely calves, deriving as much pleasure from the exploration as she was. 'I knew it,' he said. 'I just *knew* it.'

'Knew what?'

'That under those flimsy gowns there'd be two glorious legs as long as my bed. I cannot believe he never bothered to look. You are a vision, woman.'

Without shoes or stockings, she felt liberated and almost wanton, and although he had alluded to the husband he wanted her to forget, his informal and rather irreverent description of her legs and his curiosity regarding them released the remaining tensions of the day into a shy smile. 'And I'll wager you've never even noticed them, have you?' he said, recalling the nonchalant grace of her movements and the unstudied elegance of her dress.

'Only to put stockings on,' she admitted, 'and to keep me upright.'

'Huh!' Lingering, as if she had been a mare he was examining before deciding to buy, he ran one hand down her leg from crotch to toes. Then he stood and began to unbutton his coat as a half-smile played about his mouth.

Annemarie watched the businesslike disrobing with a greater enjoyment than she might have expected to, having also wondered what lay beneath the perfectly fitting coat and the tight breeches. From three sides, triangles of light played upon his torso as each part was revealed to her interested gaze, the rippling muscles of his back as the white shirt fell away, the smooth skin still faintly tanned by Spanish sun, the rounded bulge of shoulders and the powerful swell of his chest, the tapering waist and hips more beautiful than anything she had imagined, in her ignorance. Usually hidden by the tailcoat, his buttocks were now an area of particular fascination, so different from a woman's, so much neater than the wide flabbiness whose weight she had once dreaded. As he turned towards her, those same memories could not help but compare this strong virile creature with past nightmares of unseen invasion and the assault upon her senses.

Before she could continue her study of him, he was beside her on the bed, drawing her into his arms as she raised herself to meet him. Willingly. Eagerly. Fiercely, their mouths met as if even the shortest preliminaries were too long. Verne was exultant. For one who had not wanted to see, she had responded in every way as he'd hoped, shedding the inhibitions that had plagued her. Although he expected to encounter others, her softening body and questing hands told him that her curiosity would overcome any latent fears, as indeed it was already doing.

Over the undulations of his shoulders and back, her fingertips and palms made expeditions which, as well as adding to her limited knowledge, heightened the spellbinding sensation of his lips upon hers that nudged, nibbled and consumed, carrying her closer than ever to the core of him. The sense of no turning back swamped her, making her oblivious to the unbuttoning, untying, loosening and unwrapping that went on behind her, or the slipping of soft fabric from her shoulders and hips, the release of arms and breasts. As they entered a new phase of intimacy, Annemarie became half-aware that her naked body was being warmed by his skin, seductively, sending small shivers of delight along each surface as they moved in each other's arms, their mouths still wordless and hungry.

Sealed within his embrace, she surrendered herself to the new experience of being held against his chest, then of his hand cupping the luscious fullness of her breast, fondling it, passing his palm provocatively across the sensitive tip to alert her to a sudden exquisite tingle that rushed down to her secret parts, taking her completely by surprise. With a gasp and a mewing cry, she eased her mouth free of his with a hand on his chin.

Verne waited, saying nothing, understanding

that this could well be in memory of some earlier rough treatment. Tenderly, he resumed the caress, adding, as she watched, another kind of delight that he knew would not have been part of her previous experience, showering the delicate skin with moist kisses that eventually took the aching nipple into his mouth. Teasing with tongue and lips, he felt the sharp impression of Annemarie's fingernails on his back and heard her staggering breath, and knew that her fears were being replaced by ecstasy.

Constantly intrigued by this amazing woman, Verne soon realised that this occasion was going to be no exception. He had promised to take their loving slowly in response to her brutish husband's haste, but now he began to sense that it was not so much a lengthy preparation she required, but a lover who treated her with consideration and skill, with mastery as well as affection. He had brought a smile to her lips, too, which he was willing to wager Sir Richard had never done. He had overcome some of her objections and fears, and already she had attained a level of desire he'd not expected for quite some time, though her previous behaviour ought perhaps to have prepared him. Wavering between certainty and doubt, the lady was not always easy to predict.

He did not regret the leisurely pace, his self-control being what it was, for she joined him in every caress with versions of her own, enjoying his nakedness as he did hers, unashamedly seeking sensations through hands, lips, and the soles of her feet. At the same time she allowed him free access to the most hidden parts of her self, showing by her trembling stillness that her mind and body had, for those moments of bliss, parted company. For Verne, it came as a revelation to him which he could not have anticipated, having half-expected his wooing to be interrupted, now and then, by a restraining hand and the need for some reassurances, at least.

But none were necessary. His courteous unhurried lovemaking, which at first had been encouraged with sighs of pleasure, was soon goaded into something more energetic by her grasping fingers in his hair and a series of almost savage kisses that were anything but maidenly. He needed no other urging, nor did there seem to be any need, in view of her wildness, for him to enquire if she was ready. With a hand beneath her back, he pulled her under him and watched the dark gemstone eyes lock with his, reminding him that here he must proceed with care past the hurts that could not so quickly be forgotten. Her eyes remained on his as he took her that first time, searching for any indication of selfishness on his part which might imply that *her* enjoyment was not his first concern.

There was no such sign. Skilfully and with

tenderness, he accepted her silent invitation by slipping effortlessly into her warmth accompanied by the fluttering of eyelids and a soundless gasp that might, he thought, have been a combination of relief and pleasure. For her reassurance as well as his own, he watched her face for the smallest sign of discomfort but saw, with a growing sense of elation, how her sighs became moans, how her glossy hair frayed across her face as she tossed and how she continued to caress him intimately in a way, he thought, she had probably not been used to doing.

Incomprehensible murmurs escaped her, sounds of delight mingled with deeper throaty tones as the flames of her passion soon roared out of control, and here his intention to delay fell apart, for she was ahead of him, urging him with her body to satisfy some fast-growing need. Her heavy eyelids drooped over the former wariness, and now as he mastered her demands with an increased energy he saw once again the magnificent angry woman who had chosen to cross swords with him on sight. This was what he had dreamed of since that first encounter, to see her beneath him writhing in ecstasy and calling softly to him to take her without delay to a place he could swear she'd never been before. If she forgot everything else that had ever happened to her, she would remember this.

Recalling those moments, as she did many

times later, Annemarie was never able to compare the experience with anything life had offered so far: to try a comparison with what Sir Richard had offered was absurd. Exactly why her late husband had always redoubled his efforts at the conclusion of his performance, mercifully not a protracted one, had never made much sense to her. Now she understood. She remembered the incredible sensation of being overcome by wave after wave of rapture, of being swept along by her lover's fierce encouragement that shook her with its force, tumbling them both at the same time into a whirling oblivion, their cries mingling in the distance. She remembered his power and exciting energy which, rather than leaving her bruised and flattened, left her satiated, melting, trembling with a unique kind of exhilaration. She remembered his breathless words, too, while she was still wondering what had happened, yet knowing instinctively why it had not happened before.

His face was buried in the silky black tangle covering her neck, the pillow being somewhere on the floor. 'I think,' he said, 'you are the most desirable and sensational woman I've ever met. You're in a class of your own, my beauty. I think I shall keep you in a cage.'

'No,' she whispered, though her lips smiled the word. 'That would not suit. I have just been set free, my lord.'

He turned his head towards her, dark locks of hair falling over his forehead. Annemarie's heart melted at the sight of him, at the triumph in his eyes, at the heat that flowed over her from his possessive body. Could she knowingly hurt him after this, when he'd taken her to such heights? Had he not just bound her to him and caged her, if not in his heart, then at least in his command? Was she truly freed now, or would she crave more and more of him?

'Set free, are you?' he said, resting on one elbow to look down at her. 'Just now, you mean?'

He would know, she thought, how the balance of her life had now tipped and how she would need to review the quality of her new independence as a woman and as his mistress with well-laid plans. What he would not know was that, after this, she might need him more than she'd planned and more than he would need her, despite the compliments. And then who would need caging? Her? Or him? 'Yes,' she said. 'Just now. But have no fear, my lord. I have no thoughts of another escape at the present.' Softly as a feather she touched his cheek, brushing her fingertips over the strong thick hair that shielded his ears, drawing his head towards her to place a lingering seal upon her words.

She was relieved to discover that Verne did not intend to leave the decision to her. Lifting his head, he moved a strand of her hair from his chin. 'May I remind you, oh mistress mine,' he said, 'that you were not allowed to escape on previous occasions nor will you be allowed to in the future. Thank you for your acceptance, however. That simplifies matters for me.'

'Like not having to build a cage?' she said, facetiously, sensing a deepness she preferred not to fathom.

Rather than answer with words, Verne kissed her again, suspecting that she already knew the cage was built and that she had just entered it.

Chapter Seven

The talk about cages, Annemarie told herself, was not something to be taken too seriously. Men said that kind of thing and Verne had probably expressed the same sentiment to other women after making love. He would have a stock of such compliments, surely, a man of his obvious experience. Even so, he appeared to be more than satisfied with her limited repertoire, for he had made love to her again almost immediately before joining her in sleep for an hour, after which they had dressed in a state of dreaminess with hardly a word between them, walking shamelessly hand in hand across the Steyne to take tea in her cosy rooms on the corner of South Parade.

The earlier visit to the house by Samson, Verne's valet, had not been solely for his master's comfort. As well as delivering his evening dress and travelling valise, he had another more personal mission concerning the lady's maid Evie, knowing that unless he made his peace with her, he was going to be on the wrong side of the door indefinitely. So with this in mind he made himself as agreeable to Mrs Ash as he knew how, on the basis that she might sway the young lady's opinion in his favour.

Hoping to satisfy her own curiosity about the cause of the conflict, Mrs Ash lost no time in putting forwards the view that she thought the young man quite charming and what was there about him not to like? She put it to Evie within minutes of the young man's leaving. Had something happened? she wanted to know.

'Too forward, that's all,' said Evie, recalling the two incidents at Reigate, one of which was only hours old.

As soon as he'd seen the cushion-shaped brown-paper parcel under Evie's arm, he'd known the time had come for an explanation. Though he'd dodged behind a few of the Swan's guests to escape, Evie was on the warpath with no intention of letting him avoid her anger. 'You didn't mind who you landed in trouble, did you? Thief! And you making up to me all friendly, like butter wouldn't melt in your mouth. Well…*that*'s for your trouble!' The smack across his face almost knocked him into the banister and would have been bad enough by itself had not several men made matters worse by turning to watch.

'Oi!' he said. 'Steady on, miss. I can explain... honest.'

'Honest my foot!' Evie had snapped. '*That* you're not!'

Samson held his cheek to cool the sting. 'Give me a chance, then. Look, come away from this gawping crowd and I'll tell you.'

'You can start by telling me what was in that portmanteau that was valuable enough for you to help yourself to, you thieving—'

'Shh! Cut it out, Miss Evie.' The accusation hurt. He'd only obeyed orders. 'I was told it had valuables in, that's all. And I was curious. So while you were downstairs I took a peep inside.'

'And?'

'Nothing much. Only bundles of letters addressed to Lady Something; I couldn't read the writing in that light. Well, I thought they might be of interest to Lord Verne, so I took them out and put the cushion there instead.'

'Why on *earth* would Lord Verne be interested in bundles of letters?'

'Well, I dunno. I thought perhaps they might have been from Lady Golding's husband...you know...Sir Richard...'

'I *know* that!'

'To his mistress, or somebody.'

'His *what*? What mistress?'

'Oh, come off it, Miss Evie. I expect everybody knew.'

'I'm Miss Ballard to you, and no, everybody *didn't* know, Mr Samson. I didn't, for one thing, and nor did Lady Golding. And don't you go putting it about, or I'll…'

'Yes, right. No need to fly up again. Maybe I'm wrong, then.'

'You were certainly wrong to take what doesn't belong to you. So you passed these letters on to Lord Verne, did you? And what has *he* done with them?'

'No idea, Miss Ballard. He may have burnt them for all I know.' That much was true. All he'd done was to get whatever was in the portmanteau, as instructed, put something in its place and then relock it. His thieving days were over and it was rare for him to meet a victim and have to explain.

'Then you can get rid of *that*!' Evie had said, shoving the parcel at him. 'And if the room is locked, you'll know how to get into it, won't you?'

After that encounter, Samson's avoidance tactics had been more successful, but his words had lingered uncomfortably in Evie's mind like a heavy weight, reinforcing a suspicion she'd held for years about Sir Richard's behaviour. *Had* he kept a mistress? Sent her letters? Reclaimed them before his death? Bought them back to avoid blackmail?

'Mrs Ash,' she said, hanging the last of Anne-

marie's gowns on the wardrobe rail. 'Did…er…
did Sir Richard keep a mistress?'

A denial would have burst out immediately:
the hesitation provided the dreaded confirma-
tion. Mrs Ash turned to the view overlooking
the Steyne, sighing before she answered. 'He
did,' she said. 'I thought you knew.'

'No,' said Evie. She sat on the edge of the
white silk-covered bed, staring beyond the
housekeeper at the wheeling seagulls. 'No, I
didn't. Lady Golding doesn't know, either. Does
she?'

'We kept it to ourselves,' said Mrs Ash. 'The
poor lady had no need to know. She had enough
to put up with, without that. And then when all
that business blew up after he'd gone, it seemed
best to let it die a natural death. It's just a bit uncomfortable that the woman should have been
living here in Brighton, where Lady Golding
loves to be.'

'Here? Oh, no!'

'He used to come down here without her for
a few nights, telling us he'd be at Raggett's Club
when Mr Ash knew full well he wasn't. I suppose Lady Golding thought he'd be on duty at
the barracks. He never gave anyone credit for
being able to see what he was up to. Mr Ash
knows most of what goes on in Brighton. It was
one of those terraced houses on Arlington Street
where he went. A private house, not a brothel.

I don't know any more than that. It's over and done with. You'll not tell her, will you?'

'No, I certainly won't, Mrs Ash.'

'You suspected something, though. Why did you ask?'

'Oh, I'd just like her to be married again instead of a man's mistress.'

'Is that what Lady Golding is? Lord Verne's mistress?'

'Yes, that's what we have to get used to, Mrs Ash, for the time being.'

'Mind you, Lord Verne's got a bit more going for him than... Oh well, I mustn't say too much on that score, must I? I expect she knows what she's doing.'

Evie stood up, smoothing the dent made on the bed. 'Mmm,' she said. 'I hope she does.' She closed the wardrobe door gently. Samson's assumption that the letters could have been to Sir Richard's mistress was, of course, just that. An assumption. He could have been quite mistaken but, if that's what they were, then Lady Golding would have experienced yet another blow to her pride at a time when she was at her lowest ebb. Equally puzzling was the timing. Where had the letters been since Sir Richard's death? Here at Brighton? Evie thought she knew every nook and cranny of her mistress's rooms, drawers and cupboards. The idea of Lord Verne possessing incriminating material that was none of his business did not sit easily with her when he had in all other respects shown himself to be the embodiment of respectability, quite unlike the previous earwig who had laid siege to her mistress's heart. Whatever the letters were, incriminating or not, Lord Verne had no right to them and now both she herself and Mrs Cardew were involved in deceiving Lady Golding into believing they were safely disposed of. If only she could be more sure of her ground.

Later that day, while Lady Golding and Lord Verne were exploring the delights of the Royal Pavilion, Evie took a stroll in the sunshine along Marine Parade. Discreet enquiries at Donaldson's Library had assured her that Arlington Street was somewhere along here, thus setting a scene of respectability which would surely help her enquiries. It had been over two years since Sir Richard's death in the January of 1812, time enough for the occupants to have changed, but when Evie had scanned the list of subscribers to the library and discovered the familiar name of Mytchett, she felt that her prying into Lady Golding's affairs was excused. Here was a connection she had not expected. A relative of Sir Lionel Mytchett's? The late Sir Richard Golding's mistress?

Small signs of hard times were immediately apparent: an unswept step, flaking paint on the door, unpolished brass knocker and door handle. A curtain twitched at one side as Evie waited, not expecting her rat-a-tat to be answered with any promptness. When the door opened at last after the third knock, the cautious approach was close to what Evie had predicted, a weary face framed by untidy dark ringlets under a lace cap and a greeting that had obviously been prepared for a creditor rather than a friend. 'Yes? If you're from Scott and Wildings, you can tell them I'll pay on Friday.' The door began to close.

Evie put out a hand to stop it. 'No…er, no! I'm not from Scott and Wildings. This is a private visit. Personal. To see Miss…er…*Mrs* Mytchett?' Having caught sight of another face on the level of the lady's knee, most of it obscured by a sticky fist, she revised her choice of titles. 'Is this where she lives?'

'Who wants to know?'

Deception was never Evie's strong point, nor did she think to achieve anything extra by pretending to be someone she was not. 'Don't be alarmed,' she said. 'My name is Miss Ballard, lady's maid to Lady Golding. Might I have a few words with Mrs Mytchett? In private?'

Two deep-brown eyes scanned her from bonnet to shoes and back again while the wisdom and foolishness of the meeting was debated and the child turned its face into the mother's faded skirts. To be sure, Evie couldn't tell whether the little moppet was a son or a daughter when the wild halo of fair curls could have belonged to either. The woman's expression gave little away as she opened the door with reluctance, as if there was something wedging it closed. 'I wondered. Mind out the way, Richie,' she muttered, hauling the child back by one shoulder.

'Wondered?' said Evie, edging her way through the gap.

'Yes. How long it would be before something like this happened. It's *him* you want to be talking to, not me, Miss Ballard.'

'You *are* Mrs Mytchett?'

'I am.'

The light dimmed noticeably as the door was closed and Evie felt the shabby claustrophobic narrowness press inwards as the child whined to be picked up, still sucking its fist. The mother complied, grunting with the effort, then leading her guest into a room that might once have been pretty, but was now threadbare, faded and sadly in need of renovation. Glancing at Mrs Mytchett's back, Evie judged that she was probably still in her late twenties, shapely but ill served by a muslin day-dress from which a section of frill had come adrift. There was no sign of a maid, but a high pile of folded cotton garments lay upon the small side-table next to a sewing-box.

Evie settled herself in a battered old chair, noticing Mrs Mytchett's regular features and the

unfortunate down-turn about her mouth. Blotchy
skin and reddened eyelids had robbed her of any
youthful bloom there must once have been, but
Evie could well imagine that, before the child,
Mrs Mytchett would easily have attracted any
man. 'I beg your pardon for the intrusion,' she
said. 'Perhaps I ought to say that Lady Golding
did not send me here to quiz you. I came on my
own account. She doesn't know about my visit
and I don't intend to tell her, either, because—'

'Because she didn't know her husband had a
mistress? Is that it?' Mrs Mytchett said, settling
the child on her knee. 'Well, I knew it'd only be
a matter of time before she did. There are not
many secrets to be kept in a place the size of
Brighton, Miss Ballard.'

'No, I suppose not. But when you said just
now that I ought to be talking to "him", did you
mean your husband? And ought I to be address-
ing *Lady* Mytchett?'

'No. My late husband was in Sir Richard's
regiment, killed soon after we were married.
He was Sir Lionel's brother.' She almost smiled
at Evie's surprise. 'Sir Lionel Mytchett is my
brother-in-law and, no, before you jump to conclusions, we are not lovers. He stays here when
he wants to quit London, when things get too
hot for him, you understand. By that, I mean
when he runs out of money. I have my uses,' she
added in a quiet tone loaded with bitterness, her

lips touching the top of her child's head. 'Don't I, Richie love?'

'How old is he?' Evie asked.

'Almost four. He can talk well enough when he wants to. Takes after his father for that.'

'Sir Richard?'

'Yes. He doesn't remember him though.' She looked about her as if she also was struggling to remember him. 'It wasn't like this, then.'

'Forgive me for asking, but what *was* it like? Was Sir Richard generous?'

'You may as well know. The house was left to me by my husband, so Sir Richard had no expense there. In fact, he did quite well for himself to have a house bought by his wife's father and another one here owned by me. He paid for things, when he came to visit, and I suppose you could say I was kept in a modest style, though he never showed me off and I never had enough to save. He was not over-generous. Women were commodities to him, but without that support I would have fared much worse. Especially when this one came along.'

'But when Sir Richard died, surely he made provision for you both?'

Her top lip was pulled in between her teeth as, slowly, she shook her head. 'No. He didn't. Not one penny. Well, that would have been to admit that we existed, wouldn't it? And that would never do. After that, we didn't exist, Miss Ballard. I take in sewing because I can do it at home, but at the time it hit me hard, I can tell you, with his child to provide for. And my brother-in-law sponging off me as if I were a gold mine.'

'Has Sir Lionel not helped at all, with his connections?'

'He had a plan. I suppose he thought he was helping. He thought that if I'd been provided for, he could have managed my finances and done pretty well out of it. Living here cost him nothing, you see. When he realised he'd get no more help to pay for his horses and women and gambling debts, he decided to seduce Sir Richard's widow the way *he'd* seduced me. That way, if he could get Lady Golding to marry him, he'd have access to *her* funds. You're looking shocked, Miss Ballard. Did you think my brother-in-law *loved* Lady Golding?'

Evie's breath hovered in her lungs until she let it out on a sigh between parted lips. 'I don't know,' she said, 'but I think my mistress cared for him.'

'Yes, well. He's good at that, is Lionel. Has 'em eating out of his hand. I'm sorry if she got the thin end of the wedge, like me, but at least she can be miserable in comfort, can't she? From what I've heard, she sounds like a very nice lady.'

'She is,' Evie whispered. 'She's the best mistress ever. But did you say that Sir Richard *seduced* you, Mrs Mytchett?'

For the first time, her hostess smiled. 'Lord, Miss Ballard! Did you think I was a professional? No…o! I was a young broken-hearted widow. My new husband was down here at the barracks, then he was sent out to Portugal. So when he was killed in action, Sir Richard came to see if I was all right. That's when it started. That's when things like that always start, isn't it? When a woman seeks to replace something she's lost. I must have been the easiest target ever. Young. Lonely. Naïve. Flattered by the attention of a high-ranking officer. I didn't even know that mistresses usually asked for a settlement. Housekeeping money, personal allowances. That kind of thing. Lionel told me I should have fleeced him while I had the chance.'

It was on the tip of Evie's tongue to commiserate, to say how sad and how sorry before she realised that, although she was, it would not do to say so. Her mistress had also suffered badly, but what Mrs Mytchett had told her about her own callous brother-in-law was a shocking tale of heartlessness she could never have imagined, planned with a cold-bloodedness that made Evie thank Providence her mistress knew nothing of. Nor would she, ever.

But the plan had misfired, hadn't it? How much of *that* did Mrs Mytchett know? 'It sounds,' Evie said, 'as if Lady Golding had a narrow escape at your brother-in-law's hands, although he came close to breaking her heart. Did you know that he changed his mind and ran off with Lady Golding's mother instead?'

Mrs Mytchett stroked the mop of hair back from her son's sleepy forehead to plant a soft kiss upon the smooth skin. 'Yes,' she said. 'I read about it in the newspaper, but all he said when he called in at Christmas, was that he needed more money because the jewellery Lady Benistone had taken with them was not going to be enough.'

'And you couldn't help him out?'

Mrs Mytchett's eyebrows flickered upwards, her eyes searching over the mess in the squalid room. 'What do *you* think, Miss Ballard? I sit here and sew till my fingers bleed and I fall asleep over my work. I can't help myself out any more.'

'No. I'm sorry. That was thoughtless of me. You don't deserve a brother-in-law like that. So you have no idea where he and Lady Benistone are living?'

'No idea. He doesn't keep me informed.'

'Did Sir Richard ever write to you, Mrs Mytchett?'

'Heavens above, no! He used to say you can never tell what a woman would do with letters, so he never took that risk. He wouldn't have

known what to say, anyway. Talking, yes. But
not writing. So why did you come here, Miss
Ballard? To ask if I knew where Lady Benistone
might be? I can't help you, I'm afraid. If I had
any idea, I'd tell you. I have nothing to lose by it.'

So the letters now in Lord Verne's possession were *not* from Sir Richard to Lady Something, nor did his mistress have a title except
plain Mrs, and if Evie's personal opinion of Sir
Lionel Mytchett was exceedingly poor to begin
with, it was now at rock bottom after hearing of
his calculated plan concerning Lady Golding.
Even though it was prompted by Sir Richard's
brutal neglect of his son's welfare, not to mention his mistress's, Evie realised that the scheme
was essentially to feather Sir Lionel's own nest
rather than that of his brother's widow.

Any hope she had cherished of hearing news
of Lady Benistone now faded like wraiths in the
afternoon sun as she walked back to South Parade where, from the top of the stairs, she saw
the arrival of Lady Golding and Lord Verne. Before her heated conversation with Samson, she
had been inclined to look upon his lordship with
kindliness, especially in view of his impeccable
connections to royalty. Now, however, after hearing how he'd taken possession of her mistress's
private papers, doubts about *his* intentions began
to form just as they had about Sir Lionel. She
prayed she might be mistaken, for never was

there such a fine figure of a man with such caring manners. This one was certainly out of the top drawer, even if his valet *was* light-fingered.

Taking afternoon tea together, Annemarie and Lord Verne sat on opposite sides of a dainty rosewood table set in the bay window, each with a hand linked across the crisp white tablecloth, their eyes occasionally meeting in secretive smiles before returning to an idle study of passers-by and carriages. For her, everything had changed, as she had known it would, and Verne's perception of this was yet another mark in his favour—no light-hearted banter or embarrassment, no gloating, only quietness and reflection, caught and contorted in the bulbous silver teapot.

'Jacques,' she whispered, holding his eyes with her own.

'Mmm?'

'Don't ever tell me about all the others, will you? I don't want to know.'

Verne did not pretend to misunderstand. From the start of this relationship she had assumed an air of confidence that, in less than a day, had disintegrated into a storm of jealousy out of all proportion to the cause. Now she appeared to be anticipating another complication of her own which he believed had surfaced only since their ecstatic lovemaking that afternoon. She was making up comparisons to herself, not to him.

His hand tightened over hers and slid up to her wrist. 'Sweetheart,' he said, 'since you ask, I have no memory of any other except the one who was in my arms an hour or so ago. I have never had a mistress before, nor ever wanted one. I told you, no woman has ever held my attention for long enough for me to want her to myself. Until now. You, my lady, I can't get enough of.'

'You know so little about me,' she protested, half-warning him of things to come.

'Listen to me,' he said. 'Part of our agreement, if you remember, was to re-enter society with the intention of trying to locate Lady Benistone. Wasn't it?'

She nodded.

'So let's try not to throw obstacles in the way before we've begun, shall we? When we've found her, then you can show me how difficult you can be and I'll show you how well I can manage you, and we'll see who wins. Is that a deal, my lady?'

The lovely mouth widened, excited by the implied challenge. 'Deal,' she laughed, laying her free hand on top of his, light as a feather. 'More tea, my lord?'

He held out his cup and saucer. 'Good. So no more comparisons. You are beyond compare, both in bed and out of it. Another cup, if you please.'

It was so much what she wanted…needed… to hear as the realisation swirled through her like an incoming tide that she loved him, as it had done earlier when he had taken her out of her depth and brought her back safely to shore, too exhilarated to speak. Now, although he pretended not to notice it, the silver teapot shook a little as she poured.

Before he could remedy the deficiency in his knowledge of her, Verne was plied with questions about himself, his travels abroad and his time with Viscount Wellington's army, his interest in art and the classical world, in antique treasures and his work for the Prince Regent. With some shame, she remembered how he had corrected her over the plaster hand, underestimating his knowledge, which she now realised far exceeded her own. Mostly, she knew what things were, but he knew their history and provenance in detail, and although she had never before discussed the subject of her father's interest, or wanted to, with Verne it seemed to come alive as he related stories of his hunts for whatever it was his royal master thought he wanted, only to change his mind after all, or forget he'd ever wanted it.

Would this same fickleness apply also to the bureau? Annemarie wondered. Now the letters were restored to Lady Hamilton, would both master and servant eventually lose interest? It was with some trepidation that she waited to see

Verne's reaction as they entered her bedroom
to dress for dinner, half-expecting him to ask
to examine it, after all the furor. But Evie was
there to assist her mistress as Verne sat on the
chaise-longue to talk and watch, as if they had
been intimate friends of long standing, and if he
as much as glanced at the controversial bureau,
Annemarie didn't see it.

Later, however, when they returned to the
candle-lit bedroom and Evie's duties were done,
Verne sat on the wooden chest at the end of the
bed, resting his arms on his thighs. The surface
of the bureau shone like warm satin beneath the
silver candelabrum and the appreciative sweep of
his eyes. 'So *this* is it,' he said. 'You chose well,
my lady. It's a very well-made piece.'

Wearing her lace-frilled ivory negligee,
Annemarie came to sit beside him. 'Yes, I think
so, too, but wait till you see what's under the lid.
This part is even better.' Lifting the central section, she disclosed the mirror on the underside
and the array of cut-glass and silver containers,
the tools and polished wood compartments that
she had not yet had time to fill with her own po-
tions and perfumes. Together, they admired the
beautiful vessels, trying to identify the aromas
and decide on their uses as the soft light played
over Annemarie's skin and the sheen of her loose
hair. Relaxed and more at peace than she'd been

for days, she now saw no reason to keep from him the secret place where the letters had been.

She drew the drawer out and released the catch to open the extra space at the back, inviting him to put his hand inside. 'It's quite roomy. See?' she said.

He paused. 'Ah!' he said. 'So this is where she kept them. What a very forgetful lady.' His arm disappeared as far as his elbow.

'She would have had more important things on her mind,' Annemarie said. 'Like how to pay her bills, for one thing.'

Verne's hand withdrew, bearing a flat blue-leather box. 'So what can this be, I wonder? Did you know about it?'

'No, indeed I didn't. I didn't look for anything else.'

'Well,' he said, placing it on her knee. 'I think you should take a look. If it's jewellery from Prinny, it'll be worth a fortune. He was very generous with his trinkets while he was still enamoured.' He drew the candelabrum forward.

Holding it towards the light, she lifted the lid, blinking at the sudden blaze of flashing jewels that had not seen daylight for many years, set in gold, nestling on a bed of dark-blue velvet: a brooch, earrings, bracelets, a ring, a hair-comb and a deep multi-stranded necklace of massive pearls, amethysts and diamonds winking like living rainbows. Imprinted on the cream satin

on the inside of the lid was the gold lettering of
Rundell and Bridge, Ludgate Hill, London.

'His favourite jeweller,' said Verne. 'This *is*
worth a fortune.'

'If only she had remembered it, it might have
solved a few of her problems.'

'Would you wear it?'

Tipping the box this way and that under the
candles, Annemarie shook her head. 'Not I. Not
my style. Too flashy. Besides, it's not mine, is
it?'

'You bought it with the bureau.'

'A mistake. It will have to be returned.' Suddenly, she smiled. 'That's it! We'll take it back
to him. He can't have the letters now, can he, so
perhaps this will ease his disappointment.'

'Like rubbing salt into a wound, I'd say,' said
Verne. 'And anyway, he'll have forgotten all
about this. Why remind him? You could wear
the pieces separately. Or in pairs.' Taking the
box from her, he laid it on the bureau and removed the vee-shaped necklace, holding against
the peachy skin of her neck. 'No,' he said. 'Turn
round.'

She did as he asked, presenting her back to
him, but instead of fastening it round her neck,
he laid it across her forehead with the largest
pearl-drop hanging between her brows, the amethysts and diamonds encircling her black hair
like the diadem of some exotic queen of the east,

with the gemstones matching the colour of her eyes to perfection. 'There,' he said, turning her round to face him, 'that's more your style. But wait. This won't do, will it?' He eased her negligee off her shoulders, then the straps of her nightgown, letting the ivory lace fall to her waist. Taking handfuls of her hair, he spread it in tatters over her shoulders and let it fray across her breasts while she sat motionless, as entranced as any sitter whose pose is being arranged by the artist, only being able to guess at the effect. 'Now give me your feet,' he said.

'My feet?'

'Lift,' he commanded. Reaching for one of the bracelets, he fastened them around her ankles. 'Perfect. They'll look better there than on Emma Hamilton's chubby arms.'

There had been moments, during their intimate dinner, when Annemarie had speculated on the way in which he might instigate the lovemaking in her home rather than in his own apartment. Would he be inhibited by Sir Richard's stern portrait, or hindered by the absence of his valet? Would he bypass the preludes so important to her enjoyment, or would every time be specially designed to make her want more and still more? 'I don't suppose,' she said, watching him undress, 'that either the royal jeweller or their patron had this in mind, either, my lord. Will the jewellery hinder lovemaking, or enhance it, do you think?'

Magnificently naked, he drew her to her feet with his warm hands on her elbows. 'We'll soon find out,' he said, huskily.

She need not have been concerned about his memory, for the long slow raptures of his loving began even while they stood pressed together along every surface, their hands reaching and smoothing over contours denied to them since their previous encounter, every touch inflaming their desire, increasing their need of each other. Words of endearment slipped between kisses, most of which Annemarie had not heard before in this context—'superb creature...bewitching...dazzling beauty...fascinating...mismanaged woman'—words that made her feel rare, unique and desperately wanted. Once again, flimsy unstable thoughts of the reasons behind this relationship tried to break through the bliss that engulfed her in his arms, thoughts to do with that word 'mismanaged' that no doubt referred to her initial hostility and her need for retribution. But Verne's skill was such that few thoughts survived for more than a heartbeat under the burning path of his hands, caressing, lifting and stroking, sending shivers of ecstasy deep into places that no one had reached before him.

On the cool linen sheets she was covered by the warmth of his body, glowing above her in

the soft candle-light and rippling with a vigour
that bore no affinity to any of those white marble
examples in her father's collection. Verne's physique was firm and substantial, powerfully built
and in superb condition, this alone being enough
to excite Annemarie to heights that closed her
mind to everything except being possessed by
such a red-blooded male whose intelligence was
as robust as the rest of him. He was, she thought,
a complete man, more than a match for her in
every way, imposing himself upon her only so
far and allowing her to do what she believed was
what she wanted.

Her way and his fused together in deliciously
slow explorations that drew gasps of delight and
moans of pleasure, taken by him as a signal to go
further than before with hands and lips, knowing
that the whole long night lay at their disposal.
Time slipped seamlessly away as Verne taught
her things about herself that she had never suspected, tender places on her body that responded
like wildfire to his touch and melted her thighs,
spreading her legs wider. 'Now,' she whispered.
'I cannot wait any longer. Now, Jacques!'

'Shall I make you wait, my beauty?' he said,
teasing her. 'Shall I make you plead?'

'I *am* pleading,' she said. 'I'm aching for you.'

There was no more banter then as he ceased
the tantalising caress that had already worked its
magic, taking its place with his throbbing mem-

ber that threatened to rebel against his discipline.
And although, this time, his entry was rather
less gentle than before, it was what Annemarie
wanted, for now she trusted his motives as she
had never trusted her late husband's, not as anger
or disregard but as an expression of unbridled
passion. She cried out as he joined her, bringing
his head down to meet her lips in a surfeit of sensation to assure him that he had read her mind
well, that he need not hold in check the power-
house of his loins. 'Make it last…oh…make it
last,' she contradicted herself, softly.

'Ah, my love…I cannot. I want you too
much…forgive me!' He could not see her laughter. He had waited too long for her plea and now
his desire completely overwhelmed him, carrying him wildly on without knowing whether she
had kept pace with him or not.

But she had. Again, he had taken her to the
very brink of the abyss from which she had
flown and soared into unthinking space as her
body sang to its own kind of harmony and vi-
brated to her lover's insistent beat. Still pulsing
to the rhythm, her body settled back to earth
as her arms enclosed his sagging shoulders, her
lips whispering words of their own devising that
told him of her euphoria and of her amusement
at the fierce onslaught of his hunger. She did not
tell him of two words she'd heard him utter in
his undisciplined moments that might, if she'd

taken them at face value, have given her an indication of his feelings for her. Had they been
an idle slip of the tongue? Had he been holding the sentiment in check until then for fear of
seeming presumptuous? Was he now beginning
to feel for her what she could no longer ignore
in herself and, if so, where was this dangerous
game going to end and with whose heartbreak?

The amethyst necklace had long since slipped
away to tangle in Annemarie's hair, though it
had not interfered with the next sleepy lovemaking or the one after that at dawn and was anything but sleepy. As the light seeped through
the curtains, there was laughter and protest as
priceless jewels were disentangled, the kind of
mirth that had never before played any part in
her experience.

'Keep still, dammit!'

'Ouch! That's still attached.'

'Wait. I shall have to kiss you again.'

'No, that's Evie with our tea. Cover yourself!'

'Why? Hasn't she seen…?'

'Shh! Let me go! How am I going to explain
this?' Annemarie held up a tress of black hair
with a stream of sparkling brilliants clinging te-
naciously to the end.

As it turned out, there was no need for explanations. The sight that met Evie's astonished
gaze was of her naked mistress sitting cross-

legged with her back to Lord Verne, who appeared to be engaged in extracting a fistful of jewels from a very tousled head.

Two days of being almost constantly in Verne's company only made Annemarie regret that it could not have been longer. Between walks along the shore and drives through the country lanes, during which they were allowed the use of the Prince's curricles, phaetons and high-stepping horses, they visited the shops, libraries and tearooms. And at last she was shown round the ongoing renovations to the Royal Pavilion, so opulent that she came away feeling quite intoxicated by his Highness's over-decorated style. It seemed to typify the complexity of his nature: a man of contrasts and contradictions, a man who could spend thousands of pounds on baubles for his lady friends, yet ignore them when their need was greatest.

They walked towards the carriage-house where a curricle had been harnessed up for them. Annemarie went on ahead to speak to the horses just as Verne's attention was diverted by the appearance of his friend Lord Bockington who had shown off his gelding's paces to them on their first visit. 'Something you might be interested to know, sir,' said the fair-haired young man, keeping his voice low.

'Tell me?' said Verne, walking with him to the back of the curricle.

'Well, last time we met, I was very struck by Lady Golding's beauty, sir. And I suppose it stayed in my mind for quite some time.'

'I'm sure. Go on.'

'So I tried to recall when I'd last seen a woman with her looks, then I knew. It was last summer in London. The woman I saw was an older version of Lady Golding. Surely a relative, I'd have thought. She was so like her.'

'Was she alone?'

'No, she was in the company of the Marquess of Hertford. I remember it well.'

'Hertford? Are you sure, Bock?'

'Positive, sir. He was helping her into his carriage outside his house in Manchester Square as I passed by.' The note of concern had not escaped him. 'I don't know whether the Marchioness was with them or not. She may have been in the carriage. I didn't look. I had no reason to.'

'Of course not. Was it a travelling coach?'

'Four horses and…yes…come to think of it, there were trunks on the back. I thought no more about it at the time except that Lord Hertford always manages to have a beautiful woman with him, wherever he is.'

Verne noted his friend's wistful tone. 'And if you had his kind of blunt, so might you, Bock. Even if you were as ugly as sin itself. Which you're not.' Without actually saying so, Verne knew that his reference to Lord Hertford's looks would be perfectly understood. He was known as 'Red Herrings' to his acquaintances because of his fiery red hair and whiskers. 'Thank you for telling me,' he said. 'It might be useful.' Verne nodded as Lord Bockington bowed and turned to go. 'Now, my lady. Are we ready to set off?'

His lack of conversation was passed off as concentration as he took the curricle eastwards away from Brighton's traffic, but soon it became obvious that he was preoccupied. 'You're very quiet,' said Annemarie.

'I was thinking that this will be our last day here. We must start for London early, tomorrow.'

There was, she thought, the slightest hint of anticipation in his voice.

Chapter Eight

Verne pressed his lips upon the cool brow that lay against his shoulder. 'Sit up, hussy, and tidy yourself. We shall be in town soon.'

Languorously, Annemarie unwound herself from his arms, pushed a stray lock of hair back into place and yawned, taking the ruched royal-blue bonnet he offered her. 'Must be the sea air,' she murmured.

Smiling at the excuse, Verne could think of other reasons, but her sleep with her feet up on the Prince's green cushions had given him a chance to consider the implications of what he'd heard from Lord Bockington on the previous day. While any news at all must be regarded as good, he hoped his young friend might have been mistaken.

Of all men for a woman of quality to be involved with, the second Marquess of Hertford was not by any standards an ideal choice, not because of his unusual appearance or his undeniable wealth, both of which had the power to attract women from every strata of society, but because of his notorious reputation as a seducer with whom no female was safe. Age, apparently, was no obstacle to him, though it was known that he preferred married to single women, judging by the many illegitimate children he'd sired and who had been integrated into the husband's family. It was a risk women seemed willing to take, even while they regretted his utter heartlessness. As the recipient of at least eighty thousand pounds a year, Hertford could afford to live in great style, to indulge himself, his wife and his good-for-nothing son, to gamble to excess and to carve for himself a niche in the Prince Regent's exclusive circle of friends by pandering to his needs, which were mostly for flattery and finance. For a man like 'Red Herrings', this was no hardship.

However, that was not all the two men had in common, for Lady Hertford had also been an intimate of the Prince Regent for many years, so intimate, in fact, that the press lampooned the pair as overweight lovers, even though their friendship was of a more cerebral nature than that and so beyond the interest of news reporters eager to discredit them. A formidable lady of considerable presence, Lady Hertford refused to allow this to embarrass her, just as she refused to be embarrassed by her errant husband. In a position of influence with the Prince, and therefore with the rest of society, she stuck loyally to his side, fending off all would-be rivals for her special role as mentor, confidante and bountiful giver of the approval he had always wanted from his parents.

Lord Verne and the Hertfords had known each other for many years for, like the Prince, the Marquess was a multi-faceted character of great intelligence, worth fostering as a friend if only for his ability to converse on an astonishing range of subjects. As a serious connoisseur of paintings, he knew more about art than anyone else known to Verne. It was for this reason that the two men worked together on the Prince's collection, buying and selling artefacts for his new seaside retreat at Brighton and for Carlton House, his expanding mansion in central London. The money spent on these two alone was what Annemarie regarded as iniquitous, yet it was what Verne and Hertford helped him to do.

While Lord Hertford's intentions towards women, especially beautiful ones, were rarely innocent, Verne could understand how, if Lady Benistone had cut herself adrift from Sir Lionel Mytchett, any port in a storm might be preferable to being left totally unsupported. One way or another, Verne intended to make some enquiries as soon as they reached Curzon Street, which they did some moments after noon.

Lady Benistone's choice of protectors, on that dreadful day, had been made on the basis of a friendship begun in the earliest years of their marriages to very different men whose emotional support had failed to match the material benefits supplied with so little effort. Apart from Lady Hertford and Lord Benistone's cousin, Mrs Cardew, Esme had complained to no one else about the emptiness of the marriage in which she felt usurped by Elmer's other interests and by his self-absorbed lack of involvement in his family's affairs. She had sometimes wondered whether, if she'd given him sons instead of daughters, his concern for them, and her, might have been evident in more personal ways. She knew it often happened like this, but his initial passion for her had been so very great, leading her to expect it to last longer.

So it was no great surprise to Lady Hertford that the dear friend who was carried into her home that evening should have chosen the sympathy, understanding and care she could be sure of rather than risk a return to something less.

Apart from that, in the terrible trauma of her mind, Esme knew she had helped to bring this upon herself by trying to outwit a scoundrel who lived by outwitting others. The explanations that her family had a right to expect were beyond her. Lady Hertford had no such expectations.

Having already been acquainted with the details of Esme's flight from the youngest daughter's coming-out ball—social news travelled fast—Lady Hertford knew better than to suggest a return home or to inform the family of her whereabouts. That would have to come from Esme herself, when she was ready. Meanwhile, keeping the secret from everyone except her personal maid and the Marquess, who knew more than a thing or two about subterfuge, Lady Hertford tended her guest like a mother, comforting, compassionate and without blame for her foolishness or noisy outrage against the man who had wronged her, which would have served no useful purpose. Being married to a man like Hertford and the bosom-friend of the Prince Regent had prepared her well for the vagaries of human behaviour.

Lady Benistone's lingering recovery received a setback, however, only two months later when she made a horrifying discovery. 'I thought it was my courses misbehaving again,' she moaned, recovering from a bout of nausea. She sat on the edge of her bed in her nightgown, bathed in the bright morning light that hurt her eyes. 'But it's not, Isabella. Not this time. Not with the sickness, too. Oh, my dear, what on earth am I going to do?'

This was a question Lady Hertford had already asked herself. She had even discussed it with her husband who, unsurprisingly, had seen possible complications before either of them. 'Take her up to Ragley,' he'd said, 'if the worst comes to the worst. She'll be safe enough there.'

The worst had come. 'We have Ragley Hall,' Isabella said to her distressed friend. 'You can have the child there and we'll find someone suitable to adopt it. A good woman. There are plenty of them about if you know where to look.'

Once again, Esme was racked with remorse and guilt, but Isabella's reasoning was sounder than she imagined for, as long as she remained in London, the greater the risk of her whereabouts being discovered either by a revengeful Sir Lionel or by the concerned family and a return to the status quo. Or, for that matter, by the Prince Regent who had once wanted her as his mistress and whose affections were fickle, to say the least. That was a risk Isabella was not willing to take. She was persuasive and Esme knew without asking that she would be given more attention and help at Ragley Hall than she'd had for years. Warwickshire, one of the beautiful midland counties, was a peaceful place and Ragley Hall was a massive palace.

Lord Hertford was nothing less than gentlemanly, escorting her in his best coach with trunks full of clothes and everything necessary

for her comfort, even during the lengthy months
of leisure that lay ahead. Esme had never felt
anything but safe with him, for they had once
in their youth been lovers, briefly and secretly,
and now they were easy friends. He had been
furious with Lord Benistone for allowing this
catastrophe to happen to his beautiful wife. 'If
she'd been given the support she needed,' he'd
railed to his wife, 'she'd not have been forced
to go ahead with her ridiculous scheme in the
first place. Why, that young scoundrel was about
to make an offer for the daughter...what's her
name?'

'Annemarie. Lady Golding.'

'That's it. At the youngest daughter's *ball*,
would you believe? And even then Benistone
had no time to listen. Heaven only knows, I have
the greatest respect for him as a collector, but if
he'd paid as much attention to his women as he
does to his bronzes...'

'My lord,' said Isabella, 'I think perhaps one
should say no more on that.'

'Eh? Well, perhaps you're right. You usually
are. We all have our weaknesses.'

'Yes, dear. And our strengths. But Esme ought
not to be in a delicate condition at her time of
life.'

At that gently tendered opinion, Hertford had
the grace to look thoughtful. 'She'll be all right
at Ragley,' he said. 'We'll get Dr Willetts to stay

there when she's due. You've managed to keep this from Prinny, have you?'

'Not a word,' Isabella replied. 'He's too concerned about the coming celebrations to think about much else. Poor lamb.'

Once inside the house on Curzon Street, Annemarie saw that she had taken Verne's teasing too seriously when he'd implied that all would have been made ready for immediate occupation. Indignant rather than disappointed, she saw that, although the staff were in place down to the last button, the furniture and fittings were not. If she wanted to stay the night there, Verne told her, laughing at her thwarted readiness to tell him how his choices did not accord with hers, she would have to go out and buy a bed and something to put on it.

'Which,' she retorted, loftily, 'is well within my capabilities, my lord. I have never found it difficult to make that kind of choice, especially when I'm left alone to get on with it.'

'You will be,' he said as she swished past him into the echoing dining room. 'I must take my leave of you until this evening. His Highness is expecting me. I'll send the barouche round in an hour to give you time to make a list. Will that do?'

'Perfectly, I thank you. Expect a certain

amount of chaos when you return, but at least you'll have something to sit on by then.'

Stepping aside to avoid two men and a trunk, he caught the gleam of excitement in her eyes at the enjoyable task ahead. 'And something to lie on, too, I should hope. Make that a priority, won't you? Adieu, my lady.'

There was no time to ask him if that kind of talk was typical between a mistress and her lover, but she could well imagine the snappy kind of answer he would have given. Not once had she left him stuck for a reply.

By the time Lord Verne returned late that afternoon, the promised chaos was at its height with swarms of aproned delivery men peeling wrappings from walnut tables and chairs as Annemarie ordained their exact position with a graceful waving of arms. One of them was caught in mid-wave by his lordship. 'Well!' he said, holding her hand. 'This is all very impressive. For you to do this all on your own is astonishing.'

'Not alone, my lord. Mrs Cardew and my sister came with me. They're upstairs, putting the bedroom together. Better not go up. You'll see it later. Look there, we have matching sofas and easy chairs.'

'And what do they match?'

'Er...the curtains, when they arrive. Oh, and

the carpet. Oriental. You'll like it. Soft golds
and pinks. Very feminine' Alerted by the slight
widening of his eyes, she added, 'Well, not *too*
feminine, though.'

'Do we have knives and forks?'

'Of course. And a dinner service. I've invited
the family for dinner tomorrow. Our new cook
was not in the least put out.'

Verne sprawled into a deep-gold velvety sofa
with his arm along the gilded back. 'I'm glad to
hear it. But *you* might be when I tell you we're
invited to meet his Royal Highness at Carlton
House tomorrow. And before you ask if it can be
postponed, my lady, the answer is, no, it can't.'
He saw by her sudden stillness and the cool un-
seeing stare through the to-ing and fro-ing of
the servants that she had been quite unprepared
for a clash of priorities so soon. Her gaze swung
slowly round to meet his, hoping for some compromise. 'It was part of our agreement,' he reminded her softly so that no one else could hear.
'And you wanted to meet him, didn't you? Did
you think it might have been at your convenience, sweetheart? That would be asking for
a miracle.'

She came to perch beside him on the edge
of the sofa and to stroke the new pile, her ringlets trembling with the slight shake of her head.
'No,' she said. 'Not really. But it's all right, I'll
manage. I could have done with the time, that's

all. It's only family. I shall have to get used to it, I suppose.'

'To what? Adapting?'

With a turn of her lovely head, she swept him with her long black lashes and the deep gemstones of her eyes in a look intended to convey some resignation, but which he interpreted as something infinitely more tender. 'Yes,' she said. 'Adapting. I must not fail at the first hurdle, must I?'

His hand reached out to cover hers, preventing the stroking. 'That's my beauty,' he whispered. 'He's eager to meet you and I can hardly wait to show you off. He remembers you.'

Annemarie smiled down at their hands. It was an intimate gesture rarely seen before servants, but Verne was not one to care much about that. 'And Mama? Does he remember her, too?'

'He does. But we shall not take the jewellery. It would not be proper. We'll leave references to the bureau and its contents for another time, unless he brings the subject up. He's already dropped the idea of owning yours.'

'You mean, since the contents were disposed of?'

'Yes, he feels safer now. Lady Hamilton and her daughter departed for Calais one night while we were in Brighton, you see. She's escaped her creditors and that's probably the last we'll see of her.'

*Taking the letters with her. No more specula-
tion, then, about what she might do with them.
From France, probably nothing at all. The end
of an episode.*

'Well, well,' she breathed. 'So that's the end
of that.'

'Is it?' he said, watching her. 'Is it, my lady?
Are you revenged now, or is there more to come?
Eh?'

Behind her eyes, a sudden rush of hot tears
welled and prickled. Astute, mercilessly accurate, he had touched the painful core of her plan
and she could find no answer.

'Forgive me,' he said, sitting up. 'You've had
a busy day, sweetheart. Let's take one thing at
a time, shall we? Come on, show me what's upstairs before we have dinner. Has my valet arrived?'

Relieved by the change of subject, she stood
up with him. 'Half an hour ago. He and Evie are
speaking at last.'

'Glad to hear it. I wonder what that was all
about.'

'Loyalty, I suppose. Just following my lead.'

Yet with each new step she took towards this
exhilarating domestic situation, Annemarie's
own private yearnings were being met so perfectly in every respect that, if the time ever came
for her to show her hand and to walk away from

it at the height of his need for her, her world would collapse more cruelly than his, even so. He had other things to turn to for support, a world in which she would only ever be an accessory, not a significant part. Just as devastating as the loss of her new independence and the flattering involvement of being his partner would be the forfeiture of times like this when, wrapped in dressing gowns in a house of strange sounds and shadows, they sat to eat a cold finger-feast from the sheet-covered top of a large packing-case containing the new chandelier from Pellatt and Green's. Nothing too romantic, one might think, except to a woman like Annemarie who had always dressed for dinner but who, in the space of a week or so, now found herself doing whatever it took to please him and to enjoy it, too. But as they sat quietly devouring tiny pasties, salads and cold pheasant, Annemarie sensed how her heart was betraying her, instead of him, and that it was already too late to reverse the damage.

Laughing at themselves, their eyes met. 'You can't believe you're doing this, can you, Lady Golding?' he said.

Licking her fingers noisily, her mischievous sideways glance reflected the absurdity of it all. 'Don't tell Father,' she said, 'or I shall not have a leg to stand on.' They had chosen to eat in what would eventually become the morning room and, earlier, the servants had come and gone like apparitions, fading through doors as their master and mistress murmured their way round the bedroom and bathroom where the starkness was now softened by folds of linen, cotton, silk and fringed velvet brocade, white lace-edged pillows and softly shifting bed-curtains of white silk lined with pale blue.

'We'll have the oak floor polished,' Annemarie told him, 'with a large blue-and-cream Axminster over here somewhere. I've ordered it.'

'And I shall like it,' he added.

'You will like it.' She smiled, slipping an arm around him. '*Will* you?' She made no objection when he drew her closely into his arms to show her where his thoughts had been since his upstairs tour. At no time during her whirlwind shopping spree had she been unsure of pleasing him, but nor had he been left out of her choices. She had already learned to respect his tastes and preferences. 'I tried,' she whispered between his kisses, 'to please you.'

'Please me?' he growled. 'My God, woman… you please me…' Sweeping her up into his arms, he carried her across to the pale smoothness of the bed, setting her alight with the tender weight of his powerful body and the bliss of being under him, privately and peacefully, in their own place.

Items of clothing gradually littered the so-tidy room as warm skin pressed, caressed and slid silkily down long interrupted surfaces, their hands exploring as if for the first time, their sighs broken by hungry kisses that travelled the length of their bodies, each part provoking its own kind of response. Still wondering at the newness of the experience, Annemarie soaked up the long slow loving just as Verne also discovered how the uniqueness of her splendid body yielded the rarity value of a priceless find. That such a creature should have suffered so deeply from neglect and treachery in quick succession gave him every reason to offer her the best he had in the hope that her bruised heart would mend and accept him as an essential part of her future. Her tears had shown him how close he was to understanding her and how disturbed she was by the emotional turmoil he'd alluded to earlier. Skilfully, through her tiredness, he helped her to forget.

It was hunger of another kind that reminded them, after a long interval of whispered earthy compliments that, if they did not appear downstairs soon, their supper might be returned to its maker. So dressing gowns were slipped on and, giggling like barefoot children, they sat on cushioned boxes to eat their first meal at Curzon Street and to sip champagne from hastily unwrapped wine glasses, all the more enjoyable for being some way outside Annemarie's precious conventions.

'No,' said Verne, 'I may not mention this to

your father tomorrow, but I shall certainly hold
it over your head for some time, my lady.'

The appointment at Carlton House was not
until after noon, but already the rooms at Curzon
Street were busy with more delivery men and
assistants to hang the chandelier. Evie had been
to Park Lane and was now filling the new ward-
robes with gowns suitable for a royal engagement. For Verne's sake, she must look her best,
be gracious and impressed by what she would
see at Carlton House, for he had every faith in
her ability to charm her host, otherwise he would
not have risked a meeting.

Nevertheless, considering her strong views
on the Prince's extravagance, Verne thought it
might be something of a miracle if she managed to hide every one of her feelings, which
were bound to be tested to their limits, especially as they ascended the grand double curve
of the massive staircase into the Ante Room.
Her lovely eyes seemed to devour the profusion
of blue and gold, but nothing was said until he
himself remarked, 'You look stunning, my lady.'

'Thank you, my lord. I'm trying to think of
something equally complimentary to say about
all this, but grandeur and opulence seem inadequate, don't they? Not very original, either.'

'Don't try too hard,' he said as synchronised
footmen opened the double doors at the far end

of the room. 'You'll find him very easy to talk to. Ah, here he comes.'

Previous encounters, one of them two years ago, one more recent, had warned her what she would see, yet the Prince's almost fifty-three years of self-indulgence were not at once apparent as he approached, more like an affable uncle than the overweight, petulant and gouty would-be Corinthian she had expected. Close up, she could see that he had once been a handsome man and that he took some pride in his appearance. 'Ah, so you've brought the lady to see me at last, Verne,' he said, beaming with delight, his hands outstretched to raise Annemarie from her curtsy. Pulling her gently forwards, he placed a cool kiss on both her cheeks. 'And about time, too. Tell me, Lady Golding, how is Lord Benistone? Is he still snapping up all those treasures I had set my heart on?'

'He's well, your Highness, I thank you.' She hoped his notoriously uncertain memory would not lead him to questions more difficult to answer. But another figure had quietly appeared behind him, a handsome Junoesque lady of late middle age who showed by her motherly smile that she and the Prince were comfortable together. By her deep-green satin gown and matching jewels, the perfectly arranged grey hair and rouged lips, one might have mistaken her for his wife, though Annemarie knew she was not. Her cheery nod of greeting to Lord Verne widened to a smile as it reached Annemarie, though the dreaded question was already on its way.

'And Lady Benistone, too? You are *so* like her. It's quite uncanny, isn't it, Isabella?' he said, turning to his companion. 'You recall Esme Benistone, don't you? Were you not good friends once?'

Isabella, Marchioness of Hertford, deflected the question like an old hand. 'Lady Golding,' she said, kindly, 'we're so happy to see you again. Especially with our good friend Lord Verne. Jacques, my dear, you *must* bring Lady Golding up to stay with us soon. Didn't Lord Hertford wish you to see his latest shipment from the Continent before his Highness sees them? Those two,' she continued, placing a ring-loaded hand on Annemarie's arm, 'are veritable *dragons*. They won't allow his Highness to see *anything* before they do in case he—'

'My taste is *faultless*,' the Prince protested, laughing. 'Maybe a little more eclectic than theirs... I *do* love the Chinese style, don't you, Lady Golding? But wait till you've seen my... come...this way...'

The relationship crisis averted, Lady Hertford winked boldly at Annemarie as the Prince led them through the double doors, easily diverting the fickle royal attention towards safer matters. Into the Crimson Drawing Room and the tent-like Circular Room—'I simply *adore* tents, don't you, Lady Golding?'—and on into the Bow Room with its overpowering scarlet-flock wallpaper.

She fed him with questions, some of them searching, about his passion for art and his quest for more and more effective display, his answers revealing that this was a way for him to find a purpose in his life after being denied any of the responsibilities that went with his royal position. Beneath the ostentation and excess, she recognised his need to be admired and approved, like a child needing the comfort of toys in lieu of love. She saw how close he came to tears when he admitted how little he was enjoying the costly celebrations and how he recalled her smile in the park. Any thoughts she might have retained about embarrassing him further were dismissed as unworthy, a petty, pointless revenge on a man who had lost his way. Verne had been right about not bringing the jewels. Daily, one way or another, the Prince was being humiliated by his own misplaced cravings and, not knowing how else to deal with it, unable to accept advice, was trying to ignore what other men would have confronted, consoling himself instead with his own ideas of gratification.

Contributing what she could to the conversation, Annemarie was surprised how much she understood that she'd not expected to, or even wanted to. Was she not doing something very similar on a smaller scale? Was she not deriving comfort and fulfilment from spending someone else's money on her own surroundings? And had she not been trying to ignore her conscience and her heart's messages only to inflict some pain on the man who was willing to support her, for whatever reason? Did the reason matter any more? And would this be any different, in essence, from the Prince's shunning of Lady Emma Hamilton, whom he'd professed to love?

Had she, too, lost her way?

'I cannot admire him, no,' she said to Verne as they returned to Curzon Street, 'but I think I'm beginning to understand him a little more. And there are even some things I could get to like, although his blinkered attitude to spending isn't one of them. That, by the way, is something you and I may have to discuss.'

'The Prince's spending?'

'No, my lord. Mine. Ours.'

'You have not heard me grumble. Yet,' he said, softly.

'We shall not be reaching that point.'

'Then let's leave it till after the weekend, shall we? Lady Hertford has invited us up to Ragley Hall.'

'Oh dear. When? Surely not *this* weekend?'

'I'm afraid so. Hert has some purchases he wants me to see.'

'Cannot it wait? The house is barely furnished. And before you tell me again that this was all part of the bargain, allow me to point out that things are already tilting rather heavily in your favour. Two days shopping and a fleeting visit to the theatre are hardly going to help me much, are they?'

'Get used to it, Annemarie,' he said. 'There *will* be times when both of us are obliged to help the other out, with some inconvenience. It can hardly be otherwise, can it? You accepted the terms and just now you made me proud. Surely you're not going to balk at the second hurdle, are you?'

Goose-bumps began to creep along her arms. 'I made you proud? Did I ?'

'Very. Did you not notice how many times the Prince's Private Secretary came in to remind him of his next appointment? He was a good hour late, thanks to you. I've rarely seen him engrossed for so long. Even Isabella noticed it.'

'Was she annoyed?'

'Not at all. She wants the pleasure of your company. So did his Highness. Is that not worth the loss of a day or two of putting your house in order?'

'Yes, of course. I'm sorry. I shall not grumble again.'

'Come over here, woman.' His hand supported her across the swaying carriage, tucking her arm into the loop of his own, snuggling her close. 'I know how much it means to you to have everything looking as you want it, but there's plenty of time, sweetheart. And the fleeting visit to the theatre, I might remind you, was your doing, not mine. Although I didn't particularly want to watch Keane as Shylock. Posturing dandyprat!'

She lay her head on his shoulder, smiling at the way he'd already turned her annoyance and selfishness around. Even the Prince Regent shared his pleasures with duty. 'I think I quite enjoyed it,' she said.

'But we didn't see—'

'No, not Keane. My conversation with the Prince. He's very well informed, isn't he? And intelligent. And a good conversationalist.'

'That's why I enjoy working for him.'

'And not a word about the bureau, either.'

'I told you, he's forgotten all about it.'

Annemarie had not fully appreciated, even though Verne had once mentioned it to her, how closely he and Lord Hertford worked together on the Prince Regent's art collection. Nor had she quite realised the extent to which she might become involved when he'd said he needed a knowledgeable lady to accompany him on social and business occasions. Mistakenly, she had assumed that the socialising would inevitably be of use to her in her search for her mother, which a weekend at Ragley Hall in Warwickshire clearly would not. It was time she could not afford, though she was happy enough to re-acquaint herself with Lady Hertford, who had been one of her mama's closest friends.

On the surface, the two of them had had little in common except the favour of the Prince Regent and the resulting place in high society. But Lady Hertford had never been as well liked, thought by many to have too much influence, too overbearing, too wealthy, too virtuous and moralising, and when it became known that she regularly read from the Bible to her royal friend, there were those who thought it hilarious rather than beneficial. But after speaking with him that day, Annemarie had been given a glimpse of his literary tastes and saw no reason why he would reject what the Bible had to offer.

So while the forthcoming visit to the Hertfords' country seat was sure to be a time-consuming inconvenience, Annemarie hoped that the reconnection with her mama's former friend might yield some useful information. Apart from which, the unexpected pleasure she had begun to derive from humouring her lover seemed to outweigh any disruption to her own plans.

Preparations for the first family dinner at Curzon Street were in full swing by the time they returned, the competent staff being as eager to display their expertise as Annemarie was to impress. Missing details were hardly noticed by the guests when food provided every kind of tempting delicacy which the aged and conservative cook at Montague Street rarely served. Venison pasties and potted pigeon, roast duckling with oranges, artichokes with young potatoes, stuffed mushrooms with anchovy sauce and collops of hare, the latter especially for Lord Benistone. He had dressed formally for the occasion, and Annemarie was not the only one to remark how sprightly and neat he looked. Nor was she the only one to notice her sister Marguerite's unusual quietness. 'What's the matter with her?' she whispered to Cecily. 'Is she unwell? Has she been overdoing things?'

'She's been quiet since mid-day. Did she thank you for the shoes?'

'Yes, but only when I asked her if she liked them. Is she still upset by the theatre fiasco, do you think?'

'I cannot think so, dear. Not unduly. Perhaps Oriel will know.'

But Oriel did not know and was only able to suggest that Marguerite might have preferred to be out with her friends that evening. On the other hand, her lack of appetite might mean she was coming down with something.

* * *

It was past midnight when coaches were summoned and when Cecily, Oriel, and Colonel Harrow, not wishing to keep Marguerite up any longer, were the first to set off for Park Lane. As they were waved away into the night, Lord Benistone was handed a folded piece of paper by the youngest footmen who had discovered it under Miss Marguerite's chair and who was about to take it straight to his mistress. But, since Lord Benistone took it from him before he could do so, he had no choice in the matter. 'I'll see she gets it in the morning,' said his lordship, tucking it into the pocket of his coat. 'Goodnight, m'dear,' he said to his daughter, kissing her cheek. 'Wonderful evening. Thank you. And you too, Verne. Splendid. Quite splendid. Hope the visit to Hertford's place goes well tomorrow. Let me know what he's got, won't you? It's sure to be top-drawer, though I've never approved of the man himself. Still, he's a friend of yours so I'll keep my mouth buttoned, but just keep my daughter out of his reach, mind. That's a good fellow.'

Verne was quick to reassure him. 'She'll be well protected, my lord.'

'Yes, of course she will. Didn't mean…. Oh well, goodnight to you both.'

Halfway down the street, however, the notion that it was not only Annemarie who might require protection, but Marguerite also, had made Lord Benistone call out of the window to his coachman to change direction. Consequently, he arrived at his cousin's address on Park Lane only moments after Marguerite's hasty departure to her room.

Smiling at her father's concern, Annemarie and Verne turned towards the staircase. 'And how exactly are you going to keep me from the clutches of the Marquess of Hertford, my lord, if he's quite determined to have his wicked way with me?' she said. 'Better women than me have found him irresistible, I believe.'

'Do you know,' said Verne, taking her elbow to propel her up to the first step, 'that for a woman of your obvious resistance to men, your mind takes on the most astonishing reversals from time to time. Here am I, chasing you all over the place and turning somersaults to gain a smattering of your interest, and yet all it might have taken would be a reputation like Hertford's and a head of hair like a bunch of carrots. I can see I've been going about it in quite the wrong way. Where did I fail?'

'Well,' she said, allowing the propelling to continue, 'not with the hair, anyway. There's nothing wrong with the silver streak. I find it intriguing. Nothing much wrong with the reputation, either. The fact that it's not quite as celebrated as Lord Hertford's is probably because he's had a twenty-year headstart on you. He has a son, too, doesn't he? A very wicked son.'

'So he does, my lady. He also has…well… shall we say…others? Could that be an added attraction, perhaps? That he's proved his virility so many times? Alas, I have nothing in that department to boast of. Yet.'

'Then perhaps that's because you have not applied yourself to the task with the same enthusiasm, my lord. Talking about it is one thing, but there's nothing so convincing as practice, I always think. Would you not agree?' Held close by Verne's hand beneath her arm, she paused with him on the angle of the staircase, sure that she would not be allowed to get away with such blatant provocation.

'I could not agree more, Lady Golding. But are you telling me that your mind has been travelling along these lines throughout the evening while I, and probably our guests, too, believed it to be dwelling on chaste matters such as the exorbitant price of Mr Wedgwood's latest dinner service?'

She took hold of his ear to caress it and to touch the soft wave of hair she had wanted to slide through her fingers so many times while talking of mundane things. 'I think I'm telling you, Lord Verne, that my mind has been travelling in this direction for most of the day. I

watched your mouth as it ate and wished it was
on me. I watched your hands and wanted them
on me, too. Rapturously exploring. I wanted your
attention. All of it. Your smiles and your husky
laughter. I wanted your head in my arms, against
my breast…' She gasped as the image made her
voice falter, catching at her lungs. 'And…oh…
Jacques…I don't know what…what I shall do
without…without…you.'

On the shadowy staircase, he took her face
tenderly between his hands and looked deeply
into her brimming eyes. 'What is this, sweetheart? What's all this doing without me? Why?
When are you going to do without me? We've
only just started out. And if I'd been able to read
your mind better, I'd have carried you upstairs
in the middle of dinner. Our guests would have
understood and, if they didn't, well, no matter.
By the third time they might have begun to.'

'Oh, Jacques…really!'

'So what's brought all this on? Eh? This is
strange talk.'

Between his hands her head shook in denial. 'I
don't know,' she whispered. 'Just a feeling that…
oh…it cannot last. Things don't last long with
me, Jacques. I cannot expect this to, either. I'm
too happy. And I'm afraid that the more I want
you, the sooner you'll leave me.'

'Oh, no, sweetheart. Oh, no. You've got that
bit wrong. I'm not going anywhere and, what's

more, these premonitions you have about our future are based on bad experiences and best ignored. If you've been thinking I'd forgotten about our search for Lady Benistone, I haven't. Everywhere I go I'm looking and listening, picking up information just as I do on the Prince's business. I have contacts everywhere. We shall find her. As for Hertford, we've been friends for years and he knows better than to make advances to any woman in my protection. Now, where were we? Oh, yes, I remember.' Swiftly, before she could reply, his arm was beneath her knees and she was being tilted backwards to see the plasterwork ceiling pass above her at a crazy angle and she was carried up to her room, warmed by the evening sun.

Heartened by Annemarie's untypical declaration, but also concerned by her misgivings, Verne was even more responsive than usual to her desperate need of reassurance, undressing her slowly while showering her with glowing words of praise, the sincerity of which she had no reason to question. And just think, he told her, what he might have missed if that white statue in her father's hall had not chosen to move that day.

But Annemarie scarcely heard the last of the frivolity for by then, bathing in the luxury of compliments, she urged him on to more daring explorations, opening herself to him as if words had been the key. Ignited by his bold hands, her

fires blazed and demanded all his energies to
stoke them until, feeling the scorching heat
of her desire, he plunged into her at last, lifting them both to another level of bliss. There,
for what seemed like a small ecstatic capsule
of timelessness, no other world existed. Using
all his self-control, he tried to make it last as
she pleaded with him to do, but his desire was
as great as hers and would not be held back.
Too soon, the capsule shattered, whirling them
through a rapturous void where time stopped
again, and flew, and suffused them with a numb-
ing, welcome exhaustion. Arms gathered, bodies nestled and nothing was said except, 'Oh…
love!' by Annemarie in half-sleep.

Verne smiled across the tumble of her hair,
elated to have been the one to hear the word no
other man had heard from her, even though she
might not have been aware that she'd said it.

Chapter Nine

'Elmer, dear,' said Cecily, turning in surprise at her cousin's unexpected appearance. 'Have you come for a nightcap?'

Lord Benistone removed the folded note from his pocket. 'No,' he said. 'I've brought this to show you. Found under Marguerite's chair. Once she realises it's missing she'll be more blue-devilled than she was before, I expect.'

'Why ever should she be? Have you read it?'

'Not yet. But what's she doing getting letters, Cecily? Did you know about it?'

'She *is* almost seventeen, dear,' said Cecily, leading him into the dimly lit drawing room where Oriel and Colonel Harrow were alerted by the sound of his voice. 'She's not tied to my apron strings any more than she is to yours.'

'That's been one of the problems. D'ye want to read it?'

'Marguerite's personal correspondence, Father?' said Oriel. 'Ought you to?'

'If it's making her miserable, then, yes, I ought,' said her father, seating himself in the fireside wing-chair and shaking the note open.

'Might you not be coming too hastily to conclusions, my lord?' said Colonel Harrow, in a belated attempt to salvage Marguerite's privacy. But it came too late.

There was an uncomfortable silence as Lord Benistone began to read, though he could not finish it before his hand began to shake uncontrollably, and the crumpled paper was lowered hastily to his knee. 'It's…it's from *him*!' he whispered. 'That…that cowardly…*wretch*! Tch!'

'Who, Father?'

On his feet in an instant, Colonel Harrow removed the offending note that shook like a leaf in the elderly man's hand, transferring it to Cecily who was able to verify what they already suspected. 'Mytchett!' she said, unsteadily. 'What on earth is *he* doing writing to Marguerite?'

'And what is *she* up to,' Lord Benistone snapped, 'I wonder? Perhaps you should read it out loud, Cecily, and then we might have an answer.'

Cecily could not, however, quite bring herself to read it word for word, but gave them the sense of it from the most relevant phrases. 'He wants her to meet him, Elmer.'

'I'll *bet* he does! Over my dead body.'

'Yes, tomorrow night, Vauxhall Gardens, the firework display, if she wants...oh!...to see her mama...he'll take her...'

'Where?'

'Doesn't say. Eleven o'clock. But we know the man to be *such* a liar!'

A sharp cry from the doorway heralded a whirlwind of white muslin as Marguerite flung herself at Cecily, snatching the note out of her hand with a howl of distress. 'No...no! You should not have done that, Cecily. You of all people. This is *private*! How could you? Oh... this is *too* bad.'

But Oriel caught her sobbing sister before she could escape, holding her in a tight embrace as Colonel Harrow closed the door. 'Hush, dearest. Hush. You cannot keep this to yourself. We're responsible for your safety, love, and that dreadful man cannot mean a word he says. How could you ever have thought so after what happened to Annemarie? He's a *fiend*. You know he is.'

Until she was seated between Oriel and Cecily with their tender hands to soothe her, Marguerite's loud sobs drowned out much of her explanation. At last it became clear. 'I wanted to be the one to bring Mama back. You all think...' Her pretty features were contorted with anguish as she struggled to express her intentions in the face of what she perceived to be a wall of disapproval.

Cecily coaxed it out of her. 'What, love? What do we think? Come on, you can tell us. This is serious. Won't you share it with us?'

'That I haven't cared…about Mama…not being here…and I *have*…and I keep doing the wrong things…without knowing why…or what…and I *do* care so much.'

'Of *course* we know you care, silly girl,' came the irritated response from her father, ignoring the others' frowns.

Oriel would not let it pass. 'Father,' she said, sternly, 'if you could bring yourself to think of Marguerite as a young lady instead of a silly girl, it might help matters. You may not fully understand why she feels as she does, but Cecily and I can see why she is anxious to make a personal contribution, even by putting herself in danger to do it. Her motives are commendable, even though rather rash. Marguerite, how did you come by this letter?'

'It was delivered by hand this morning, while you were out. I don't know who by. I haven't spoken to the man, or even seen him. That's the truth, Oriel.'

'We believe you, love,' said Cecily. 'So how did he…?'

'If you read the rest, you'll see he was at the theatre when we were there and he saw Annemarie with Lord Verne, so he knows she's back in society again. He saw me there, too.'

'So he writes to *you*?'

'Well, he wouldn't write to her, would he? Or to Father. So he's asked me to meet him tomorrow at the fireworks because he's assuming I'll be there. He promises to take me to Mama. He *must* know where she is.'

'And you believe him? A man of *his* sort?'

As her good intentions shattered before her eyes, Marguerite's sobs burst out once more and were controlled only with some difficulty. 'What choice is there?' she howled. 'I want her back! I don't *care* how.'

'Yes, dearest,' Cecily said. 'No wonder you've been out of sorts all day with this on your mind. Have you replied to him?'

'I couldn't, there's no address to reply to. I suppose he thinks…'

'You'll swallow his silly story,' said Lord Benistone. 'Listen to me, Marguerite. When a scoundrel behaves the way he's done, he forfeits all rights to be believed. If he knows where Mama is, which I doubt, he'd have sent a letter to me direct. But this is all about a ransom. It's all about money, m'dear. It must have always been about money, right from the start.'

'I thought I might be the one to bring her back, Papa.'

'Well then, since I must now begin to regard my little girl as a young lady, I think you ought to be the one to meet him, too.'

'Elmer!' Cecily cried. 'What are you saying?'

'I'm saying, Cec, that Marguerite can keep the rendezvous.'

'Not alone, surely?'

'Of course not alone. We'll all go.'

'May I come too, my lord?' said Colonel Harrow. 'I can make myself useful.'

Lord Benistone eased himself out of the chair as if everything was settled. 'Certainly, William. You're family now.'

Cecily had hardly recovered from the shock. 'What about Annemarie and Lord Verne? Shouldn't they know about this?'

'Indeed not, Cecily. They're off to Warwickshire tomorrow. What's the point of upsetting her when there's no need? We can handle this on our own. Anyway, this is Marguerite's concern, is it not, young lady?'

'Yes, Papa. Thank you.'

'Then we'll thrash out the details tomorrow. No more tears now.'

'Elmer,' said Cecily, when Marguerite had left them, 'ought you to be doing this?'

'Yes, Cec. I ought. I know exactly what the bastard's about and I've been waiting for a chance to get at him for a year. If it's fireworks he wants, that's what he'll get.'

* * *

The reputation of Vauxhall Gardens as a safe place to spend an evening had suffered in recent years and now, although there were still many attractions to be enjoyed, a rowdy element often spoiled the peace, the music and especially the drinking. For this reason, and also because of the extra thousands expected to turn up for the spectacle of a firework display, neither Cecily nor Lord Benistone had wanted Marguerite to go. He had relented when Oriel and Colonel Harrow had offered to stay by her side all evening. Revised plans now augmented her original escort to include Cecily, Lord Benistone, and no less than three of his lordship's burly assistants more used to handling bodies of marble and stone than living ones. Packed into two coaches, they set off through dense crowds towards Vauxhall, the horses being forced to a standstill many times before they reached the gates.

Once out of the coaches, however, they had to shout to make themselves heard above the racket. 'This is impossible,' Oriel yelled, clinging to Colonel Harrow's arm. 'We shall be trampled to death. How shall we ever find him?'

'He mentioned Milton's statue,' her fiancé replied, 'over on the Rural Downs overlooking the river. Perhaps it'll be less of a crush over there.'

Jostling, dodging and surging on a tide of shouting people, they made slow progress through the mass of revellers along the tree-lined avenues, passing temples and rotundas, pavilions, picture galleries and booths selling gifts, all brilliantly lit by festoons of coloured gas-lamps. Dance floors bounced in time to the crash of orchestras, the aroma of food from the intimate supper boxes around the sides mingling with the sour stench of sweating bodies and spilt ale.

Cecily grumbled about having to buy expensive tickets to meet a villain like Mytchett. It was not, she said, her idea of a bargain, and why could he not have met Marguerite in a more civilised venue?

'It's the crowds who'll cover his tracks,' shouted Lord Benistone. 'If he saw her with a crowd of her friends at the theatre, he'll assume she'll be with them here, too, with no one to take care of her properly. Keep her close, Cecily. Don't let her out of your grasp.'

There was no chance of that. Marguerite had wanted to come with only Oriel and Colonel Harrow as chaperons, but had had no conception of the potential danger from the rowdies who, like packs of hounds, bayed their way through the alleys and gardens, scattering families on all sides. Having been allowed to take a lead part in the plan, she was determined to be the one to find Mytchett amongst so many, though by now she could no longer believe that he would lead her directly to her mother. She stayed close, hemmed in by the solid black defence of the three bodyguards, her eyes darting and blinking at the mirrored reflections on all sides.

Past the large orchestra and sparkling fountain, they eventually managed to reach the Rural Downs, an open area of wild garden with the river in the background where grottos, caves, waterfalls and marble statues had been erected between dark conifers to represent an idyllic countryside. 'Keep your eyes peeled,' Lord Benistone told them. 'The fireworks are due to start soon and that's when he'll appear, when everyone's attention is diverted. Marguerite, he'll only be looking for you, not us. You go towards him, but not too close. We shall surround him. Cecily, you and Oriel stay beside this tree with William.'

Still muttering, Cecily thought the chances of finding Mytchett in this throng must be slender indeed, but she had not reckoned on Marguerite's doggedness. 'There!' she cried, grabbing her father's arm. 'Look, Papa! There, by Milton's statue. He's leaning on it. See?'

'Are you sure? Is that him? I can't make out his face.'

Marguerite was convinced. 'Yes, I *am* sure. I'm going…no…let me go. I'm going to speak to him.' Before her father could change his mind about her safety, she pushed herself forwards into the crowd towards the lounging figure whose dark-grey coat blended perfectly with the leaden statue, a camouflage that surely could not have been accidental. At that same moment, an ear-splitting scream of fireworks burst into the night sky from a tower erected at the far end of the field. Accompanied by squeals from the crowd and a seemingly orchestrated lifting of heads, the first rocket exploded, effectively redirecting all attention from below to above. The crowds came to an awe-inspired standstill.

Fearlessly, Marguerite stood her ground with only a few yards between them, confronting the young man before he could do more than push himself upright to meet her. 'No!' she yelled at him. 'Don't come any nearer. Just tell me… where is Mama?'

One could see the attraction, even in such an unlikely situation: tall and well proportioned, the pleasing flash of white teeth as he recognised her, the confident tilt of his head where a grey beaver sat respectably straight on fair wavy hair. The smooth voice was the same too, silky and calming, the voice with which he'd charmed Annemarie. 'Miss Marguerite,' he called, holding out a hand towards her, already expecting too much. 'I'll take you to her. I know how she's missed you. Come. You did well to get here on time. Where are your friends? Gave them the slip, did you?'

The whoops and squeals of excitement rose

and fell around them, but Marguerite's attention remained firmly on her mission. 'Stay there! Tell me where she is. Give me her address. We... I can find her,' she called.

Mytchett's eyes darted from side to side, searching the crowd. 'We? Who've you brought with you? Come with me, quickly! I'll take you there,' he persisted, pushing towards her, reaching out for a hand, an elbow. Anything. There was now a tone of desperation in his voice.

But a steel hand darted out of the crowd to grasp Mychett's own elbow, swinging him round with a force that took him unawares. Thinking it was some hooligan, he shook himself angrily, bouncing off nearby revellers. At the same time, Marguerite was aware of the bulky presence of her father's man beside her, offering her his arm. 'Better come back now, Miss Benistone. His lordship will deal with this,' he said. 'Let's leave it to him. See, he's not alone.'

Peering through the crowd, she saw that her father's other two men had placed themselves on each side of Mytchett, preventing his escape, and that her father had come face to face, at last, with the man who had blighted their lives for a year. In the circumstances, it would have been unrealistic to expect Lord Benistone to retain his usual composure after so long struggling to accept his wife's absence. Now the sight of Mytchett and the sound of his seductive offer to Marguerite ignited some kind of primitive response in the elderly man that no one had encountered for years.

'*Where is she?*' The sound of his bull-like bellow could be heard above the yells of the crowd, turning heads in surprise, holding their attention at the enticing possibility of a brawl. Especially one between toffs.

Mytchett appeared to shrink with the shock. 'I…I…er…don't know, my lord,' he shouted, though his words hardly mattered. 'I wanted… er…to…'

'Yes, you vile turd, you thought it was time to get your filthy hands on my youngest daughter, didn't you? Not satisfied with the damage you've done, you thought you'd fleece me for a few grand, didn't you? Eh? How much were you going to hold her for? Ten grand? Twenty? Well?'

Totally unprepared for this verbal assault, Mytchett tried to back away from the furiously aggressive lord. 'No…no, sir. My lord, I can explain.' But his retreat was prevented by the two solid Benistone men and also by a deepening audience whose interest had begun to grow and even to take the side of the white-haired man whose courage they admired. Oblivious to the loud explosions and the flood of light from overhead, they closed in, shouting encouragement.

They were not, however, ready for Lord Benistone's response to Mytchett's whining denial, which was to catch the long thin horse-whip thrown to him by one of his henchmen and to crack it expertly across the space between them. Even Cecily had forgotten what a dashing young horseman he had once been. Then, far too suddenly for Mytchett to see it coming, he brought the lash down across the man's face with a wicked crack that made him scream, drawing a line of blood from brow to chin. Bending double, he covered the wound with his hands.

Marguerite's escort became more insistent. 'Come, Miss Benistone, please. Come away to your sister. This is not going to be pretty.' Firmly, he moved her back to the tree where Cecily tried to shield her from the scene.

'He ought not to have allowed her to come,' she said crossly to Oriel. 'This is not the kind of thing a young girl ought to see.'

'She's a woman now, Cecily dear,' said Oriel. 'She may as well know that this is what happens. Father knew what he was doing.'

'I cannot approve, all the same.'

Nevertheless, approving or not, the five of them watched as his lordship raised the cruel whip again to bring the lash accurately across Mytchett's bent back, his legs, arms and head. Held back by the two Benistone men and the cheering crowd, he could only double over to protect himself from the punishing cut that made ribbons of his coat and covered his face and hands with blood. Howling with pain, he barged blindly about trying to evade the next blow until Colonel Harrow came forwards to grasp Lord Benistone's wrist. 'Enough, my lord! Enough.... Please, no more. He's got the message and you're tiring. Here, allow me to take this.' Turning him away, Colonel Harrow supported him through the onlookers and back to his group, none of whom paid any further attention to the ensuing plight of Sir Lionel Mytchett.

The excitable crowd had not had enough. Blood had been drawn and they wanted more. Howling and hooting, they leapt after the terrified man who staggered through the throng, hoping to disappear. But, blinded and half-fainting with pain, he headed for the bright reflections of fireworks on the surface of the River Thames, lurching down its precipitous bank with a sickening thud into the stinging coldness that numbed his senses and rolled him like a weed into its strong night current. Still not satisfied, the mob followed with yelps of blood lust, splashing and churning the water and scattering a kaleidoscope of exploding colours into the deep-black satin depths. Then, when they could neither reach nor see anything of their prey, they waded back to the bank, laughing at the fun and the applause as the river's surface broke for one last time, gurgling and smoothing like streamers of coloured silk.

Chapter Ten

By the time they arrived at Ragley Hall, Annemarie was sufficiently briefed to know what to expect from the seriously wealthy Hertfords. The Marchioness came down the wide stone steps in a froth of mauve chiffon and satin that stopped on the very low neckline, her free hand waving her greetings well before the carriage had rocked to a standstill. Bewigged and liveried, the footman opened the door and let down the folding steps in front of a mansion considerably larger than Carlton House, and grander. Annemarie was no stranger to grandeur and opulence, but this ancestral home was one of the most magnificent she'd ever seen, built to reflect the family's position in society. If Annemarie had wondered what common ground there could possibly be between Lady Hertford and her badly behaved husband, she soon saw that, while he knew what treasures to buy, she knew exactly how to display them to advantage without turning the place into a museum.

The Marquess was not far behind his wife, older than her by some fifteen years yet stylish and sprightly and still the proud owner of a fuzz of brick-red hair and profuse side-whiskers that showed no sign of greying. Ostentation and excess in all their forms came more naturally to him than restraint, and certainly earned him more countenance than he might otherwise have had, not being a particularly handsome man. To make up for this, he had the most charming manner.

'So this is what it takes to get you here, Verne,' he said quite seriously. 'If only I'd known.' As if to put Annemarie at her ease after the scolding, he turned a twinkling smile upon her, sharing the joke. 'My lady,' he said, taking her hand, 'I can now see why he waited so long. A very discriminating man, our friend Jacques. Now I forgive him.'

No ordinary welcome could have pleased her more. He was, as Verne had told her, actually a very likeable fellow. The unsavoury and very disparaging remarks her father had occasionally let fall about the Marquess's adulterous escapades wandered through her mind as they were led into the Great Hall, yet her recent meeting with the Prince Regent had taught her, if anything, that she would do well to reserve her judgement of people's characters.

The motherly Lady Hertford linked her arm through hers. 'It's been a long journey for you, my dear. You must be tired. I'll take you straight up to your room and have some refreshments sent up. Your maid arrived last night with Jacques's valet, so all will be ready for you. We usually eat at seven. Plenty of time to relax.'

To their delight, they had been given adjoining rooms connected by a door, an acknowledgement of their relationship that Verne had assured her would cause not the slightest lift of an eyebrow amongst the Hertfords. Yet it had been very late that night when they made good use of the convenience after hours that passed too quickly in talk and being shown art treasures which, they were told, were only a fraction of what the house contained. Wrapped in each others' arms, she and Verne had slept between monogrammed silk sheets under a pale yellow canopy embroidered with buttercups, dandelions and daffodils, waking only once in the early hours to make love and then to sleep again until Evie had drawn the curtains.

The tall sash windows looked out across endless views of landscaped parkland that rolled away from the house over lawns, lakes and carefully placed trees into the morning haze of Warwickshire. Verne threw up the window-pane and placed an arm around Annemarie's shoulders. 'Would you like to go riding this morning? Hart has a well-stocked stable. I expect he'll—' He stopped, glancing at Annemarie's expression. 'What? What is it?'

'Over there...*there*...by that clump of trees. On horseback. See?'

'Yes, it looks as if Hert is already out there.'

'With a woman, Jacques. And it's not Lady Hertford, either. They didn't say they had another guest staying. Surely he doesn't have a mistress here, does he? Lady Hertford would not allow that.'

'Out of the question,' said Verne, turning her away. 'Let's get dressed and go down to breakfast. I'm hungry.'

Annemarie was reluctant to move. 'Yes, but who is she?'

'We'll find out soon enough. We'll join them when we've eaten.' He disappeared into his room and closed the door, leaving her with the impression that he knew who the guest was, but would not say.

'Do you know who she is, Evie?'

'No, m'lady. I haven't seen anyone else. No maid, either.'

'Strange.'

After breakfast, at which their hostess was not present, they rode with Lord Hertford on thoroughbred horses through the parkland, during which Annemarie broached the subject of guests in the hope that her host would elaborate. But he was as evasive as Verne, saying only that the lady was recovering from a slight indisposition and preferred to avoid company, and that they might meet her later on, if she was willing. With that, Annemarie had to be satisfied, and tried to put it out of her mind during their tour of the vast house and the family portraits by Sir Joshua Reynolds.

In the evening, after a memorable dinner and excellent conversation, Lady Hertford and Annemarie left the men to their port while they took tea in the drawing room, browsing through scrapbooks and several ancient account books belonging to the estate in its earliest days. Annemarie had not quite reached that level of familiarity that permitted her to ask, point-blank, about the extra unseen guest, so she was relieved when the Marchioness tugged at the bell-pull, whispered to the footman and told Annemarie that she had requested her other guest to join them, at last. 'You may be surprised to see her here,' she said, unaware of how much she understated the case after Annemarie's year of anguish.

The door opened to allow a tall graceful woman to enter, her bearing so elegant and poised that, even though she had once been more shapely than this, her identity was impossible to mistake. 'Lady Benistone, m'lady,' said the footman, bowing out.

In retrospect, Annemarie thought, it might have been kinder if she'd been given some warning, or an option on where and how best to meet. Suddenly, like this, not only had her mind to adjust to the shock of seeing her mother after a whole year of absence and such a traumatic parting, but also to the change in the one she had last seen as a beauty in the full flower of maturity, rounded and luscious and brimming with good health. The woman was the same, and the beauty too, but now it filtered through months of grief and desperate worry, thinning her down to a shadow, saddening her lovely eyes and pinching her cheeks.

She was hesitant, unsure of her reception, fearful of instant rejection. Her soft voice reflected her anxiety. 'Annemarie,' she said. 'Dearest…oh, *dearest*!' Holding out her arms, she pleaded for physical comfort and prayed that her daughter, at least for a moment or two, would grant it her.

With a cry, Annemarie was on her feet, her face drained of all colour. 'Mama…Mama!' she whispered. 'It *is* you. Tell me I'm not dreaming.'

'It's me, love. Forgive me. Hold me…oh, hold me.'

It was only a few steps into the motherly arms

Annemarie had longed for, even while she had struggled to understand the treachery, the abandonment and the lack of communication: a year's worth of anger and misery which, in these last few weeks, had changed to a greater need to know that Mama was safe and well. And now, that seemed not to be enough. In her arms, she wanted explanations that would justify her terrible period of pain. She wanted to know of Mama's sufferings, too, for it was obvious that she *had* suffered, and to make her aware of the damage she had done for the sake of one mad Season of lust, excitement and a younger man's admiration. That was what it was all about, wasn't it? His admiration and her remaining power to attract a man away from a younger woman. And now, Mama was in the protection of an older man, a hardened womaniser whose misdemeanours, in Annemarie's mind, all at once took precedence over his attributes. How could Mama have stooped so low? Again.

Annemarie clung and sobbed, her face buried in the long neck that still gave off the familiar perfume of a rose garden. 'Why?' she cried. 'Why did you?'

Gently stroking her daughter's back, Lady Benistone hardly knew where to start. 'It's a long story, my darling. It's not at all what you think.'

'What am I supposed to think, Mama, when

you're here with…?' She could hardly say what she meant with Lady Hertford standing by.

'Hush, love. Don't weep. Please don't weep any more. I can tell you everything, then you may begin to understand better. But will you tell me about my dear ones…the girls…and Papa? Are they well? I long for news of them. Shall we sit and talk?'

She could not deny her mother this, although there was a side of her, the hurt side, that questioned whether this concern was truly genuine or whether it had emerged through a recent conscience. Lady Hertford must have suspected Annemarie's cynicism. 'That would be a good start, my dears,' she said, laying a kindly hand on the young shoulder. 'I've told your mama all I know, but that's not a great deal. She needs to hear it from you. Be kind to her. She's had a hard time. Perhaps I ought to have warned you.'

So they sat close together, holding both hands and sharing a small handkerchief as names wove in and out, not happily, but forlorn, puzzled and cast adrift, with Father going through some kind of inexplicable change rather like an adolescent in love. When she added, with conviction, that he needed his wife back, Lady Benistone's tears flowed faster. 'I cannot,' she cried, shaking her head. 'Don't you see? I can never return, Annemarie.'

'Why not? Is it the state of the house? It still upsets you?'

'No…oh, no! Not that. I'd go back to live anywhere with Papa, if I dared. But after what's happened, how could I ever face him? I am quite disgraced now. I've dragged my lord's name through the mud and made all society pity him. And my family, too. He's always been so very good to me. How can I return now, as if nothing had happened?'

The questions were left unanswered, interrupted by the return of the men, neither of them disconcerted to find three tear-streaked faces. Being a stickler for etiquette, the Marquess insisted on introducing Lord Verne to Lady Benistone, who could not otherwise have acknowledged him. Her apologies for her appearance at such a time were immediately set aside by Verne's delight at meeting the mother of his mistress, and if she was rather puzzled when he said that this moment fulfilled an ambition of his, she did not pursue it when there were more pressing questions to be asked.

Annemarie kept up the pressure, still certain that her mama must be rescued from Lord Hertford's attentions as a matter of some priority, while not actually saying anything to insult her kind hosts. 'Marguerite needs you, Mama,' she said. 'She's sorely in need of your influence. Cecily has been a wonderful chaperon, but you know what Marguerite is like. So headstrong. And dear Oriel won't set a date for her wedding until things are back to normal once more. You *must* put aside your fears, Mama. Papa grieves for you. I can hardly bear it. He's sold some of the collection to the British Museum recently, but he won't tell us why. I'm wondering if he intends to sell the house.'

With downcast eyes, Lady Benistone shook her head. 'It's not possible,' she whispered. 'Too much has happened. I cannot believe he'll take me back.'

Frowning, Annemarie glanced across at the Marquess, who sat totally relaxed in his deep wing chair, following the conversation with interest and showing no sign of responsibility for any distress. The man was inhuman, she thought, convinced of his guilt. Verne came to the rescue, bringing the sad exchange round to a point where explanations could replace imminent accusations. Taking Annemarie's hand in his, he held it on his knee and gave a gentle squeeze to indicate his support. 'Lady Benistone,' he said, 'I think it would help your daughter to know something of the circumstances surrounding your decision to leave your family. If you'd rather I left the room…?'

'No, Lord Verne, please don't. I cannot tell you how grateful I am for your support of Annemarie. Isabella has told me what you've done for her and I think you all ought to know what happened and how.'

'I *know* what happened,' said Annemarie. 'I was there, Mama.'

'Yes,' said Lord Verne, gently, 'but there are usually two sides to a story. I think you should hear your mother's version.'

'I'm sorry, Mama. Please go on.'

To revive the memories of the incident she had tried hard to forget was so painful that there were moments when Lady Benistone had to stop to recover herself. She had known there would have to be explanations and that Annemarie would be hurt all over again, but the Hertfords, the lady's maid and their doctor were the only ones who knew about the stillbirth of a son at eight months, for they had disguised the pregnancy well, and the resulting illness was explained as 'a problem common to women of a certain age'. No one else, they said, needed to know and this part of the sorry story she would spare her daughter.

Nevertheless, there was yet another shock in store for Annemarie, which her mother believed could come from no one but herself, concerning the reason why Mytchett was so eager to lay his hands on Annemarie's legacy from her late husband in retaliation for leaving a mistress, his sister-in-law, and her child without a penny to live on. 'You would have seen it in your husband's will, dearest, if he ever intended to leave them anything,' said her mother. 'And he obviously wanted you never to find out.'

'Mytchett?' said Annemarie, horrified. '*Mrs* Mytchett?'

'Sir Lionel's brother's widow. Cecily and I found it out.'

'Then why could you not have told me, Mama?'

'Just before Marguerite's ball, dearest? How could I do that? I thought it was best for all the attention to be on your sister than on your distress over your late husband's scandal. Could you have concealed it? I doubt it. I had to prevent Mytchett declaring himself somehow, for I know you'd have accepted him in the excitement of the moment, only to regret it later.' To her credit, she did not add, as she could have done, that there would have been no need to take matters into her own hands if she could have obtained Elmer's attention. At that time, they had almost stopped discussing anything and certainly nothing personal or domestic, although she had tried. 'I thought I was doing the right thing,' she whispered through her tears, 'but I see now that my plan was flawed from the start. In the end, we were all hurt, weren't we? *Do* forgive me. I've missed your papa and his funny ways so much and I've never stopped loving him.'

The hairs on Annemarie's arms prickled as

her mother voiced the same unsound scheme of getting a man to commit and then leaving him, which she, too, had thought of in her secret heart, except that Verne was no villain and had done nothing to deserve such shabby treatment. Nor would it be money he'd be left without, but her love, newly found and unconditional, a far more precious and rare commodity. How strange that their strategy had been so similar, and stranger still that they were doomed to failure. The startling news of Sir Richard's mistress had been a shock, but less than it might have been if their marriage had been as sweet as her relationship with Verne. That would have been unbearable.

'Don't weep, Mama,' she said, weeping herself. 'Please don't weep. If only we'd known. Could you not have sent us a message?'

'I was ill for weeks, dearest, and terribly ashamed. I pleaded with Isabella not to say where I was until I'd had time to recover. I knew what you and papa would be thinking, that I didn't care about my loved ones, that I'd wrecked Marguerite's big day and that I'd stolen the man you loved.'

'I did not love him, Mama. I didn't know what love was, then.'

Lady Hertford intervened. 'I wanted to let you know she was safe, my dear, but I had to respect her wishes. I knew there would come a time.'

Lady Benistone looked fondly at her friend.

'She and Francis have been Good Samaritans,' she said. 'I could not have been better cared for.'

Annemarie's spontaneous admission that she now knew what it felt like to be in love was received by Verne with something like jubilation. In one respect, he thought it was a pity that it had taken such heartache within a family to expose the direction of her gentle heart. But such was the way love appeared. 'Lady Hertford,' he said, 'could you not assure Lady Benistone that her family would gladly receive her with open arms just as her daughter has done? You and Hart have showered her with kindness, nursed her back to health and brought her up here for safety. Mytchett can have no more interest in her now.'

'Lord Verne,' said Lady Benistone, 'I know you mean well, but I have stretched the generosity of my family too far. Too much time has passed for me to expect forgiveness from them. I've done too much damage by my foolishness. People talk. The scandal will take years to die down. As for thinking Sir Lionel will let matters rest where they are…well…he won't. It's a matter of pride. He'll make a nuisance of himself and my darling lord must not be any further humiliated or harassed than he has been already. Ragley Hall is safe. London isn't.'

On the last point, Annemarie was obliged to agree. Both Ragley Hall and the Hertfords *were* safe. No longer could she assume that the Marquess had designs on her mama's virtue. Sadly, she had been guilty of misjudging almost everyone involved in this heartbreaking episode. She had learned that her parents adored each other and that it had taken this to remind them of it.

The talking continued far into the evening with so much to tell, so many misconceptions to untangle, so many hurts to salve. Eventually, when stifled yawns made conversation difficult to follow, they went their separate ways although, for Annemarie, too much had emerged for her to let go of it easily in soothing sleep. No sooner had Samson and Evie been dismissed than she began a series of questions that soon began to sound more like protests. 'You knew about Mama being here, didn't you? You knew before we set off. Lady Hertford told you, didn't she, and she had promised Mama not to betray her confidence. You could have told me, to spare me the shock. *Couldn't* you?'

'Lady Hertford,' said Verne, lounging half-naked across the end of the bed, 'promised not to tell your family. Well, she didn't. She told me instead. And what would *you* have done if I'd told you beforehand? You'd have dashed straight round to your family and told them. Wouldn't you?'

'Of course I would. They…'

'Which is exactly what Lady Benistone

wanted to avoid. So.' He ducked as a sandal hurtled towards his head.

'So don't be so damned *logical*!' she said crisply. 'I can't stand it when you're logical at this time of the night. And I expect you knew about the mistress, too, *didn't* you? Don't prevaricate.'

'I was not going to prevaricate. I did know, yes.' Turning the sandal over in his hands, he appeared not to be taking her question seriously enough. 'Can't imagine how you keep these things on your feet. It looks more like a—'

'I *thought* as much.' The second sandal flew, was caught and held against the other. 'And you might put those *down* when I'm talking to you.'

Lazily, he placed them on the floor and then, without the slightest warning, swooped across the space and picked her up like a feather, falling back with her in his arms into the soft embrace of a very large easy chair. Trapping one of her arms behind him, he caught her other hand before she could use it as a lever. 'All right, that's enough, my beauty. You're upset and angry, and you're quite entitled to be. But not with me. Be still now!'

Wearing only a fine silk nightgown, her loose hair half-covering her tear-stained face, she struggled against the indignity and the severity of his command, thinking that a sympathetic hearing would have been more welcome than reasoning, at this late hour. But she was held in an iron grip with tears of helplessness and relief rolling off the end of her chin. Eventually, she buried her face in the smooth warm skin of his chest as she had wanted to do all evening, sobbing out things she could not have said before. 'Poor…poor Mama…suffered so much…and we didn't know. And…all for my sake…she's not well…so thin and sad. We must get her home, Jacques. She needs us and we need her.'

'She'll need time to get used to the idea, sweetheart. This is as much a shock to her as it is to you, remember. She can't have known long that we were coming.'

'I feel so…so *stupid*,' she whispered. 'Why could I not…?'

'Not what?'

'Not have seen what a money-grabbing scoundrel the man was. And Sir Richard. What on *earth* was I thinking of not to know about… her? I've been so naïve, Jacques. And everyone laughing at my stupidity. And Mama and Cecily not telling me because they thought I was in love and not able to handle the truth. And I wasn't. I only wanted to be married, with a house, and children, and…'

'Hush now. No more weeping. You can stop berating yourself. I dare say most women desire those things without knowing what love is. Most men, too. But if it's taken all this to show you how it really feels, then none of it was wasted, was it? Do you know how it feels now?'

The mass of black shining hair nodded below his chin and he felt the warmth of her lips upon his skin as she kissed his chest, sending vibrations tingling into his heart. 'Good,' he whispered. 'That's all right then.'

'How did you find out….about her…the Mytchett woman?'

'Barracks' talk. Soldiers have little to do but gossip and her husband had been one of them. I hear what goes on.'

'I wish you'd told me.'

'There was no need for you to know at the time. It certainly would not have done *my* cause any good to malign your late husband. Your mama had a reason for telling you. I didn't.'

'What cause?'

'To make you mine, my beauty. What else?' he said, stroking back a sheet of hair from her face. 'I told you at our first meeting, but you were not listening.'

'I *was* listening, but I assumed it was bravado. You came for the bureau.'

His deep groaning sigh made her lift away from his chest to look up at him, but when she saw the twitch of his mouth at the corners she sank back again. 'Tch!' he said. 'There's nothing for it, is there? I shall simply have to take an axe to that damned bureau before we can get it out of the reckoning. Can we establish here and now, my darling girl, that after my first glance at you that day, I decided that you were going to be mine and that the bureau was no more than an excuse to stay close? And if you need it any plainer than that, I intended there and then that the title of Lady Verne would suit you better than Lady Golding. Since that moment, I've been crazily in love with you. Truly. So can we now forget the bureau and its contents? Good grief… you're not weeping again, are you?'

'Oh, Jacques,' she said, sitting up. 'Doe. I'b dot weeping. But this was dot supposed to happen and dow my plan isn't going to work.'

'Ah, the plan. Do you want to tell me about it?'

'It's dot a very dice one.'

'I gathered as much. Tell me anyway. I promise not to co-operate.'

'Doe. I suppose I hoped you might dot. I was dot intending to fall in love with you, you see, and—'

'No one *intends* to fall in love, sweetheart.'

'No, I know. But I was intending *not* to fall in love with you.'

'Oh, I see.'

'And now I have. So I can't walk off and leave you, which is what I planned to do, without hurting myself very badly. And you were not supposed to fall in love with me for months.'

'Months?' he exclaimed. 'As long as that?'

'Yes, by which time we'd have got the house up and running and you'd have invested a lot of money in it and in me, too, and you'd have been hurt and angry, and then I'd have been revenged for *my* hurts.'

'And that was the plan? To say goodbye and go back to Montague Street or your house in Brighton?'

'Well…yes.'

'You and your mama are more alike than I thought. I have to say, my love, that as plans go, they don't come much dafter than that. Quite addle-brained, in fact. Was that really the best you could come up with? Eh?' Tipping her back again into his arms, he kissed her soundly until she cried to be released.

'It's not going to work, is it?' she said, lamely, touching his lips with her fingertips. 'Do you really want me to be your wife instead of your mistress, Jacques?'

'Could you ever doubt it, sweetheart? Your plan never stood a chance. And as for this need for retribution, I think you may have to let it go. You cannot punish the whole of mankind… well, me anyway…for the sins of other people. What's done is done and one has to put it down to experience. I went along with the mistress thing because I could see from the beginning what that was all about. After all the resistance, it could only be about wanting my commitment and raising my expectations, and then the pleasure of ruining them. I could see your jealousy, too, sweetheart. That told me quite a lot.'

'I'm ashamed, Jacques. I thought love would be sweet and comfortable, but it can be painful, can't it? I've never felt jealousy like that before. It was much worse than having Mama go off with that man. I felt humiliated by that, but it was nothing like the black despair I felt after the theatre débâcle. And I knew then that I adored you. Don't ever leave me, Jacques. Please. Don't hold this against me. I want to be your wife, but I don't deserve you.'

'My tigress!' His hand slipped beneath the loose silk and found the soft fullness of her breast, holding it possessively as he bent to kiss her again, dispelling any lingering doubts about who deserved who most. In her lover's embrace, the heavy blanket of foreboding and uncertainty that had already begun to slip away now faded like a wintry fog, leaving her heart to overflow with a new lightness. Not knowing how, when, or even if she could safely readjust her plans for their future, she had kept all indications of her adoration concealed from him as far as she was able, not being as sure of his feelings as she would like to have been. Now, her doubts had flown. He loved her, wanted her and would be faithful to her. Of that she was sure. He had been waiting for her capitulation and who could blame him after all that defiance? His tigress, he had called her.

Even so, he refrained from teasing her about her earlier resistance for he knew of the reasons, and there was so much more to content them than the abolition of problems. His loving that night was careful, slow, and perfectly tailored to her needs, her overworked emotions, her re-adjustment to personal security and the relief of the reunion with her beloved mother. She did not reach a climax of the same previous intensity, but he knew by her sighs and caresses that her enjoyment was in no way diminished when there were untold years of loving to look forward to. Sleep overcame them long before the list of urgent topics could be discussed, most of them to do with Mama and her return to the family who needed her. But their last words before sleep, mumbled into hair and against warm moist skin, were of a more personal nature, all the more treasured for being withheld on so many other occasions. Liberated, Annemarie's sleep consoled her for all her foolishness while Verne's dreamless sleep was more like a reward for his confidence and tenacity.

Their last day at Ragley Hall was spent in talks with Lady Benistone intended to persuade her of an ecstatic welcome at Montague Street, although Annemarie was not able to say with any conviction how much, or little, the living conditions had changed to make her future comfort greater than before. But with a year's news to catch up on, the day flew past easily, with breakfast on the following day, a Monday, their last meal together for some time. Neither of them knew for how long.

Just like Lord Benistone, Lord Hertford's addiction to *The Times* at breakfast was excused; one was rarely expected to converse at such times, even with guests present. Spontaneous outbursts of information *did* emerge, however, when it was thought worth sharing. 'Oh, listen to this,' he said from behind the double pages.

Annemarie exchanged glances with her mother and smiled. 'My lord?' she said, politely.

'Four people killed,' he said. 'That's appalling!'

'Where is this?' said Verne, mopping up his egg yolk.

'Vauxhall Gardens. Saturday night. The fireworks, you know. Prinny's latest attempt to entertain the masses. Well, no one expected them to turn up in their thousands, apparently. Dreadful crush. Dangerous conditions,' he read, picking through the most evocative words. 'Carriages smashed. Clothing ripped to shreds. Two women crushed against the barriers. One man badly burned by a firework, died from injuries. Another fell into the river. Oh! What's this? Good heavens above, Verne. You're not going to believe it.' The newspaper collapsed in a heap upon the Marquess's empty plate, revealing a shocked expression and a pallor in stark contrast to the red hair. 'Perhaps…?' Deep with concern, his eyes indicated that the ladies might prefer to leave rather than hear the details.

'What is it, Francis?' said Lady Benistone. 'I'm not going to be shocked and nor is Annemarie. Read it to us, if you please.'

'I think you are,' he said, lifting the newspaper. 'A body, found downstream from Vauxhall, was identified as that of Sir Lionel Mytchett, well-known gamester and member of White's Club. Well, they've got *that* wrong. He was thrown out last year. The body was badly lacerated, it says. Fell into the river and drowned. No witnesses. So that's the last we'll be seeing of him, then. Can't say I'm heartbroken.'

When there was no response from across the table, his lordship let *The Times* fall again to look at his guests before folding it up and laying it quietly down. Lady Benistone was being held in her daughter's arms, with only one hand smoothing over her back to indicate the direction of their thoughts. Then, still with their arms around each other, they turned and left the room.

'No witnesses?' said Verne, frowning. 'At Vauxhall?'

'That's what it says.'

'Rubbish! What do *you* make of it?'

'I think,' said the Marquess, pulling at his whiskers, 'that this makes the problem of Esme's return to London a little less complicated. Wouldn't you say so?'

'Imminent, Francis. I'll do what I can to make it happen.'

'So Benistone's selling up, is he?'

'I have yet to find out. He's playing his cards very close to his chest, these days. What he'll do when he finds she'd been under *your* roof for the last few months I cannot imagine. I hope he doesn't jump to the same conclusions as Annemarie.'

That idea gave the Marquess several moments of very loud and irreverent amusement, his wife not being in the room, entirely inappropriate to the news just imparted, ending with the flippant suggestion that he might have to go into hiding.

Chapter Eleven

For some reason, neither Evie nor Samson knew what, their master and mistress were delayed at Ragley Hall while they had been sent off at the appointed time a little after dawn with instructions to contact Lady Golding's family and invite them to Curzon Street without delay. Both Evie and Samson knew what that was about. Lady Benistone had been found. So, with leather bags and boxes piled on the opposite seat of the coach, trunks behind and on top, and the groom sitting up there with the coachman, they'd been told to change horses as often as necessary to reach London before dinner. It was just as well, Evie said to herself, that she had begun to like Mr Samson again when such proximity for a whole day could be a severe test of one's inclinations. She was pleased to find that her original opinions of the smart young man had been, on the whole, correct.

Samson's opinion of Miss Evie Ballard, despite the peppery encounter at the inn, was rather more basic than hers of him. In his book, she was a little cracker with a temper like a wildcat and a pair of eyes that flashed like lightning, a figure as trim as any stage-moll and a pair of lips that just skimmed a row of pearls, just ripe for kissing. In short, it had been worth his ride on the box with the supercilious groom and the outrageous fib he'd concocted to explain away the stinging handprint on his cheek. By the end of this journey, Samson was reasonably sure he could turn the fib into a reality.

Since then, he had adhered strictly to 'Miss Ballard' but now, for no apparent reason, she had responded to 'Evie' without a murmur. 'I suggest we take Lady Golding's luggage to Curzon Street first,' he said, 'and then I'll go on to Montague Street and Park Lane before I take his lordship's things to Bedford Square.'

'Except for his overnight valise,' said Evie. 'I expect he'll be staying…'

'He's not spent one night at home since…'

'Since Brighton.' They had changed horses for the third time and were now on the last stage of the journey, having taken cold food into the coach to save every last moment. Evie brushed the crumbs from her skirt and folded away the linen napkin.

Passing her the water bottle, Samson adopted

his helpless expression. 'Where does this go?' he said.

'Tch! Here.' She leaned forwards to push it into one of the bags and found that, when she leaned back again, Samson's arm was around her waist, pulling her gently to his side.

'There, that's better,' he said.

With only the slightest hesitation, Evie relaxed against him.

The coach rocked and bumped along the roads to London with only the briefest of halts at the turnpikes or to let a wide wagon squeeze past. Evie untied the ribbons under her chin and eased the bonnet off her head, allowing her dark curls to brush against Samson's cheek. 'Nice,' he whispered. 'Very nice.'

Behind Evie and Samson by about one hour, the occupants of the other more luxurious coach were similarly disposed to go over old ground, in the light of recent revelations, and then to nestle together for a few more miles of comfortable silence until the need for another discussion. Having no doubt at all of the family's forthcoming delight at the news of Mama's safety, Annemarie's main concern was that her comfort at Montague Street would not be any more designed around her wishes than it was before. Although Mama's sudden walkout was, on the face of it, for a very unselfish reason, there was also an ele-

ment of desperation behind it which, the women
of the family knew, had been growing through
years of neglect from the man she adored. His
insistence on using their home as a museum,
where visitors to his collection were more important than his wife and daughters, had con-
tributed in no small part to Lady Benistone's
assumption that her husband would hardly miss
her. She had told them so last night. Without his
help, her plan had been the best she could de-
vise and not a very clever one at that. Annemarie found it hard to anticipate any expression of
joy on her Mama's lovely face when she returned
to Montague Street after Papa's recent changes,
whatever they were. Annemarie had not had a
chance to look, nor had the others been inclined.

The news of Sir Lionel Mytchett's death had
been a shock to both mother and daughter, not a
cause for rejoicing, but creating a kind of numb-
ness. His not being there would take some getting used to. There had been many times, they
said, when no death could have been too painful for him in their minds. Now, their relief was
tinged with a sadness that any man's death could
be so ignominious. A fall into the river. What a
lonely way to go.

Verne's thoughts ran along rather different
lines. Lacerations on the body, *The Times* had
reported. To him, that meant only one thing. A
horsewhipping. In public. By whom? Another

cuckolded husband, more recent than Benistone?
Or Benistone himself? Almost certainly, the
family would have read the report by now. The
forthcoming meeting at Curzon Street promised
to be interesting.

Sipping brandy from one of Annemarie's
new crystal glasses, Lord Benistone had already made up his mind that the hasty summons
to Curzon Street could only be to discuss the
news in *The Times* that morning. He would, of
course, have to explain to Annemarie his part in
the tragedy, if that's what it was, and hope that
she would understand their reasons for leaving
Vauxhall Gardens without delay. In the circumstances, it would have been quite impossible in
such a crush to find any witnesses willing to de-
scribe exactly what had happened without impli-
cating themselves at the same time. Nor was he
himself inclined to volunteer any information.
Without going into all the painful reasons for his
being there, that would be out of the question. If
Esme had also seen the news, he wondered what
effect it would have on her decisions for the future. Sighing, he took another sip.

'Elmer, my dear,' said Cecily, entering the
dining room as if the effort of responding to
Annemarie's message had been a little incon-
venient, to say the least, 'I wonder why this
couldn't have waited until tomorrow? What can

there be to discuss? We had only just finished dining. Have you eaten yet?'

'No.'

'Then you ought not to be drinking that on an empty—'

'Leave him alone, Cecily,' said Oriel. 'Hello, Papa. You all right?' With a kiss to both cheeks, her smile lingered as she searched his face for signs of tiredness. Marguerite followed, hugging her father without a word, saying more in that one embrace than she'd said in a year. He could see that she had slept badly, that the fidgeting and simpering was missing, that her gown was without the usual frill and fuss, her hair swept upwards from her neck into the tall crown of her bonnet, her eyelids still puffy with weeping, yet the blue eyes bold with a new wisdom. She had been given a brief view of a man's world and it had both frightened and sobered her for, as her father's man had told her, it was not a pretty sight to see her peaceable parent in such a vengeful role. She had never thought him capable of it. She had never heard a man scream before, either, nor the howling of a crowd for the blood of a man they didn't even know. Had they thrown him into the river, too?

Annemarie and Lord Verne were not far behind, their own news temporarily engulfed by hugs and handshakes and questions about who had read what and how that news was affecting them. 'More than you might think, dear,' said Cecily, helping herself from a plate of warm shortbread biscuits. 'We were there, at Vauxhall Gardens. Elmer will tell you.'

'What, all of you?' said Annemarie.

'Yes, all of us,' said her father. 'I *was* about to explain, thank you, Cecily. It was our Marguerite who orchestrated it. She's the heroine in this.'

Attention was immediately switched to Marguerite, but the young lady's attention was firmly fixed on the complicated pattern of the Axminster and it was clear, after a pause, that she was not going to take advantage of the situation to explain what had happened. So Cecily and Oriel gave a very detailed account of what had occurred on that night and the one before, adding that no one other than themselves, Lord Benistone's three men and a very uncaring crowd of hooligans knew exactly what part Father had played in causing Mytchett's injuries, which he had apparently tried to bathe in the river. It was not, they said, a very sensible thing to do, was it? However, said Cecily as an afterthought, they could hardly be expected to help him, so they had hurried away from the scene without knowing what became of him. It had taken them almost as long to get home as it had to get there, and she had lost a shoe and Elmer, poor dear, was exhausted by his rage.

And Marguerite, thought Annemarie, must

have been shaken to the core to witness the brutality, however deserved. What was Father thinking of to allow her to see it? Was this more of the blindness that afflicted him where his family were concerned? Would he always put his own needs first? In a sudden outpouring of motherliness, she went to kneel before Marguerite, taking her into her arms and feeling the immediate response of softness in place of the resistance she had half-expected. Pressing her cheek against Marguerite's, she crooned her sympathy as their mama had often done. 'Oh, my sweet… oh, how dreadful for you…I'm so sorry it had to come to this.'

She felt the head shake against hers. 'No, don't be, Annemarie. Really. It was not like that. I *wanted* to be there. I wanted to do my part. Papa knew how much I wanted to make amends.'

'Amends for what, love?'

'For all the times I've not behaved like a lady,' she whispered, 'and said the wrong things without thinking.'

'Oh, dearest. That's all over now. But you should not have seen what you did.'

'It has not harmed me, Annemarie. Papa knew what he was doing. We were well protected and what I saw may not have got Mama back, but it's made me very proud of my papa.' Reaching out with one hand, she sought her father's and was immediately clasped, warmed and caressed.

'You're very courageous,' said Annemarie, 'and Mama will be proud of you.'

There was something in the way she said 'will be' that made Lord Benistone focus intently on her face to watch the smile radiate like the sun from behind a cloud. 'Will be?' he said. 'Annemarie?'

'Yes, Papa. Lord Verne and I have found her. Safe and well.'

Incomprehension played around his eyes. 'But you've been to Ragley Hall.' He looked across to Verne for verification. 'Haven't you?'

'Yes, my lord,' said Verne. 'Lady Benistone is there. She's been cared for by the Marchioness of Hertford since last year.' There was never going to be an easy way to say this other than by leaving the Marquess's name out of it, Verne thought, watching how his lordship's eyes changed, hardened and challenged his.

'*Has* she, indeed?' Lord Benistone said, quietly. 'And how safe is *safe*, exactly? In the Hertfords' care? Yes, well I can guess what *that* means.' He stood up, dropping Marguerite's hand, visibly shaking.

'She *is* safe, my lord,' said Verne, glancing at Annemarie for help.

'Papa,' she said. 'Are you not glad?'

He had turned white like parchment and, to hide his shock, held his face in his hands, his gnarled knuckles quivering. 'Yes,' he growled,

'but I did not expect *this*, to be cuckolded
twice…by…'

'Papa! Stop! Listen! Please listen!'

But he was not listening. 'I shall *thrash* the
mangy little red-haired lecher!' he yelled. 'I shall
take that whip to him and do as I did to—'

'Papa…please…no, you're not listening to me.
You're wrong. Mama has not been in any way
unfaithful to you, nor has Lord Hertford acted
dishonourably towards her. Please sit down and
let Jacques and me tell you about it. Come on,
Papa darling. You're tired and distraught, and
jumping to all the wrong conclusions. There, sit
down while I pour you another brandy. And for
pity's sake eat something. Have you eaten anything since yesterday?'

The question was ignored as Lord Benistone's
confused emotions were engulfed in three pairs
of loving arms that hugged and comforted, the
sound of the women's joyful cries eventually
calming the fury that had not quite dissipated
since Vauxhall. There were tears in his eyes, too,
when he emerged, unashamedly sobbing. 'Will
she come back to us?' he said. 'Tell us what happened. Where's she been all this time?'

Between them, Annemarie and Lord Verne
gave them the full story of what, how and why
their mama's plan had failed, including Lady
Benistone's own interpretation of her incompe-
tence that took care not to direct any of the blame

towards her husband, although his nods showed
them how he suffered. 'My fault,' he murmured
more than once. 'My fault entirely. She'd rather
go to Hertford than to me. Too bad...too bad!'

'It was *Lady* Hertford she needed,' said
Annemarie. 'Her old friend. She was ashamed.
She still is. She doesn't believe you'll take her
back.'

'Not take her *back*?' his lordship roared. 'How
could she ever think that?'

'Quite easily, my lord,' said Verne, 'after what
happened to her. Mytchett made sure of her disgrace and now she doesn't feel she deserves to
be forgiven for it.'

'God's truth, man! It's not a question of *my*
forgiveness, is it? She must come home to us.
She belongs here. The longer she stays away,
the more talk there'll be. I'm the one who needs
her forgiveness. Me. I've treated her shamefully,
poor woman. Just imagine going to *those* lengths
to protect her daughter when I could have done it
with two well-chosen words. I shall go up there
myself and demand—'

'Papa,' said Marguerite, 'do you think it might
be better to *ask* rather than demand? Plead with
her? Beg her? Tell her how we love and long for
her? Tell her that in future you'll pay her more
attention, perhaps? And thank the Hertfords gra-
ciously for their care of her. You'll have to ac-

cept their hospitality, remember, unless you stay overnight at the local inn.'

'Then I should take you with me, young lady. With that kind of diplomacy, you can stop me flying off the handle, can't you?' Since none of them had ever seen, or heard, Lord Benistone so much as raise his voice before he horsewhipped Sir Lionel Mytchett, this excuse sounded implausible, though they were heartily in favour of Marguerite escorting her father on this delicate mission. It was testament to her transformation that she was now being given the role of diplomat when, only a few days before, she might have been their last choice.

'Yes, Papa. I'll go with you. We'll bring her back together,' she said.

'But not until you've had something to eat, Elmer,' Cecily said, observing the arrival of plates of food. 'Come on, there's enough here to feed an army.'

'But I'm not dressed for dinner,' his lordship said with a sideways glance at Annemarie. 'Nor is Verne, I see.'

'Papa,' said Oriel, severely. 'Let this be the last time, then.'

With the issue of Lady Benistone's return taking precedence, the astonishing drama at Vauxhall Gardens had been pushed to one side of the discussions that passed between mouthfuls at

the informal dinner table. For Annemarie, however, her father's violence towards Sir Lionel
Mytchett was just about the most uncharacteristic response she could ever have imagined when,
for a whole year, his manner had been more quietly grieving than boiling anger. Which made
her aware, yet again, of how she had misjudged
his feelings on the subject and how deeply he
had been affected. Before Oriel, Cecily and Marguerite returned to Park Lane, she managed to
have a quiet word with them while Papa was
talking to Lord Verne.

'Something will have to be done about Montague Street,' she said. 'We cannot allow Mama
to see it as it is, can we?'

'Well, how *is* it?' said Cecily. 'Have you been
there lately?'

'No, I've been busy at Curzon Street and so
have you. Then the four days in Warwickshire.'

'So while Papa and I are away, why not go and
see if you can make it habitable?' said Marguerite. 'Make two or three rooms fit for their use,
at least. And the kitchens. There won't be any
food. There never is. And I don't suppose she'll
have much in the way of luggage, except what
Lady Hertford has provided.'

'That's what I thought, too,' said Oriel. 'We
should go round there as soon as you've gone
and see what's to be done. Cecily?'

'Certainly, dearest. I know your papa has

moved some stuff out, but no more than that. I could hardly bring myself to look at what he's left behind. We'll go. If he can persuade her to return, things will have to change.'

'I'll persuade her,' said Marguerite, quietly. 'She'll come.'

Oriel hugged her sister. 'Of course she will, love. Of course she'll come.'

Verne was not quite as astonished by Lord Benistone's merciless punishment of Sir Lionel as Annemarie was. Nor was he as surprised as she was to discover that the father who had allowed his marriage to deteriorate so badly should suddenly have found the energy and motivation to retaliate. 'It's as if he's been thinking about it all this time,' she said, 'to see how long he could bear it.'

'It takes some men longer than others to realise what they must do about it, sweetheart.' In the peace of their bedroom, shuttered but still curtainless, they rolled towards each other between herb-scented sheets to seek the warm comfort of arms, soft skin and accommodating curves.

'You don't think the authorities will start asking questions about what happened that night, do you?' Annemarie said, snuggling into him.

'They'll do their best, I expect. But I would not be too concerned, if I were you. For one thing, Sir Lionel was found well downstream of Vauxhall, so they have no way of knowing exactly where he fell in. For another, even though they believe he'd been at Vauxhall, they'll never find anyone to witness it in a crowd like that. They were all watching the fireworks, weren't they? I don't think your father is in any danger of being questioned. Accidental death, they'll call it. Like the others.'

'Mama could hardly believe it. Sir Lionel's death, I mean.'

'So wait till she hears what part your father played. I'll wager she's never seen that side of him.'

'I think, dear heart, that at least four of the Benistone family have revealed a different side of themselves recently. Don't you?' she said, sleepily.

Verne slid his warm hand over the silky skin of her buttocks. 'So might there yet be another side of this particular Benistone to be revealed, do you think? Or have I seen it all?'

Teasingly, she smoothed the sole of her foot down his leg. 'I have no objection to you investigating further,' she whispered, 'just to make sure. If I'm to be the new Lady Verne, it's only fair that you should know these things before you commit yourself.'

'Sweetheart,' he said, lifting himself up to rest on one elbow, 'I was committed on that first day, even before you'd stopped snarling at me. Nothing's changed. Nor will it.'

Despite the late hour, their tiredness and the highly charged emotions of the last few days, their loving was raised to yet another level of ecstasy that night, with so many of Annemarie's personal dilemmas now solved, easily, gracefully, as if there had never been a good reason for them in the first place. Released from the debilitating revenge which had drained her zest for life and kept her friends at arm's length, she saw how foolish and unnecessary her plans had been, how unfair and unworthy. Verne was everything she had ever wanted and now she was able to tell him so in words of love and in the liberal giving of her lovely body. After such lavish generosity, he could not have doubted for a moment that her love for him was genuine, all-consuming and free at last from self-imposed obstacles.

There was still much to be done at Curzon Street for which Annemarie had expected to have plenty of time between shopping expeditions, excursions and visits to exhibitions and, in the evenings, dinners, theatres and balls. It now looked as if she might have to spend two or three more days at the family home on Montague Street in order to restore some kind of order before Lady Benistone's return, though she could not resent the effort that would be needed to achieve this. With Evie beside her and two housemaids trotting behind, she reached the newly painted, red front door at the same time as Cecily and Oriel.

Inside her former home, Annemarie found herself being one of an awestruck group who wandered slowly through room after room to admire and wonder at the space and light, the fashionable colours and handsome furnishings, the tasteful paintings of flowers, the sumptuous cushions, polished surfaces not seen for years and graceful ornaments that until now had been hidden behind the conglomeration of years. The spaciousness was almost overwhelming after the claustrophobic surroundings and the uncomfortable invasion of Lord Benistone's treasures into their rooms. Her parents' room had been transformed into a white haven of flowing curtains, lace, linen, brocade and silk, like a new page of a diary waiting to be written upon. A large bowl of white, cream and apricot roses stood on a low table by the sash window where the light caught the velvet petals, and Annemarie knew that this must have been described in detail by her father, for the colour scheme was Mama's favourite, until it, too, had been swamped.

She felt a lump form in her throat and, glancing at her sister, saw tears glistening in her eyes.

'Oh, Oriel,' she whispered, 'I never…ever… thought he'd do this.'

Oriel's voice trembled. 'He's done it for Mama,' she said. 'Perhaps he thought that if he actually *did* something, something would happen for him, too.'

'And it has,' said Cecily, 'hasn't it? Have you ever seen him so full of energy? It's as if clearing his house out has cleared his mind at the same time. I would never have thought he'd thrash a younger man the way he did. And then threaten to do the same to Lord Hertford. He really does care, doesn't he?'

'We just didn't know what lengths he'd go to, to prove it. We may as well go home now. We're not needed here.'

'More flowers?' said Oriel. 'She loves flowers everywhere.'

'Shall we go and interfere in the kitchen?' said Cecily, impishly.

'Just to check the menus? Well, someone has to do it,' said Annemarie.

As it happened, they stayed the whole of the morning to check on things, to note the more personal details: soap, tissue-lined drawers, hangers in the wardrobe, her left-behind jewellery that needed a polish, her favourite tea in the caddy, her bone-china tea set, her music on the piano. They cast their eyes around Marguerite's room, too, which she had not occupied for some time and which now had a beautiful Wilton carpet and matching curtains.

The three of them went into town to buy her a new white quilted-satin bedspread, a very daring pink satin negligee and slippers to match, and new towels embroidered with M and pink butterflies that seemed to represent a passing phase in her young life..

'In Brighton,' Annemarie said, 'I met a rather dashing young cavalry officer. I think I shall ask Verne to invite him up to London. I would not be at all surprised if he took a shine to our new Marguerite.'

Cecily was not so sure. 'I cannot see Lord Verne going along with *that* plan,' she said, pulling on her gloves. On this point, however, she was mistaken.

'He's already here,' said Verne that evening.

'What, in London?'

'In London. Shall you invite him to dine with us? I owe him a favour.'

'By all means, if you think he'd regard it as a favour to dine with us. I could include him with the family,' she added, with a studied nonchalance, 'to chat with Marguerite? That would be doing *me* a favour.'

The smile that had been held back suddenly broke. 'Little schemer.' He laughed. 'You think they might get along together, don't you? Well,

I think so, too. Bock's a very level-headed chap.
He'd be better company for her than those niffy-
naffy types she was with at the theatre. He's
been around a bit, too.'

'By which you mean he knows about women,'
said Annemarie, rather primly. She made as if
to move away from his side, but was prevented
by his arm slowly pushing her back into the sofa
cushions, helplessly unbalanced, his body keeping her there.

'You have a problem with that, my lady? Men
knowing about women?' he said, taunting her
with a serious face much too close for argument.

'No,' she whispered.

'Good.'

Hazily, at the back of her mind, she recalled
how his own obvious experience had antago-
nised her, made her afraid and determined to
be an exception to his rule, whatever that was.
At the same time, it was useless to deny that his
arrogance had excited and intrigued her, even
while she tried to make it appear otherwise. And
though she had never wished to know the details
of his conquests, there was something tantalising
about a man who had 'been around a bit' that had
made her want to be the last one, the best, the
hardest to catch. The prize. 'Arrogant man,' she
said, just before his mouth slanted across hers,
sending wave after wave of desire down to her
womb, melting it, readying it for him.

'Confident,' he replied, allowing her a breathing space. 'I had to be confident or I'd have got nowhere near you, would I? I knew you'd be difficult. Volatile. Defensive. Worth all the effort, though.'

'Effort? *What* effort?' she scoffed, anticipating his response. She had expected to be lifted up into his arms and carried upstairs, but not to be swung along the sofa with her legs somehow enclosing him, her head upon the tasselled bolster from which there was no escape. As she twisted and writhed under him, her struggle was used as fuel to feed her challenge, to move on past the tender preliminaries towards the effort she had just derided.

Without a word, he contained her flailing arms in one hand, his other hand knowing the quickest route to the softness of her thighs and the shadowy moistening folds whose ache demanded instant satisfaction. His kisses emptied her mind as his deft and skilful fingers worked their magic, preparing her to the last possible moment before his entry, causing her to mew at the sweetness of it and the urgency they were sharing. He released her hands only after the last wild surge of power and the shuddering climax, the directionless rapture, his groan of emptiness and her long sigh of completion. Then it passed through his mind, no more than that, how she had once suffered such impulsive lovemaking at the hands of her late husband, and how much she had learned since then about love in all its forms, from him. He did not remind her of it, the moment being too delicate to hold such un-happy recollections.

After three days and with no communication from Lord Benistone concerning the success of his mission, or otherwise, they could only wait patiently, and hope, and make what small last-minute preparations they could without in any way changing those made by his lordship. But by mutual consent, Annemarie and Lord Verne, Cecily, Oriel and Colonel Harrow gathered at Number Eighteen Montague Street in the late afternoon on the off chance that, if they were coming at all, it would be about then.

Their prediction was astonishingly accurate for, as the grandfather clock in the hall struck five, the sound of hooves and wheels rattled on the cobbles and came to a stop. Mr Quibly would have had the—mostly new—staff lined up to greet their master and mistress, but had been persuaded that Lady Benistone would prefer to be seen only by the closest members of her fam-ily, until later. It was Marguerite who emerged first with the happiest of smiles. In marked con-trast to her previous childish manner, she stood back to allow them to see how Lord Benistone almost lifted his wife down the steps on to the pavement, setting her feet down safely, crooking his arm for her support and smiling like a bridegroom with his new bride.

The embraces and cries of joy, although intended for the privacy of the hall, could not wait so long and, by the time they had moved inside, a small crowd of pedestrians were politely applauding Lady Benistone's return before they could move on. Inevitably, tears flowed through laughter, relief and some considerable amazement concerning Lord Benistone's secret renovations, a surprise to Marguerite as much as to her mama who, led by the hand into the drawing room, hardly recognised it. 'The space...the light...ah, here's my little china dog...and my music, too. Ah, this is...oh, Elmer!' Unreserved, she threw her arms around his lordship's neck and wept. 'I don't deserve it,' she cried. 'You are too kind, my love. Too...*too* kind.'

'Of course you do,' he said, holding her close, like a lover. 'I should have done this years ago, sweetness. I should have seen what was happening.'

'But all your treasures. What will you do without them? They meant so much to you.'

'Not as much as my lovely wife and daughters,' he said, holding her elbows. 'It began to look as if I was losing all of you at once. Even our dear Cecily didn't call as often as she used to. And I missed you so,' he said, plaintively. 'I thought it was time I grew up, so Marguerite and I have done it together, haven't we, love?' Holding out his hand, he took his daughter's fingers and kissed their tips. 'We've had time to talk. Journeys are good for that. Neither of us could walk off. And now our lovely Oriel can marry her William, and Annemarie will….well, who knows what Annemarie will do next?'

'Papa! That's unfair!'

Verne came to her rescue with a possessive arm around her waist, laughing at her confusion. 'With respect, my lord, we *do* know what Lady Golding will do next. She'll marry me.'

'Weddings from Montague Street,' said Lord Benistone. 'I like the sound of that. But perhaps we might precede them with a pre-wedding ball, since the last event was not the unqualified success it ought to have been. We'll do it again, properly this time. With Cecily to help, of course.' Turning to Marguerite with a gentle shake of her hand, he exchanged smiles. 'Happy now?' he whispered.

With a younger and more innovative chef to replace the former one whose weariness had begun to show, dinner at Montague Street that evening was special in every way, from the carefully prepared menu with Lady Benistone's favourite dishes to the elegance of the table setting and the meticulous evening dress of the diners.

There were so many thoughts to express, so much to discuss, news to exchange, plans to be revealed for a future that had once seemed so bleak, that it was late when the family dispersed, happier than they'd been for far too long.

Clinging together until the last moment, Annemarie and her mother had reached the point of intimate chatter that follows so easily after a surfeit of happiness, good company and wine, little exchanges that would be half-forgotten next day and would need to be elaborated on. The Prince Regent was always a source of such tales, though Lady Benistone had been touched, and amused, that he'd asked about her. 'After all these years,' she giggled, linking arms. 'Perhaps it's time he saw for himself, dearest. Lady Hertford told me… No, perhaps I ought not to say. Who he wrote to is not our concern, is it?'

'Who *did* he write to, Mama? Anyone we know?'

'He's had his letters returned to him now. And what a good thing, too. Can you imagine, what a scandal if they'd been made public like Lord Nelson's were in April? Poor dear. It would've been the end of him.' Her arm squeezed against Annemarie's. 'Don't you remember what a furor it caused?'

'For Emma Hamilton, you mean?'

'Of course. She's been so indiscreet. But don't

for heaven's sake let on that you know. Isabella only told me to make me smile.'

'And did you, Mama?'

'Well, yes. But not as much as Prinny, I expect. Goodnight, my love.'

Embracing, and with a glance over her mother's shoulder, Annemarie saw that Verne had been standing close enough to hear what had been said and that his face reflected all the concern she might have expected. Hardly able to believe her ears, she stared at him, shaking her head, then turning away, feeling her goodwill dissipate in a haze of confusion. Despite all she'd done to help, all she'd lost and gained, all she had believed in and the friends she'd trusted, her plan had come to nothing. Without her knowing it. Until now. 'Cecily!' she called across the hallway. 'Don't go yet. I need to speak—'

But Verne was there before her, reading her intentions. 'No,' he said, softly. 'Not now. Let her go. I'll explain. *Please*, Annemarie.' His emphatic plea was enough to prevent the confrontation that would surely have ensued before Cecily swirled out into the night air and the waiting carriage.

'I needed to speak to her,' Annemarie said, angrily. 'It's important.'

'Yes, I know. We'll discuss it alone.'

'*Discuss?*' she retorted. 'We'll have to do better than that, my lord. I need some answers.'

Verne had always hoped, with varying degrees of justification, that in time the letters would have been forgotten or, at least, pushed to the bottom of Annemarie's list of important things to remember. Realistically, he realised that it was still too soon for this kind of miracle and that he might one day have to make up a convincing story that would exonerate Cecily from all blame. After her assistance, he could not allow that to happen. If lies were a bad thing, then surely the protection of a friend was some kind of excuse.

Back at Curzon Street, he was quite prepared for her first salvo fired as soon as the bedroom door was closed behind them.

'It was Cecily, wasn't it?' Annemarie began. 'She was the one I gave them to. I trusted her and she unlocked my portmanteau and passed them on to *you* to give to the Prince Regent. So much for my trust. And all this time you've led me to believe I was doing a poor woman a good turn by returning what was *her* property. Laughing at me…the two of you…how *could* you do that? How else have you deceived me, my lord? No… let me guess…' White faced, pacing the room while pulling off her earrings, she was about to launch into another series of assumptions when she felt Evie's nimble fingers unhooking the high bodice of her evening gown. 'You'd better leave us, Evie,' she said, pulling away. 'I'll manage.'

Evie had been hoping to remain invisible for as long as possible but now, almost as white-faced as her mistress, she could not allow this tirade to develop so far in the wrong direction, even if it cost her her position. 'My lady,' she whispered, avoiding Lord Verne's frowns, 'please may I speak? I can explain what happened.'

'Evie,' said his lordship, 'I think you'd better do as Lady Golding says.'

'But it was not Mrs Cardew's fault, m'lady. Please let me tell you,' Evie whispered, caught between the two of them. 'It was all *my* fault.'

'You, Evie? What did you have to do with it? Surely it was—'

'No, m'lady. There was only a cushion in the portmanteau when Mrs Cardew took it out that afternoon. I don't know where she was supposed to be taking it, but I know it wasn't full of letters. She'd have got such a surprise when she opened it. Just that blue cushion from the inn. It weighed about the same, you see.'

Half-undone with her bodice falling off one shoulder, Annemarie sat on the bed, looking from Evie's distressed face to Verne's combined expressions of disbelief and resignation. Clearly, this was not the story he'd been going to tell. 'Exactly what are you telling me, Evie?'

Annemarie said. 'That *you* unlocked my port-manteau?'

'Not me, m'lady. Not personally. But some-body did. You remember how the inn was packed with passengers from the mail coach? And how I had to go down and get my supper, and how long I had to wait? Well, it's my belief that somebody got in and had a go at the portmanteau while I was out, m'lady, because when I returned it was open. Well, you were too tired and upset to be bothered about it that night, so I just took the cushion and put it inside. You said it had some jewellery in and I knew you'd discover the theft, sooner or later, but I thought it was best to say nothing until morning.' Evie's eyes filled with tears as she fumbled in her apron pocket for a handkerchief. 'But I couldn't. Not then.'

'And you locked the portmanteau up again?' said Annemarie. 'How?'

'The lock wasn't broken, m'lady. Somebody knew what they were doing. I used your key to lock it. I'd have told you about it, only there didn't seem to be a suitable time.'

'So you don't know where the letters went, Evie?' Verne asked.

'I didn't see any letters, m'lord. Lady Golding told me it was jewellery, you see. And then Mrs Cardew was to take it somewhere, but nothing was said after that so I assumed Mrs Cardew had resolved the problem.'

'Yes, quite. So you think the contents were stolen by one of the guests?'

'Must've been, m'lord.'

'So,' said Annemarie, ominously quiet, 'how did the…er…contents…find their way to the Prince Regent, I wonder?'

Evie glanced at Lord Verne while doing her utmost to clear her expression of all misgivings. 'I can only suggest, m'lady, that whoever took them must have sent them on. Perhaps there'd be a reward of some kind.'

'Ye-es. I'm sure there would be. Indeed, it sounds extremely likely.'

'Rings true enough to me,' said Verne. 'Evie took every care…'

'Thank you, Evie. I think you should go now. It's getting late.'

'Thank you, m'lady. You'll not blame Mrs Cardew, will you?'

'Not at all, Evie. I've rarely heard such a concerted effort to save Mrs Cardew from any responsibility in the matter as I have just now. It's almost too good to be true. Goodnight, Evie.'

'Goodnight, m'lady. M'lord.'

Verne watched the door close, shaking his head and wondering whether Evie's valiant story had made matters worse or better. He suspected the former, especially as the question of how the Prince got his letters back sounded as implausible as an honest thief. A squeak from the bed made him look up sharply. Annemarie had rolled over, face down into the white linen sheet, her arms bunched beneath her shaking body from which muffled sobs and yelps emerged, with the occasional moan.

'Sweetheart…oh, my darling girl. Don't… don't weep. Let me explain.'

Another yelp. 'Ah…not you, too,' she squeaked. 'I can't *bear* it.'

'What?' he said, placing a hand softly on her back to still the convulsions. 'Can't bear what? She meant to protect Cecily, that's all. I knew you'd not believe her.'

It was then, when she turned towards him in the foetal position to ease her aching ribs, that he saw how she could hardly speak for laughter and that the wailing and squeaking were the beginnings and endings of words with no middles. For it was if an unyielding barrier had disappeared, leaving behind an empty space, totally without substance, meaning or importance. As Evie's ridiculously flawed explanation had been intended to excuse everyone except herself, even the thief, Annemarie was able to piece together the picture of that time in the Swan at Reigate when all was confusion and emotional turmoil, and an inexcusable unconcern for her maid's personal comforts which had always mattered to her. She had not asked about her supper, she had left her in charge of 'valuables', and poor devoted

Evie had had to fend for herself or find someone willing to help. The answer was obvious, wasn't it? The young man she'd had a fierce argument with, had cold-shouldered, warmed to, and was now protecting from extreme anger. Verne's own valet, following his master's instructions, who was following *his* royal master's instructions. How utterly absurd. What a comedy.

For some moments longer, Annemarie could only gasp out the explanations Evie had offered, 'Evie protecting you…and Samson…you protecting Cecily….Cecily protecting…me, and me protecting…Lady Hamilton. Oh, Jacques! It's a wonder you could all keep track…of who…was protecting…whom! Oh dear. I've never heard anything so silly in all my life.' Mopping at her eyes, she sat up and flopped her arms about his neck. 'Can we forget about it now, please?'

'Darling, beloved! Do you mean that you don't care that the Prince has them instead of *her*? Really?'

'Not any more, my love. I wanted to hurt him, but now I don't. I wanted to help her, but it was already too late, wasn't it? She was leaving.'

'You sent her money, Cecily says.'

'At least I know she got that. It would have paid for something.'

'But don't lay any of the blame at Cecily's door. She never saw the letters either. I had them by the time we left Reigate. She's a loyal friend.'

'And I'm now protecting the disloyal one, am I not? The Prince who deserves it less than any of us. I could have ruined him. But I'm glad you stopped me.'

'Are you, love? Am I forgiven? I had to do something drastic.'

'I know. So maybe if you go and remove *your* evening clothes without your valet, we could do something drastic together before we sleep. Yes?' She put up her face for his kiss, made all the sweeter for knowing that, after all her efforts, he was the one who held the reins. A man above men. A man whose direction she would enjoy. A man she would love for ever.

Moments later, Verne emerged from his dressing room, tying the cord of his silk gown that concealed neither legs nor chest. Her lingering stare at the gaps made him smile. 'Well?' he said. 'Waiting for me?'

Annemarie pulled her own sheer negligee more tightly across her breasts. 'No,' she said, picking up her hairbrush. 'I'm waiting for an exquisitely mannered gentleman to invite me, with some deference, to spend an hour or two in polite conversation with him. But I fear that life is scattered with such disappointments.' She sighed, noisily.

'Is that so, my beauty?' he replied, taking the brush from her hand as it rose to make the first sweep. 'Then you'll have to make do with me until he appears, won't you?' He sat himself behind her astride the long stool and took a fistful of her hair, sweeping down it expertly with the brush. 'So what is this polite conversation to do with?'

'You wouldn't understand.'

'Try me.'

'No. It's to do with some jewellery I own.'

'Amethysts and diamonds, by any chance?'

'Could be.'

'You want them reset? Is that it?'

'No. I want to give them to someone.'

'I told you. I don't think he'd appreciate the gesture.'

'I was intending them for a *her*, not a *him*.'

'Do I know her?'

'Apparently, you knew of her before I did. She must be sorely in need of funds. She has a small child. Children are expensive. She has no protector, as far as I know. She could make better use of the jewels than me. They must be worth thousands.'

'Very commendable, sweetheart,' he said, brushing tenderly away from her temple. 'But has it occurred to you that, if Mrs Mytchett were to take them to any jeweller, there would be questions asked about how she came by them? She'd be hard-pressed for a convincing answer, I should think.'

'Then I'd better sell them myself, hadn't I?'

'Better still, let me take them back to Rundell and Bridges. They'll give you a good price and they'll be glad to see them again. There'll be no questions asked.'

'You agree that it would be a good thing to do? To help her out?'

The brushing continued. 'An excellent thing. Generous. Typically charitable.'

'She's been badly used, but I hope she won't regard it as charity.'

'What, then?'

'Recompense. Her deserts. I bear her no grudges. She need not know who the money comes from. In fact, I'd rather she didn't.'

'She might guess, though.'

'I don't see how. It's worth a try.'

The brushing stopped as his arms enclosed her, his face nuzzling into her neck where he held the hair away. 'It is indeed, sweetheart,' he said. 'Now, are you still waiting for that exquisitely mannered gentleman to turn up?'

'Too late,' she murmured. 'Perhaps I should make do with you, after all.'

'Come to bed, then,' he said, sliding the silk negligee off her shoulders. 'We've had enough polite conversation for one night. Don't you agree?'

'Mmm,' she said, leaning her head back to receive his kiss.

* * *

In her own white bedroom, Esme Benistone also made use of her husband's services as lady's maid, a task stretching way beyond the usual time with each detail of the room to be examined and reflected upon. 'This thing,' said his lordship, referring to her corset, 'is not going to come off unless you stand still and allow me to unlace it. Is it?'

'Dearest, I can unhook it from the front. Didn't you know?'

He sighed. 'How am I supposed to know that, after…?'

She turned to face him. 'Don't say it, love. We have some catching up to do, don't we? It'll be like old times when we were just finding out about each other.'

'And loving what we found.'

'I never stopped loving you, Elmer. I so wanted your love.'

'Oh, dear heart, you never lost it. I've been so foolish. Please forgive me.'

'We both have. Come to bed. Just your arms, your warmth, your love. The rest will come, in time. Will you give me some time, dearest?'

'All the time in the world. I shall not lose you again. Come, lass.'

With so much else happening that summer—fêtes and garden parties, processions and massively over-subscribed dinners followed by balls, displays and exhibitions—the Benistone Ball, as it came to be known, was an exclusive affair to which only family and good friends were invited to celebrate the restoration of a divided generation. The Hertfords found it a perfect opportunity to reconnect with Verne's family from Salisbury, the Marquess and Marchioness of Simonstoke, their younger sons, Robbie and Christopher, and the elder sister, her husband and young ones all of whom were overjoyed to know that, at last, Jacques had found a woman for whom he'd had to make rather more effort than usual. The scandal attached to her and her mama only added to their fascination, particularly in the case of the two young men whose immediate interest in Lady Golding's younger sister caused a certain rivalry with Lord Bockington.

Bock had already won an advantage by being present at several family dinners in the preceding weeks, since when he had called on Marguerite almost daily, with her parents' approval, to take her driving, with and without Cecily. By this time Marguerite's affections were fully engaged by the handsome cavalry officer who had seen some action and who now understood the value of his information to Lord Verne. Smitten by Marguerite's good looks, and already in love with her, he found himself enchanted by the fusion of innocence and finesse which had begun to show and which, quite naturally, she was learning to cultivate as a far more successful and attractive lure than her previous gaucherie.

'I can hardly believe the change in her,' said Verne, throwing down his riding gloves and whip. 'She's actually talking sense at last. She'll be quite a woman in a year or two.'

Untying the veil knotted behind her head, Annemarie lifted off her riding hat to loose a river of black silk over her shoulders, at once softening the austere dark brown of her habit. Unbidden, the memory of that terrible episode after the theatre reminded her of how far she, too, had come when even something as meaningless as Marguerite's girlish boast had set her afire with jealousy. Now, she could accept Verne's praise of her sister without a qualm. She took his hand and led him into the morning room, recalling how her fortunes had changed so dramatically and how proud she had been riding beside him in the park, how striking he looked, how attentive, well liked by everyone and loved by her. 'Have I told you…recently…?' she said, closing the door and placing a hand on his lapel.

'No,' he said, automatically. 'What?'

'That I love you. Adore you. Is there another grade upwards of that?'

'If there is, sweetheart,' he said, taking her waist between his hands, 'I don't need to hear it. Love and adoration will do very nicely, thank you. It's more than I ever expected, more than I ever dared to hope for and much more than I deserve.'

'Oh…' she smiled, tracing a line round his jaw with her thumb '…nobody said anything about *deserving*, my lord. No, you probably don't deserve it, but there it is. Unconditional. Free. All yours.'

'All mine,' he whispered. 'My glorious, scandalous woman.' There was more than a hint of laughter behind the kiss that surfaced once before being submerged in a deeper passion that told them both how permanent their love had grown.

'And there's more,' she said.

She had no need to elaborate when the way she said it, half-shyly, half-proud, gave him all the clue he needed. Sliding one hand down between them, he rested it below her waist, his eyes searching hers, questioning. 'Truly?' he said. 'You're sure?'

'Fairly sure. Yes.'

'Oh, my darling…sweetest…most wonderful creature!' Tenderly, he held her close to him, the finest and rarest treasure he had ever beheld in all his searches.

Epilogue

The summer of 1814, as the story indicates, was packed with events to celebrate Napoleon's defeat, although no one at the time believed he would ever escape from his confinement on Elba to organise another army in 1815. Annemarie had partly relied on these hectic celebrations to help her find her mother, thinking that, somewhere in the crowds, there would surely be a sighting. The discontent of the Prince Regent and his unpopularity is no exaggeration, and I chose to pity him rather than to mock, his unloving parents having a lot to answer for in making him the irresponsible man he became. It was part of Annemarie's transformation to find in him the opposite of what she had expected.

His friend, the Marquess of Hertford, was in many ways the same, living a life of dissipation while indulging in a genuine love and appreciation of art, and Ragley Hall in Warwickshire is now open to the public, still full of the treasures Annemarie would have seen. The Hertfords' London home is known as Manchester House, though Carlton House was demolished, after all the money spent on it. Brighton Pavilion is still there, thriving, recently renovated and utterly splendid.

Montague Street lies behind the British Museum, which was then a fledgling institute, and the recipient of several collections, including Lord Townley's and the library of the Prince Regent's father, George III. In 1814, the British Museum was not quite the thriving organised place I have made it out to be. The public were only reluctantly admitted on certain days and in limited numbers, hustled round by guides far less knowledgeable than those of today. However, it suited my story to endow them with an eagerness to acquire Lord Benistone's treasures which, only a few years later, they would have deserved.

Lady Emma Hamilton spent some years, on and off, in various debtors' prisons after the demise of her protector, Lord Nelson in 1805. The story of the publication of letters from him to her is true, though she gained only publicity and scorn by it. But then, I do not believe she was responsible for that catastrophe, except by neglecting to keep them more safely. There is no record of any letters from the Prince Regent to

Lady Hamilton; I have invented that because it sounded like a possibility. After the Prince's death, thousands of trinkets, jewellery, letters and locks of hair were discovered amongst his belongings, most of which were destroyed.

On July 1st 1814, Lady Emma Hamilton and her daughter Horatia escaped by night on a chartered boat to Calais. She died in the following January, penniless and suffering from a debilitating illness.

Lord and Lady Verne's marriage took place on the same day as that of her elder sister to Colonel Harrow, though it was Annemarie's son who was born only a month before Oriel's. The Vernes had two more sons after that.

Marguerite and Lord Bockington married in the following year on her eighteenth birthday, by which time the scandal surrounding the Benistones had been well and truly eclipsed by the Battle of Waterloo and all its repercussions.

* * * * *

The Regency Ballroom Collection

A twelve-book collection led by Louise Allen
and written by the top authors and rising
stars of historical romance!

Classic tales of scandal and seduction in
the Regency ballroom

Take your place on the ballroom floor now, at:
www.millsandboon.co.uk

MILLS & BOON®
Book Club

Join the Mills & Boon Book Club

Want to read more **Historical** books?
We're offering you **2 more** absolutely **FREE!**

We'll also treat you to these fabulous extras:

- Exclusive offers and much more!

- FREE home delivery

- FREE books and gifts with our special rewards scheme

Get your free books now!

visit www.millsandboon.co.uk/bookclub
or call Customer Relations on 020 8288 2888

Discover more romance at

www.millsandboon.co.uk

- ♥ WIN great prizes in our exclusive competitions
- ♥ BUY new titles before they hit the shops
- ♥ BROWSE new books and REVIEW your favourites
- ♥ SAVE on new books with the Mills & Boon® Bookclub™
- ♥ DISCOVER new authors

PLUS, to chat about your favourite reads, get the latest news and find special offers:

- 🔲 Find us on facebook.com/millsandboon
- 🔰 Follow us on twitter.com/millsandboonuk
- ♥ Sign up to our newsletter at millsandboon.co.uk

_SD

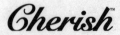